WWW.BLOODOFZEUS.COM

WWW.BLOODOFZEUS.COM

WWW.BLOODOFZEUS.COM

HEART *of* FIRE

HEART *of* FIRE

BLOOD OF ZEUS: BOOK TWO

MEREDITH WILD
& ANGEL PAYNE

This book is an original publication of Waterhouse Press.

This is a work of fiction. Names, characters, places, and incidents either are the product of the author's imagination or are used fictitiously, and any resemblance to actual persons, living or dead, business establishments, events, or locales is entirely coincidental. The publisher does not assume any responsibility for third-party websites or their content.

Cover Design & Images by Regina Wamba
Interior Cover Images: Shutterstock

ISBN: 978-1-64263-246-0

For Aedan, my little fire

— Meredith

For Thomas, who sees all my blazes
and still isn't afraid of the heat

— Angel

Just so my wilted spirits rose again
And such a heat of zeal surged through my veins
That I was born anew. Thus I began:
– Dante Alighieri, *Inferno II*

CHAPTER 1

MAXIMUS

"*HERE BEGINS A NEW LIFE.*"

My rough whisper is absorbed by the still air of Kara's bedroom, which has become a perfect haven for the last twenty-four hours.

It didn't feel right, let alone safe, to hang out at my place downtown after the man claiming to be my long-lost father—and, oh yeah, the allfather of Olympus and every immortal being in it—came for a casual drop-in last night. Not long after, the paparazzi were spreading like an oil spill along my street, making the view of the Hollywood Hills a pastoral scene by comparison.

The stars over the sleepy slopes are slowly consumed by the approaching dawn as I repeat the line once more. Dante's words have always felt like those of a soulmate, but not once in the hundreds of times I've read from *La Vita Nuova* has the sentiment resonated so strongly. Or inspired such a yearning to fight it.

But fight what? I'm where I've begged fate to bring me, for days and months and years. But I was never specific about those pleas. Maybe that was my slip. I never said the truth had to be sane. Or logical. Or believable.

Because it's absolutely none of those.

I blink hard, expecting to wake up and laugh off this bizarre fever dream. When I do, it'll still be yesterday morning at my place, when my naked body was warmly wrapped around the woman who's taken over so much of my heart, mind, and soul. No stranger will knock at my apartment door, saunter in, and make a claim so wacky I should be wondering what flophouse he's wandered in from and how much crap he's pumped into his bloodstream before doing so. Because that's the logical thing to think when a guy tells you he's the king of the gods. Worse, that you and he have twenty-seven years of Father's Days to catch up on.

Then Z had to drop his third bomb—a smaller explosion by comparison but a stunner all the same. Even now. Perhaps even more so, considering how small, innocent, and soft Kara seems in the big bed behind me. That peaceful tilt of her lips. The sprawl of her dark, thick waves against the luxurious white linens. The wistful way she curls her hands. Even the symmetrical, slender ovals of her fingernails.

She looks like an angel.

But she's my perfect little demon.

And I'm beginning to truly believe that she's all mine.

I turn back to the window, my mind wrestling with the possibility. It's bad enough that the claim is so dominant in my senses and my blood...the blood that shouldn't want her. Thanks to my DNA, I crave nothing *but* her.

And there's fate, toying with me again. Because any second now, I could lose her because of the DNA that's *her* curse and the destiny to which it's bound her. Spitting on that covenant hasn't won us any favors, despite how my father—or whoever the hell he is—has offered to intervene on our behalf. Yesterday morning, I was desperate enough to trust the man. I didn't have any other choice. I still don't. Unless...I do. Unless all of this really *isn't* happening. Unless Z really is just a tweaker in a Skid Row trash bin right now instead of negotiating with Hades like he promised.

But do I really want to test that theory?

"Maximus Kane, please tell me you aren't awake before the birds."

There's the answer to my query. Right here on the air, in all the sweet edges of Kara's sleepy rasp. In the sight of her, filling my hungry gaze, silky and curvy beneath the sheet as she stretches. Most of all, in every exquisite angle of her inquisitive stare, conveying that she's missed nothing about my brooding silence.

Beneath the track pants I slid into a few hours ago, things start to stir. Needless to say, I don't feel like brooding anymore. Not by a long shot, now that she's awake and focusing on me again. That expression makes yesterday's rushed escape all worth it. True, as safe houses go, I could ask for a lot worse, considering the sprawling patio, good-sized library, every conceivable modern amenity, and this killer view. But at this moment I'm not referring to the trees, the hills, or the *Hollywood* sign.

Being here, with this breathtaking beauty, is like a dream. Right down to this very second, in which I'm as excited as the first time she ever touched me, then changed me.

I shrug, attempting a show of casual charm. "More worms for me. I'll even share."

Kara sits up, curling her knees into her chest. "Trade you the worms for what's going on in that beautiful head of yours."

Another shrug, making up for more flustered vibes. I can lecture to hundreds of students at a time, but this sole female can undo me with one damn look. "Sleep and I have never been best friends," I finally say. "Few hours a night, and I'm good to go."

"Hmm." She tilts her head. "That makes sense, I guess."

"You guess? Why?"

"Well, considering everything."

"Everything like what?" My intention isn't a confrontation, but I need to hear it from another source besides the inside of my mind. "Just say it again, Kara. For me."

She jogs up her chin. "Everything, like you being a demigod."

Her gaze glitters now, reminding me of the sparklers Jesse and I played with during our boyhood summers. I want to smile, slammed by memories of happiness and hope, but right here and now, the memories are disjointed. *Different.*

"You can say it too, Maximus. And if you need to talk about it . . . well, I won't be freaked out."

"No." I lower to the mattress with an audible heave. "*I'll* be freaked out."

"Why?" Her confusion is sincere. I feel that as fully as her warmth, spreading through me as soon as she uncurls and presses against my side. "You had to have an idea. At least a small one. You were already asking questions. You openly shared them with me."

I wrap a hand around her wrists. "From now on, I share everything with you."

She sets a sigh free, heating the ball of my shoulder. "Even now?" she presses. "Even knowing what I am?"

I'm compelled to turn, dragging her in at the same time, until she's nestled in my lap and engulfed by my embrace. The sheets, which are the texture of spun butter, gather even tighter around her. "Especially now," I tell her, stroking my knuckles along her cheek. "Knowing *who* you are."

Though she quirks her lips, the spark of levity doesn't make it to her eyes. "Right," she mutters. "Who I am. Kara Valari, spawn of the demons who royally messed up your existence."

"No." I extend my grip to her nape, squeezing gently to demand her attention. "You're Kara Valari, the brave and brilliant creature who defied her family and the fate they were dooming you to. You're the demoness who dared to say that wasn't okay, but you're also the human being who stood up for so much more. You stood up for *us*."

At last, her big eyes and full lips get warm with confidence. Not a lot but enough to make me relax my grip.

"So . . . you really believe it? That we're—that *I'm*—"

"A demon?" I smile at once, then lift my upturned lips to her smooth forehead. "I was halfway to figuring that out already, beautiful. I'm the guy who read all your grandfather's screenplays to get to the bottom of it, remember?"

I'm rewarded for that with a musical Kara giggle. "Now *that* deserves a medal of valor. Or a knighthood. Perhaps both."

"Do either get me a few more hours in bed with you?" I flash a roguish smirk. "Maybe a few days? Weeks?"

Her own gaze flares. "I doubt Alameda will approve a Kara sabbatical, Professor."

There's the flirtation killer. Still, I work to keep my tone light while replying, "Oh, I strongly doubt they'll refuse."

Her eyes widen more. "Wait. What?" she charges. "What's going on?"

I grunt and twist my lips. "It's probably nothing. Just an email that came in overnight."

"An email from who?" she demands.

My grunt turns into a low, protesting rumble. Still I reply, "Chairperson of the university's board."

"Who said what?"

She's quieter about that one. I abhor being the cause of her overly cautious tone.

"They think a few days away from my duties might be a good idea."

She gasps. It's *not* quiet. Or cautious. "Why?"

"It's just a suggestion. Not an order, per se. But I'm not in much of a position to challenge them at this point. Not if I want to keep my job."

She pushes up and away, out of my lap. She doesn't go far but gets in enough inches to show me all the energy of her frustration. "You *love* your job."

I resist the urge to kiss her. This woman... how she knows so much of me already. How she values what she sees too.

"Yeah," I say gently. "You're right. I do love my job."

"And they're issuing this decree, keeping you from it."

"Not a decree." I push out a heavy breath. "A *suggestion*. Remember?"

Kara's having none of it. "What the hell are they thinking? This isn't the first 'celebrityship' that campus has seen. Don't you remember them rerouting the cafeteria lines when that Microbio grad student had her boy-band lover in for a visit? And when they closed the locker rooms when everyone thought he'd dumped her for the volleyball team coach? You want me to go on with the examples?"

"I could probably do the same thing," I return. "Hell, I've been on staff at Alameda for a bunch of them. But this is different and we both know it."

"Because of me." She pushes back even farther, taking the sheet with her like a protective force field. "Because of my getting sloppy about watching for cameras and thinking we were flying under the radar."

"All the things that make it just as much my fault." I turn and crawl up the mattress until I'm resting on my haunches in front of her. "You get that, right? There are *two* of us here, Kara. Two halves of the magnet. Two bands of the storm. Two people who were in the control booth that day and not being more careful... about everything."

She regards me with an incisive expression. "You'd still do it all again?"

I run my fingers up the outside of her leg and celebrate the tremors I cause beneath the luxurious sheet. "I wouldn't change a goddamned thing."

"Funny... *You're* the god they should fear."

I sit back again, shaking my head, betraying the chaos in my head. I can't fully wrap my mind around her words, despite my intuition that they're true. "I mean, even if half of this insanity is real, that's not what I'm about."

Kara cocks her head once more. "*If* this insanity is real?"

I tighten my jaw. "You know what I mean. We have to admit that maybe I'm not..." I falter for half a second. "That Z isn't... Well, that he won't come back. That he was just some cleaned-up bum off the alley, looking to case out some of the apartments in the building."

"Right," she rebuts as the tension climbs up her face. "Because bums off the street wear bespoke Italian suits and smell like their cologne cost just as much."

"Sure. If they've recently rolled someone, it's a possibility."

"A possibility you're going to believe, other than the truth that's staring you in the face."

"Not exactly in my face," I reply and sweep an arm out toward the peach and green mosaic of the hills. Across the ravine, a few early-riser joggers make their way along the Montlake Drive trail. "It's been twenty-four hours, Kara." Not that I'm keeping track or anything. "And we still haven't heard from him."

Maybe that's me being judgmental. And unreasonable. It's not like I could text the guy, telling him I'm here instead of the apartment. But if he's really Zeus, does he need an address?

"Which gives you the perfect excuse not to believe a word he told you?"

"Well, I don't *disbelieve* him."

"But it's easier for you to write him off as a random crazy instead of believing his claim. It's even easier for you to believe *I'm* a *demon* than to admit his truth about your heritage."

As soon as I lower my hand, I encase her other knee with my palm. Without giving it another thought, I push back on her legs, giving me room to occupy the space between them.

I keep going until the fit is flawless. Until it's all so, *so* right again. Until I can feel her heartbeat with my own, our pulses perfectly matched. Until she's circling her arms around my neck and her legs around my waist and her core against my erection.

The DNA in my blood doesn't matter anymore because there's nothing in it but her.

My silent assertion from before? About her being all mine? I was wrong. So wrong. So twisted around.

Because I'm all hers.

"I think the only truth that matters is right here," I tell her. "And right now." I dip in, meshing her mouth beneath mine with slow, adoring rolls, until we drag apart with reluctant sighs. "I also hope *nobody* comes looking for us.

Not ever again."

"Hmm." Her breaths take on a dreamy lilt. "What a nice thing to wish for." She delves her hands into my hair, kneading my scalp with steady languor. "We could be hippies. Live on the beach. In a yurt."

With my face pressed against her neck, I chuckle. "With our dog named Bubba?"

"Well, of course. But Bubba will have to get lost when I want to have my way with you."

"Who says we're doing that inside the yurt?"

"Ohhh." Her laugh is high but husky as I bite and nuzzle my way to her ear. "So, right out on the sand? I enjoy how your mind works, Maximus Kane."

Her praise inspires me to new action. After a decisive yank and a forceful swoop, I roll us both all the way over, off the mattress and onto the floor. My wicked laugh mingles with Kara's stunned shriek, and we kiss with deeper passion as the white fabric billows then settles around us. Her mouth is warm and wide, ready for me to explore and savor. Her body is bare and beautiful, ready for me to touch and tantalize. But the best part of it all is her passion, returned to me with fullness and fire . . . especially the flames that call to me from her eyes.

Surrounded by that awesome blaze, I'm able to find words to fill my parched throat. "I think we should pretend this is the sand."

"And now I *adore* how your mind works."

I pull her close, guiding one of her thighs around mine while cushioning her head with my bicep. I need another kiss, and I take it. Her mouth is as hot and succulent as ever, matching the decadent dew between her legs, telling me she's more than ready for me. And holy hell, am I ready for her.

She moans as if she's received every detail of that message from my psyche. Yet again I'm grateful for the woman's hyper empathy. *Go, little demon, go.*

No.

Stay, little demon, stay.

She smiles against my lips. "Well," she whispers, pushing incessantly at the waistband of my pants. "If you insist . . . "

I don't get the chance to answer her. A pronounced slam of the front door does it for me.

I go still. Kara tenses too, but not in the same who's-barging-in-at-six-a.m. way.

"Take it down a notch, Olympian," she chides before kissing me softly. "It's just Kell. She's clearly been out canoodling."

I kiss her back but keep my eyes open, kicking up a brow. "'Canoodling'?"

"It's what she does. But back to what *we* were doing. Something about pretend sand . . . and having my way with you . . . "

I let her kiss me once more, but I still can't relax into her desire. Something—instinct, sixth sense, premonition, whatever—eats at my libido. Something about the rhythm of the footsteps out in the living room. Footsteps that don't track toward Kell's bedroom . . . or even the kitchen.

"Kara? You awake?"

I breathe a little easier. Okay, it *is* Kell.

"*Kara*."

Holy shit. *That's* not. But I recognize the voice instantly.

"Kara!" Veronica Valari's repetition seems to push at the walls themselves. "I need to see you out here. Now."

CHAPTER 2

Kara

THE BEST THING ABOUT seeing my mother at this hour is that Z is standing right beside her. For all Maximus's doubts, for everything he's feeling about this man that's far from resolved, Z's presence here gives me hope. My mother's icy stare adds to my surety that he's found a way out of this mess. She wouldn't look so miserable otherwise.

Her arms are folded tightly across her chest, accentuating her heavy bust through the leopard fabric of her blouse. Silence hangs in the room like the early morning fog. Except this is more eerie than peaceful.

Kell shifts on her feet, her gaze fixed on some imaginary point of interest outside. Everything about her posture betrays her guilt.

"You told her I was here," I utter with bitter resignation.

Her eyes are wide and dark, nearly a mirror of my own. "It wasn't like that."

"I only asked for a little time to lay low," I remind her.

"Lay low? After the warhead button you've pushed?" my mother scoffs, hiking one of her etched black brows. "Besides, there were only so many places to look, darling." She utters the last word with sugary sweetness that doesn't match the rest of her tense posture. "You haven't been answering my calls, which simply isn't like you." She lifts her gaze, narrowing it on the man beside me. Her regard slides south of Maximus's waist before her nostrils flare slightly. "At least you have discriminating tastes, Kara. He could have been human."

Z answers with a low chuckle as he casually paces the living room, curiously checking out the decor. "That's my boy." The perusal and the remark feel like an invasion.

I don't know whether to feel defensive or downright embarrassed by the conversation. "I don't see how it matters, all things considered."

"Oh, darling. It *matters*."

"Why?" I bite back.

"Maximus is a demigod," she says, unfolding her arms haughtily. "It's not good, but it changes things."

"What things?" My voice wavers, giving away the worry that's been plaguing me every hour since I broke my vow. "Are they coming for me?"

Maximus catches my hand in his, warm and possessive. I yearn to tuck in closer to him but don't dare.

"I've managed to work something out with Arden." My mother tucks her short black hair behind her ear, her expensive bracelets tinkling with the motion. "Though you left him in quite a *mood* when you ran off the other night. I had no idea how taken he was with you already."

Maximus tightens his grasp, shifting himself in front of me a fraction, as if he can protect me from the mere mention of my betrothed.

"He's not coming anywhere near her."

"Why would he? She has nothing to offer him. You made sure of that," she snaps.

If this topic wasn't so awkward already, I'd correct her. Maximus didn't seduce me, unless the weeks in his class listening to him passionately read page after page of Dante counts. Of course, it was so much more than that. A thousand little moments that twined our souls, tighter and tighter, until I couldn't imagine giving myself to anyone else.

But none of it matters if I don't survive our relationship. Before this moment, I doubted that I would. But now, there's something about my mother's stance, something defined and different about her attitude, that infuses my spirit with real hope.

"So what does this mean? Are we safe?"

"As for Maximus, I pulled some strings at the university. They've agreed to let the matter go." She levels an even stare at the man I adore. "You should be able to start back on Friday, Professor."

A whoosh of air spills from me. While the threat of having to pay the ultimate price for our affair has weighed on me, so has the prospect that Maximus would lose everything he's worked so hard for because I couldn't stay away. His livelihood. His passion.

"Does that mean . . ." I'm afraid to even ask, but the

relief singing through my veins and flowing into my hopeful heart is too much to resist. "Can I go back too?"

My mother's nostrils twitch again. "You can. For now."

I can't help the broad smile taking over my face.

"For now?" Maximus's question cuts through the elated moment.

My mother interjects before I can explain. "Kara agreed to quit her studies at Alameda. To protect you and your career, of course. We couldn't have the two of you creating any more newsworthy scenes. Someone had to go. It was her or you."

Maximus's expression is torn with confusion. "Kara, why didn't you tell me?"

I turn in to him, mold my palm over his pectoral, and stare up into his tortured gaze. "It didn't matter. Nothing mattered," I whisper. Nothing but Maximus and the night I thought would be my last.

"Kara." My mother's sharp tone severs our connection, pulling my attention back to her. "This isn't sentimental. Sending you back to Alameda has nothing to do with my approval or lack of it—and everything to do with your ultimate safety."

"I don't understand."

"Being seen together before threatened to destroy the path you were born for. Had Maximus been a mere mortal, I doubt there's anything I could have done to protect you. You could say we're in limbo until this is sorted out, but we might be able to use the visibility to our advantage."

Maximus laughs roughly. "Visibility? As in, having a

relationship in the public eye?"

Z halts his pacing. "That's exactly what she means."

"But . . . isn't that dangerous?" I ask.

Z shrugs. "Call it PR. Call it *politics*. And sure, while you're at it, you could call it a Hail Mary."

My eyes bulge at that. "Excuse me?"

"Think of it this way," he goes on. "Disobedient subjects are easier to dispose of when very few know they even exist. Extinguish the problem. Poof." He snaps his fingers, causing tiny snaps of electricity to leap from them. "You, Kara, are a Valari—which means you have the unique ability to position yourself directly under the limelight. And until this is resolved, the limelight is the safest place you can be. If anyone makes a move, all eyes are on you. On both of you, in fact."

I disconnect from Maximus's embrace and step toward Z. I'm struggling for words. While I should be grateful for the advantage fate has given Maximus and me, I'm still reaching for some reasonable argument that will let us go about our lives peacefully. Something better than the media spectacle I've grown up in. "Please. There has to be another way. Can't we just stay under the radar for a while longer? Until you work things out?"

Z tugs on the collar of his pale-blue shirt, which perfectly matches the brilliance of his eyes. "Like Veronica said, we're in limbo at the moment."

"You said you'd make calls," I remind him more accusingly than I probably have the right to.

"I have and I will. My brothers and I, we're due for a

family reunion. There's a reason why people organize these dreadful things. Too much time goes by, things get lost in translation. Grudges go deeper. People take the rules a touch too seriously. We just need to clear the air is all."

"If it's that simple—"

"It's not simple at all," he replies with the quick confidence of a god who knows everything. "But nothing ever is. In the entire history of time, not a single thing has ever been simple. This I can promise you."

I release a tense sigh. "And you really think this will work?"

"Darling," my mother chimes in, "there's nothing I do better than publicity. The good, the bad, and the ugly. If it's a media frenzy we need to whip up to keep the gods at bay, I'm the best person for the job."

I pause to take in her promises and her determination, even wrapped in her arrogance. "Why would you help me?"

She winces. "Are you seriously asking me that?"

"The last time we spoke, your designs for my life were very different. You were pushing me out of Alameda, forbidding me from seeing Maximus ever again, forcing me onto Arden—"

"My purpose here has never been to ensure your happiness. It's always been secondary to your safety, to setting you on the path you were meant for. You defied me, but here I am once again, doing what I need to do to keep you safe. I'm not standing here in defense of love and romance. To hell with all of that nonsense. I'm doing this because you're my daughter, and I won't have you taken from me."

She exhales her breath with a soft hiss. "At least not without a fight."

I have to measure my own breaths. They're nearly painful from the unexpected emotion sawing through me. All this time, I never thought she cared that much for me. But perhaps we've simply been seeing the world differently—focusing on such divergent things that I discounted her love. Maybe she couldn't offer me the warmth and sweetness one might expect from a mother. But for all her biting words and self-absorption, there's something about her ready stance now that I can't ignore. Her teeth are bared slightly, and she has the distinct look of a feral creature ready to attack to protect her young.

Though we've rarely seen eye-to-eye, I believe what I see now. I trust it. Enough to go along with this plan that defies all my instincts and shatters all my safety zones. A plan that will forever change Maximus's life too, because being associated with a Valari for more than a single news cycle will have implications he can't possibly understand now.

But we have no other choice. If this is the only plan, then I have to show up for it.

"What do we have to do?" I finally say.

"Well." My mother glances to Z briefly, then back to me. "You'll be seen together, obviously. And casually, with the rest of us too."

"And Arden . . . He's just going to let this go?" I hedge. "Just like that?"

My mother's lips purse slightly. "Not exactly."

"Meaning what?" I press.

"He obviously had his sights set on you, but in the end, we came to an agreement. He was able to readjust his expectations, given some perspective."

In the few seconds between taking in her subtle glance at Kell and my sister's nervous shifting, I piece it all together. With horror. With the teeth-baring fury that clearly runs through our demon veins.

"No!"

My mother's jaw tightens. "It was the only way."

"No," I growl it this time and step between the two women, taking a protective stance in front of my little sister. The moment I do, my shoulders are caught beneath her clamping hold.

"K-Demon," she rasps. "Please don't make this any worse—"

"Kell, this disaster isn't yours to fix."

My mother rolls her eyes. "You're being dramatic. Please. She could do far worse than Arden Prieto."

"He's a snake!"

"He's a demon, and he was promised something he now can never have. He's furious, and your existence hangs in the balance. What did you expect, Kara? That you could follow your heart and no one would have to face the consequences?"

"I didn't *expect* anything. I was born into this nightmare, forced to live under these laws against my will. So was she."

My mother huffs. "Well, if your grandfather hadn't—"

"If Gramps hadn't done what he did, none of us would be here making him pay for it. Right?"

She stiffens her spine, crosses her arms, all eyes on her. "We all have our part to play, don't we?"

"It's fine, Kara," Kell utters with a softness that betrays the lie on her lips.

I whip my stare back to her. "It's not fine."

"Yes, damn it. It *is*. I'm not like you." She swallows hard. "I'll do whatever I have to do. Especially if it buys you time."

CHAPTER 3

MAXIMUS

"WHY DON'T WE TAKE a drive?"

I battle, unsuccessfully, to hide my lack of enthusiasm about the suggestion from the man standing next to me. Z doesn't flinch, except for the higher tilt of his roguish grin. We're on the deck outside Kara and Kell's living room, isolated from the others, for now. The chilly morning fights to stick to the air, but in these hills, the Southern California sun is persistent. Its heat spreads rapidly across the stone slab beneath my bare feet.

But that's the only warm part of me.

I don't anticipate a de-thaw anytime soon, since the deep freeze stretches into the marrow of my bones and cells of my blood. All the visceral parts of me that are waging a war worse than the battles of the wrathful in the marshes of Styx. My spirit should be welded with relief and gratitude, but I can't stop thinking of Veronica Valari's arrangement as an ultimatum instead of a solution. A mandate that—surprise, surprise—will likely brighten the gleam on her empire by a few million notches.

But bitterness is no good to me right now. No matter how strongly I yearn to race back inside, grab Kara, and whisk her away to a corner of the world where we'll never be found, I have to let logic prevail. That also means conceding to the reality of our situation. If we're to survive the underworld's backlash, maybe we do have to fight fire with fire. Even if that blaze is made of headlines, spotlights, and paparazzi flashes.

In short, it's my worst nightmare—though as soon as I look back inside, it's eclipsed in the space of one breath. There's a plate of glass separating Kara and me, but our gazes lock in sublime synchronicity. At once, I notice the reflection of my face staring at hers. I don't recognize the man I see because he's never existed before. I'm beyond smitten. I'm devoted. Entirely fixated on her happiness and her safety.

Especially that.

So for now, I'm all-in with Mama Valari and her bold strategy. That also means upholding my promise to Z. It's time for quality father-and-son bonding time if I'm to believe what everyone around me seems to. That I'm the son of a god. The son of Zeus himself.

At the very least, this reunion should be interesting.

With gritted effort, I shift my regard back to the man who smiles at the burgeoning sunlight as if he created the giant fireball himself.

"A drive," I say. "You mean you can't snap your fingers

and transport us anywhere you want to go?"

He lifts a hand and turns it over. With a wiggle of his fingers, silvery light forms iridescent webs between them. "Always an option," Z returns. "But I've heard that taking a drive is a good excuse for talking things out."

"Is that what you want to do, then? Talk?"

"You'd rather stay here?"

"You're mistaking me for someone who wants to do any of this." I shrug. "Guess I just had different expectations."

His return expression also walks the line between serious and humorous. "Like what?"

I eye him carefully and really debate just yanking the cork in the dam. To seriously tell him every thought barreling through my brain. But this isn't the time or place. The sooner I get this father-son visit over with, the better.

"Not important," I finally say. "So where are we going?"

"Also not important. Why don't we just get in the car and go?" He hones his gaze, as if he's trying to read me again. "Is there someplace special you want to go?"

Yes. The most remote place on earth. With the woman I'm leaving behind. On a day when she needs me most.

I shove the conviction aside. It's not constructive right now. It only reminds me of the torment that my sweet little demon must be enduring. She's escaped a lifetime beneath Prieto's thumb, only to have catapulted her sister to the same awful fate.

She's heartbroken. Vulnerable. I shouldn't be leaving her.

But I must.

I'm bitter about that, and it's impossible to sift every

note of that from my voice. "Someplace special? You mean like a park where you never played catch with me, or the schools where you weren't around for ice cream social nights. Someplace like that?"

Z curls his fingers back into his palm. The result isn't exactly a fist, but his new tension is palpable. "You're a little frustrated. I get that."

"Frustrated?" I shake my head. "I gave up on frustrated in fifth grade, okay?"

"Fine, then. Angry. Confused. I get those too. As a matter of fact, I share them."

"Thanks. That's so validating."

His soft, almost approving chuckle makes me feel strange things, but I push them away. I can't afford to bask in his pride right now. The temptation is ludicrous. Frivolous. The sooner Z gets what he wants from me, the faster I can be back at Kara's side.

"Let's get out of here," he says with a warm lilt. "Why don't you drive?"

I always feel a little better behind the wheel of my truck. Several minutes later, the silence that stretches between us until we're well into the suburban sprawl of Encino, Woodland Hills, and Calabasas is an added bonus.

Z finally cracks the air with his musing. "Markets of 'whole' foods. As if they'll be more complete with spirulina smoothies and grinding their own almond butter. Why don't more of them realize a walk in the sun and an afternoon orgasm will do the same thing?"

I want to laugh but don't. "Are you serious?"

"I'm serious, and I'm right."

No arguing with that one. If I had a choice about what to do with my day, it'd be a hike with Kara, my hand twined with hers, followed by hours of tangling our other body parts.

With piqued curiosity, I reply, "Surely you have the power to share this kind of wisdom. I mean, you're Zeus, right? Allfather of Olympus, chief of the gods, etcetera?"

"It doesn't work that way."

He sounds irked, which makes me more intrigued.

"So what way *does* it work? I mean, you can literally rule elements." And what a field day Jesse's going to have when I tell him. *If* I tell him. What little information I've already leaked has absolutely piqued his interest. The fire in Kara's eyes. Her grandfather's screenplays about demons and crawling back from hell. If he knew I was descended from someone powerful enough to spin the weather— "Holy shit," I whisper. "It wasn't just the other night. All those freak storms over the last couple of weeks." I tear my eyes from the road long enough to stare him down a moment. "That was you, wasn't it?"

"No." Z cocks a brow. "That was *you*."

My stunned silence and refocus on the road ahead is the only response I can manage.

"You're a creature of great passions, Maximus." He beams his intense stare at my profile. "You've simply been keeping it all under tight lock and key until now."

"No kidding." All over again, I marvel at how swiftly Kara has done just that—unlocked pieces of me I'd forgotten or refused to accept. But having control over the elements? I've let myself believe Z could do it, but accepting that I'd have a similar kind of control? That's another matter entirely. One I'm not fully comfortable with. Not even by half.

"Why have you kept yourself so pent-up all these years?"

His query is soft and sure, scraping at the edge of accusation. But I'm still too consumed by my curiosity.

"Last week, Kara and I were at the observatory. This storm came out of nowhere. If your logic is right about me, about my . . . passions . . . I get it, but Kell saw this crazy constellation from their place when it rolled in."

"Oh, *that* was me."

"Doing what?" My perplexity practically mashes the two words into one. "Stopping off in LA before heading out to seduce another unsuspecting mortal?"

For a second, he's visibly disturbed by my disdain. But I won't apologize. There are years of frustration behind it. Years of confusion, isolation, and desperate hope for my father's return, wondering how many questions he'd finally answer. Eventually, those were replaced by the other years. The ones filled with resigned anger—and, finally, grim acceptance.

Where *was* he?

As Z pulls in a long breath through his nose, I already know I'm not getting that answer so easily. "Perhaps it's best that we step back a bit here."

My knuckles go white against the steering wheel. It's a paltry show for the real storm that gathers beneath my breastbone and behind my frontal lobe. "Now you're beginning to sound like Mom."

As soon as the observation is out, my thoughts darken along with the gunmetal gray clouds that blow down from Hidden Valley, promising heavy rain. Mom's secrecy has been its own betrayal. Was Z complicit in it too? That would explain a lot but then crack open even more questions. I'm deeper in the dark than before.

"I loved your mother, Maximus." His declaration, firm and quiet, is oddly audible above the pelting drops on the windshield. "I still do."

"The same way you love every other female you set your sights on?"

"And now *you're* sounding like my wife."

"Maybe she's on to something."

"Or maybe she's a queen who thinks her crown is a free pass for cruelty."

No need to wonder if he's joking about that, because he clearly isn't. We hit some traffic, affording me the chance to assess his expression in more detail. What's nearly as unnerving as his sudden virulence is my new notice of certain features. The blue rings in his irises. The way his brows nearly meet as he scowls. Even the way he compresses his lips, pursing more than thinning. Traits I see in the mirror every morning.

He picks at the invisible lint on his slacks before breaking the silence again. "Look. I'm the king of a world so ancient, no one believes it's real anymore. The thrill of the conquest is one of the few interesting things I have left. Well, short of starting a war with one of my brothers—which wouldn't be pretty for all of your human friends."

"How so?"

The question falls out before I can examine the wisdom—or not—of asking. Z doesn't seem so troubled.

"Because we can't contain the violence to our realms. So bad things happen in yours."

"Bad things? Like what?"

When Z's initial reaction is a soft snort, the hairs on the back of my neck comprehend his chilling inference.

"Let's just say that the world *thinks* Pompeii was wiped out by a volcano," he offers. "And that the Great Chicago Fire was due to Mrs. O'Leary's restless cow. We're most prone to causing earthquakes, though. Shensi, Damghan, Aleppo, and Kanto were all us. And a few of the more spectacular hurricanes—"

"Okay, okay," I cut in. "I got it." Especially while driving on a freeway within significant shaking distance of the San Andreas Fault.

Traffic picks up, and we travel a few more miles in silence that's not entirely awkward. As we start nearing the ocean again, Z returns to his inquisition. "Do you remember anything from your childhood? A single memory about where you lived before Los Angeles?" There's a hitch at the end of his query, like he has more to say. "Do you remember any of the time that you spent... with me?"

Damn. That's a major piece of more. I drum my fingers along the wheel, suddenly unsure about being stuck in the vehicle with him and this conversation. Except he has answers to questions I've been asking my whole life. I'm more sure of it than ever.

"I've never seen you before yesterday." *Dad*. I almost choke from how badly I want to add it, so I force myself to say something less biting. "I'm serious. Not until the second you walked into my apartment."

His silent reply doubles my tension. The deep grooves that create dark moguls in his forehead aren't any easier to witness. "I can't say that surprises me."

"Though it pisses you off."

"No." He braces an elbow to the window ledge and brings the back of his fist to his lips. "I'm not angry, son. I'm sad. And baffled."

"I think I'm missing part of the story here."

Though my eyes are on the road, his new stiffness is palpable enough in my periphery. "I may be a rake, a hothead, and a capricious son of a bitch, but one thing I am *not* is a bad father. And if you don't believe another word from me today, give credence to this. Your mother and you could have lived in a golden palace in Olympus, had she but asked. But she didn't, and I thought her happy with the home I did bestow to her for raising you, until—"

"What the hell are you telling me?" I demand through locked teeth, but Z meets my stare with the calm of a man who knows better than to respond. "Are you saying that before we moved to LA, we were living in the land of... what? The gods and goddesses?"

"Well... yes." Z lifts half a smile. "More or less, that's what I'm saying."

"More or less?" I cock a brow. "Which means what?"

"That Olympus isn't just 'gods and goddesses land,'" he explains. "It's also home to the titans, the muses, the graces, the demigods, and even a few elevated oracles." His grin inches up a bit more. "In many ways, it's just like LA. A melting pot of cultures."

"A melting pot of—" I stop short again, unable to speak when my thoughts are riding out a hurricane in my head. How can he be so casual about this? So accepting?

Maybe because . . . it's his truth?

Because he's telling *me* the truth?

"Fuck," I finally croak. The word stands in for the billion and one questions that crash my mind's servers. Until I can properly reboot, I'm just a blank screen of bewildered mush. Useless for much else.

Thankfully, Z seems to get it. In full. He gives me the pause, and then another, before saying, "You all right there? You need another minute?"

"No. I need a beer."

Maybe two.

Or ten.

If I'm seeing double by then, the world's greatest pop can drive me home. But I doubt any alcohol infusion is going to dull the jolt of whatever Z's got to tell me.

CHAPTER 4

"NOW WE HAVE TO sort out your schedule." My mother unsnaps her crocodile Stalvey handbag and retrieves her phone as if she didn't doom my sister to an eternity with a vicious demon moments ago.

I haven't stopped vibrating from the news. Meanwhile, Kell seems to have accepted it with frightening ease. At least that's what she's selling on the surface as she drops onto our sofa and pulls out her own phone.

"So, I made you reservations tonight at Yamashiro," my mother says quickly. "That should be subtle but definitely put you out there a little more. We can tip some people off that you'll be there. Just be prepared for it. Get caught in the photo storm on your way in, and have a car collect you out the back afterwards. Then Friday is Piper's premiere at the Chinese Theatre, so we *have* to do that. It'll be the perfect red carpet introduction for Maximus." She frowns suddenly. "He'll need some wardrobe help."

"He has a tux."

She hesitates. "Do you know the designer?"

"The man could be wearing the latest in brown paper bags and no one would care," Kell mutters.

"Oh, never mind." Mother scowls and flaps a hand. "I'll just send someone over to get his measurements and have some options delivered. We have time."

I force in a few deep breaths until I'm finally fortified enough to cut in, "Mother, please just—"

"Don't *Mother, please* me, Kara. I know what I'm doing, and you know enough to let me. He has to look the part, or those reporters will rip you to shreds."

I ball my hands into tight fists, as if the concentrations of pressure might keep me from totally losing my shit right now. "But he's not *like* us."

She flashes me an unimpressed look from under her thick lashes. "He's not like *any* of us, sweetheart. But in the interest of keeping you from a fiery eternity down below, I'd suggest he start acting like he is. This is going to be a quiet week comparatively. We're just getting started—"

I raise my hand to shut her up. "Listen to me. He grew up downtown to a single mom who worked more hours than she didn't. His life then, and honestly now, could not be more different than ours. No level of pretending and no amount of wardrobe help is going to change that reality."

She rotates a thin stylus through her fingers a few times before pointing it at me. "I like that. Handsome intellectual with modest upbringing falls for his famous student. It's very reverse Cinderella. I can work with that." She taps a few more notes into her phone. "So we'll keep it understated but sophisticated."

I exhale an exasperated sigh and look to Kell. She shrugs with her usual resignation. Maybe my sister is right—she isn't like me. At all. I don't know what that says about either of us. I could never manage to feel comfortable in a life that demanded such public displays of wealth and celebrity. She's always acted like she was born for this. At least born to tolerate it. At the moment, I wish some of that knack would seep into me by osmosis. Even just for a few weeks. Long enough to get me through the storm to come.

"Speaking of that modest upbringing, you should definitely schedule some appearances at his place."

My mother's comment has me gaping back at her.

"And be sure to wear some of your vintage pieces when you do. Sustainable is the new black, you know. The paps will be delirious. Oh!" Her dark eyes brighten and her lips form a plush *O*. "The farmer's market in Pershing Square. What day is that?"

"Wednesday, I think," Kell supplies in her bored monotone.

"Perfect. That'll be a nice midweek sighting. And so very domestic. If there's any question you're serious about each other, that should remove all doubt. If you're going to a farmer's market together, you're practically married already."

I press my fingertips to my throbbing temples and pray for patience.

With a soft and sympathetic look, Kell pats the cushion beside her. I take the invitation, plunk down, and stare at the ceiling while our mother prattles on about the rest of her plans for my week.

I remind myself that her heart is actually in the right place. She's hyper-focused on my safety and protecting me by doing what she does best. I pray again, beseeching the universe that Maximus will survive the chaos I've done my best to avoid, even if I've also grown adept at handling it over the years. But this is another world for him. I'm terrified of what he'll think. How he'll react.

If he'll stay.

"Saturday might be a little tricky..."

At my mother's hesitant tone, I dip my stare back to hers. "I'm afraid to ask."

She crosses her arms and flickers a brief look to Kell. "Well, it's a university event."

"Another one?" I tilt my head, openly dazed. They've hardly finished taking down the decorations from Conquistador Crush.

"It's exclusive this time," she explains. "Smaller and off-campus. A private dinner with the president and select guests at her estate, which I hear is stunning. They're fundraising for the art center. It'll be an important finale to your coming-out week with Maximus. I'll be there, of course, so there will be some press. It'll fully validate your affair. With all of us there, you'll essentially be getting the university's public stamp of approval."

For a long second, I don't say anything. Though I hate the sound of it at first, I like the idea of Maximus having a clean slate with the university after this circus is over. I'll jump through whatever hoops are necessary to reinstate his good name at Alameda.

"That sounds manageable," I admit at last. "What's so tricky about it?"

"Arden will be there," she says, clutching the tip of her stylus between her canines.

But she's not uneasy on my account. This has to do with Arden and everything she's done to appease him. Offering my sister to him should be enough, but I'm sure it's not. The mere thought of Kell's inevitable sacrifice sends a fresh shot of hot rage through my veins.

I straighten my posture. "No."

My mother tips her head to the side. "Kara."

"You expect things to go well with Maximus and Arden in the same room?"

"Well, no. Arden's understandably furious. But we're about to be family—at least if this all goes well for you—so we'll need to rip the Band-Aid off eventually. Plus, if there *does* happen to be a certain degree of drama, I can always work with it. Imagine . . . Successful art dealer and penniless professor fighting over Kara Valari." She smirks. "It'll do wonders for Kell's social accounts, with her being caught in the middle of it all. Uh, I love it!" She drops her phone back into her purse with a satisfied sigh. "If that doesn't keep the gods' heads spinning, I don't know what will."

"Thanks, Mom," Kell says with a forced smile.

Our mother walks to her, her heels clicking on the marble, and bends to give her a kiss on the cheek. "You're welcome, dear. I'll be in touch." She straightens and points to me. "And you'd better start picking up your phone, young lady. We have a busy week. I can't keep chasing you down like this."

I nod wordlessly. I'm not sure I'm capable of anything more than stunned silence after this morning. Still, there is hope in this situation now, where before there was nothing but grim anticipation. Slivers of it are caught between otherwise terrible circumstances. Worst of all, Kell's. I can't seem to dislodge her dilemma from my thoughts—or my soul. I feel like a rabbit that's dodged a wolf, only to turn around and see the beast has sunk its teeth into someone truly dear to me.

I have to help stop the bleeding. No matter how helpless I feel about it now.

When I turn, I'm almost taken aback. My sister's simply thumbing through her social feed, seemingly lost in the glare of technology.

"Hey," I venture softly . . . timidly.

"Hmm?" Kell's still only half here. Or so she wants me to think.

"Are you okay?"

"I'm fine. Why?"

I tilt my head. "Kell . . . Mom's gone. You can cut the act."

She finally looks up. "I'm fine, okay? We knew this was coming."

"Not with Arden, we didn't."

"Kara—"

"This is my fault."

"*Kara.*"

"You have every right to be furious with me." I pause a beat, debating whether to voice the plan that's already been forming in my brain. "We need to figure out a way to get you out of this."

Her laugh is dry, maybe even bitter. "Just stop there, okay? They're not going to let us both off the hook. And I doubt Zeus has any more sons in LA. If you find out differently, let me know. I'll be more than happy to seduce one of those fine boys into getting me out of this."

"I didn't seduce Maximus."

At once I regret the defensiveness in my tone, but I'm finding it hard to hold much back lately. Especially with Kell. For the first time in my life, I almost feel like I could trust her with every confidence. Almost.

Which is why I still keep a few thoughts to myself. In the deepest, darkest parts of myself.

Did I actually seduce Maximus?

Maybe. But only a little . . .

Kell releases a tired sigh and traces the piping along the sofa's arm. "Whatever. Doesn't really matter, right? He's obviously madly in love with you. I doubt I could pull that off as quickly anyway."

That renders me quiet, because acknowledging that she could be right aloud is its own kind of terrifying. All my life, I never imagined love was in the cards for me. If I'd been forced into Arden's bed, forced to give him children, I'm certain love would have nothing to do with it. Hell, maybe that's why my mother wants no part of the stuff. She's all instinct now, no sentimentality.

But with Maximus, I'm starting to think it's possible. In those blissful moments when we were tangled up in his bed, whispering promises and adorations, and when we were so lost to our passions we were no longer ourselves, I almost let myself believe our connection could be love.

The perilousness of our situation should make it easier to confess everything he makes me feel. But I can't bring myself to say the words or even take stock in them. Because with all our tomorrows so uncertain, what if loving him is the most selfish thing I could possibly do? What if saying the words means he'll start loving me back? Worse, what if he *doesn't* say it back?

There's an answer that's easy to grasp.

Because it's too soon and this has been such a crazy pace of feeling and passion and risking everything to have more of it.

But would I have made the sacrifice for any other reason? If I didn't love him, how could I have come this far with him . . . and he with me?

"What's he like?"

Kell's question has me blinking out of my frenzied thoughts. "Maximus?"

"No, dummy. Arden. I met him at the fundraiser at Alameda, but it was really brief. I have no idea what he's like. And we're having dinner tonight, so I'd appreciate knowing what I'm getting into."

I clench my jaw, biting back the hateful things I truly want to say. I'm not giving up on getting Kell out of this, but if she's resigned to her fate with him already, maybe painting him in the worst possible light isn't the best choice. I struggle to isolate his best qualities. Or even one.

"He's not hard to look at."

She grins. "I gathered that for myself."

"All right, well . . . you obviously can't trust him."

Her dark brows draw together. "In what ways?"

All of them.

That stays inside. Aloud, I phrase it more diplomatically. "He's smart," I tell her. "Dangerously smart and dangerously perceptive. I honestly don't think there's any outmaneuvering him, so remember that. Everything is strategic. A power play or careful negotiation, whether you realize that's the game you're playing or not."

Remarkably, her posture relaxes. "Okay. That's . . . interesting."

"And he'll know when you're lying."

She lifts a curious brow. "Really?"

"You can sniff out what people are feeling, and I guess he's got a built-in lie-detector or something. You'd never know it, though. He's that calculating. He never called me out on it a single time until he told me why he was here."

"For you . . . "

I nod. "For me."

"I know you despise him, but there must have been something about you that truly interested him."

"I certainly didn't encourage him."

"Then what *did* you do?"

I shrug. "Nothing. I was just . . . me."

I lock my stare with hers. Kell wants to know what makes him tick. Maybe I need to give her exactly what she's asking for.

"Between us, he thinks our mother is vapid and shallow."

Kell winces. "Well, she is. Someone doesn't need to be wildly perceptive to pick up on that."

"Fair enough, but I get the impression he's not a fan, even if he can use her bad taste to his advantage with the work he does. The whole endeavor with building the collections was a joke to him." I weigh my next words. "All I'm saying is whether you want him to like you more, or like you less, maybe keep it in mind."

She stares at me for a long moment. "So you're saying if I play dumb, he'll see right through it."

"Exactly." I don't have to hesitate about that one.

"And then he'll hate me for it."

"Or worse." Or that one either.

She pulls in a long breath. I'm glad to watch it. For the first time, I'm detecting her serious care in considering the incubus she's now destined to exchange vows with. I want to hope that she and Arden will come to a friendly arrangement with each other, but her healthy respect for his domineering side will only help my headstrong sister in the long run.

"Look, Kell," I say after a long pause. "I just don't want you to get hurt. And if he's as upset as Mom says . . . "

"I can handle it."

"All right," I say, merely as a placation, while praying like crazy that she can. But I'm terrified she can't. More that she'll hate me for putting her in this position before she's ready. Before she's due to give up life as she knew it to serve a relentless demon and his ferocious whims.

But everything about the way she says it, down to the confident set of her shoulders, makes me believe she can.

CHAPTER 5

MAXIMUS

"BEER. NOW THERE'S A good plan."

I swear not to make too much out of the warmth brought on by my father's compliment as I exit the freeway just before San Buenaventura Beach. "I know a great place," I say.

"Great. So do I."

"Yeah, but mine's right on the water."

"Crazy coincidence." He dots that with a single snap of his fingers. "So's mine."

And my truck is no longer heading up the access road along the Ventura sand.

It's stopped. And parked. Right on the sand. But on what beach, I'm not sure. Nothing looks familiar. There are no lifeguard stands, surfers' showers, or seaside snack shacks for reference either.

What there is . . . is a bar, just like he promised. But this place looks like no local joint I've ever laid eyes on before. Not that I'm the expert in the new and hip Southern California hangouts, but I surely would have heard about this one through Jesse, who is. From first glance, it's a sleek building of contemporary lines, neutral paint blocks, and natural wood accents. Tropical flowers are well-kept in box planters, and a dozen species of palms provide shade. An open-air patio overlooks the sand.

Inside, things are a much different story. It's like the Parthenon and Atlantis invited Las Vegas in for a three-way, and this is the oddly beautiful child that happened. Greek columns surround luxury seating areas. A gilded bar wraps around a giant tube of multicolored fire. Past the main room, a wide patio stretches along a huge saltwater fountain, where dolphins and tropical fish are swimming freely.

It's almost humanly impossible to take it all in. For once, I take solace in the new reality that I'm not entirely human.

The early October sun, still situated where it should be in the sky that hasn't changed, gleams on the water as we enter the main lounge. The place is relatively uncrowded. Z and I grab a couple of barstools, though we've definitely caught the attention of every eye in the place before the bartender strolls up.

"Your *Majesty*," he says, beaming a smile from the midst of a white-gold beard. His long hair, as well as the suns, moons, stars, and flames tattooed along his dark hickory arms, are the same arresting color. "Welcome back. Labyrinth has missed you."

"Honey, you know the drill." Z removes his hat and

shakes back the thick mop on his own head. "Cut the 'Majesty' nonsense if you know what's good for you."

The guy kicks up a bushy blond brow. "Understood. Wouldn't want you to embarrass me in front of my newest customer." He turns his focus to me, looking me over with unabashed curiosity. "Name's Honey. What can I get you, buddy?"

I hesitate. "Honey?"

His barrel laugh confirms it before his words do. "Honey Bacchus. Proprietor of this fine establishment for three thousand years." He offers me his hand. "And you are?"

"Doesn't matter." Z's interjection is a command couched in gentility, though he has to realize that the man is already parsing the truth. "We'll have two pints of Medusa's Revenge."

Honey dips his head and walks off to pour our brews while my thoughts battle to stick to the mold of my brain. My logic struggles to grasp the simple basics right now—like time and reality.

It's official. I've had some crazy days in my life, but the top prize now goes to the last twenty-four hours. This little field trip, to the bar of all cocktail bars, has been the clincher.

"What is this place? Some sort of watering hole for the gods?"

Z smirks. "Something like that."

As Honey brings us the beers, I entertain a small hope that the fragrant wheat liquid will, for once, soothe the edge on my nerves. But I'm not expanding those expectations. "Pleasantly buzzed" is a term in everyone else's vocabulary, not mine. Apparently I can add "only human" and "merely mortal" to that list now too.

Am I any of those things anymore? Human? Mortal? Even a man?

Was I ever?

The most reliable source for my answers is sitting on the barstool next to mine, filling a long moment by grimacing at his beverage.

"What's wrong?" I mutter.

"Not to sound like an entitled god on high, but under different circumstances, I'd have ordered some of Honey's special nectar from the back."

"So why didn't you?"

He rubs his fingertips together, causing subtle sparks, but halts as quickly as he's started. "As I said, different circumstances. Another time, I promise. As for now . . . I assume you want to remember this conversation."

I snort softly. It's not a full laugh but enough to convey the sentiment. "That'd be nice, considering the prologue you dropped back on the freeway."

Z pushes his mug away. The free counter space gives him room to park his elbows and fold his hands. He's well-practiced at the commanding pose, as if he's had thousands of years perfecting it. "Maybe we should start with what you already know."

"You mean next to nothing?" I copy his position, cradling my mug between my hands.

He sits with that for a few seconds. It doesn't seem to surprise him, nor do I expect it to. "Has your mother told you anything about me, then?"

"Her story is that you met in Egypt while she was there doing humanitarian work. She didn't realize she was pregnant with me until you'd both gone your separate ways, and she never saw you again."

He makes a small snort of acknowledgment. "That's *almost* true."

"Almost? Okay... Which part?"

It spills from me more like a demand than a request. I don't pause to apologize. The pressure in my senses is too intense. Under the painful sting of having to accept that Mom has been lying to me for nearly ten years, I yearn for the details she never gave me. Everything Z already knows.

My origins. My truth.

My *identity*.

"We did meet in Egypt." He reaches out to wipe some dew off his mug thoughtfully. "It was one of those moments that's incredibly brief but somehow lasts forever. A permanent imprint on a person's soul."

He glances over for a second, almost as if he needs my reassurance that he's not sounding crazy. He doesn't. I know that now, with just two seconds of remembering the moment I first touched Kara.

Not wanting to interrupt his reminiscing, I simply give him a silent nod, wordlessly urging him to continue.

"She'd just landed in Cairo days prior and had ventured out from the hotel she was staying at. Our paths crossed in the marketplace. Me being me, I asked her out for a drink the second I laid eyes on her. She was shy but accepted." He winks with a crooked smirk. "I can be very charming."

"I've heard." I swallow down another gulp of my beer, preparing to scrub the image of my young mother being seduced from the story once I hear it.

"One bottle of *Cru des Ptolmees* turned into two," he goes on. "We drank the second one in the park after night fell. The gardens were quiet. The sky was clear. The air smelled like jasmine. And we talked all night." He exhales softly. "Well . . . we talked most of the night."

I finish my beer, hoping he'll skip over the finer details of my conception.

"So . . . that was it?" I query into his pause filled with simplicity and complexity in the same three seconds. "One night of passion, and then you disappeared?"

He frowns. "You're determined to think the worst of me, aren't you?"

I let out a dry laugh. "I'm just trying to piece this together, Z. You were there one minute, and then you weren't."

His scowl deepens. "And I can understand what that must look like, from the outside."

"Damn right, from the outside." I'm able to keep the words even. I have no idea how. I've been "on the outside" of this whole story for as long as I can remember.

At last, he pushes on.

"After a couple of days, some serious safety concerns came up for their group—so the authorities had her team transferred to a new location."

"Did she tell you about it?"

"Of course." He keeps meeting my gaze, barely blinking. "We could barely stand to be apart," he adds in a husky murmur. "I followed her to Alexandria without thinking twice. But once I knew she was safe and settled again, I had to return home to attend to some other matters."

"Home," I echo. "To Olympus?"

"Yes."

"For some 'other matters.'" I'm terse.

"Yes." He's terser.

"Like what?"

His lips thin. "It's not relevant now. But I did try to get back to your mother. You need to know that. By the time I could get back, Nancy had left the program. Like I said, everything happened quickly. She wasn't in the country more than a month."

Another pause that's thick with so much meaning, I'm surprised we're in a mystically shrouded bar and not a crumbling manmade church. The juxtaposition aside, I'm compelled to accept his account. So far, Z's confession isn't remarkably different than my mother's.

The realization brings on some new confusion. "You said her version was almost true," I remind him.

"Indeed I did."

"So . . . what's so drastically divergent here?"

"She told you she never saw me again."

Which brings us back to the revelation that floored me moments ago. The one that accounted for the nothingness of my childhood memories.

"Let me guess," I venture. "She left out that eight-year

stint in Olympus. Because I sure as hell never heard about that."

He steeples his hands in a moment of contemplation. "In a number of ways, I understand her secrecy. It's not exactly easy to explain all that to a young boy, especially because it seems your memories of those years have been blocked or wiped, but there'd also be nothing to explain had she stayed."

"Why didn't she?"

He lifts his brows. "I'd love to ask her the same question."

I tense. Everywhere. My shoulders. My gut. I look down to where my hand clenches my mug, threatening to shatter the thing. But I need the liquid too badly. My throat is dry from rampaging nerves. The thought of getting Z and my mother in the same room is concerning. But also oddly intriguing.

"You'd want that? To see her again?"

His face changes in a different way. His irises sharpen, ice on steel. "Why wouldn't I?"

"It doesn't sound like you were exactly on good terms if she snuck out of Olympus to get away from you."

"Who said she was trying to get away from me?" His eyes narrow with concern, maybe even real fear that my mother left for that very reason.

"Valid question." I look down again, wondering why my mind went to that explanation first. But that answer feels too complicated to delve into. Not right now.

I finish my beer and exhale a tired sigh. We've not even been here an hour, and I'm drained as a damn dishrag.

Who knew filling in the gaps of my past would be so complicated... and exhausting? On the other hand, my past isn't exactly the stuff of a standard fill-in-the-blank.

"If nothing else, I suppose she'll have to come clean once and for all," I say. "To both of us."

"Maybe your mother isn't the refreshingly honest woman with whom I was first smitten," he says. "But there might be another explanation."

"Such as?"

"My brother."

I wince. "Poseidon?"

He sighs calmly. "It seems he's twisted his trident deeper into my business than I thought. I can't put the blame squarely on her, even if she was complicit in stealing you away."

"Why would he meddle in this?"

"I'm not sure, but I intend to find out." He downs the last of his drink, glaring at the loud waves crashing into the sand as he does.

"I think Mom's covering," I declare bluntly. "But not because she wants to. It's like she's been compelled to." I grimace, already hating how ridiculous that sounds. "Like she's... afraid."

I hope to hell she's not afraid of Z. My trepidation swells when his irises darken. His casual demeanor seems to solemnify.

"If she'd been made to feel afraid," he says, his words low and measured, "trust that I'll be getting to the bottom of it soon enough. What's done is done. But now that I've found you, I'll be damned if I'm going to let anyone keep you from me again. We've already lost too much time."

For a long second, I'm just as unmoving as him. How many times have I had daydreams about a moment like this, drenched in the intensity of my father's pride and possessiveness? It's here now, feeling just as awesome as I've hoped—but a thousand times more awkward.

He seems to take in some of the meaning in my silence. His gaze is filled with scorching blue strength as he leans in, unflinching now. "No matter what she says, no matter what she's told you or hasn't, you're my son. Nothing can change it. I *know* you. Better than any mortal ever will."

His declaration—and its implications—hit me harder than possibly anything ever has.

I'm really his son.

His demigod offspring.

The phrase resonates through my senses, turning the moment into something surreal. My nerve endings crackle. My equilibrium is my enemy. I seek out focal points to banish it. The wind along the deck outside. The rhythm of the waves against the sand. The core of my own heartbeat...

Which brings me the answer I need most.

The person I need most.

The single creature in this universe who, in all her half-demon perfection, will restore my humanity better than anything or anyone else right now.

No matter what's happened in my past, no matter how unbelievable or tragic or strange, Kara's the future. *My* future. She's the one who's unlocked all of this. She's turned my curses into something I can live with. Something I can embrace.

And as much as I crave more answers from Z, something tells me he won't be hard to track down.

"We should head back," I say.

He sighs loudly. "Good idea. I have a feeling Veronica Valari has big plans for you this week."

I stifle an answering groan. Barely. "Can't wait."

He grins. "If it buys you a lifetime with your little devil, I'd say it's worth it, wouldn't you?"

I nod without thinking. I don't have to for this one. I'll do anything to have Kara safe. To earn more days with her. To have a lifetime with her... The possibility makes my breath snag painfully in my chest, but it's a welcome discomfort. I don't have to ponder how much I already want it. I just know. The way I know it'll rain. The way I know how incomplete I feel without her by my side. The way I knew, from the moment we touched, that she was going to change me forever.

CHAPTER 6

"WHERE HAVE YOU BEEN?"

The second the words fly out of my mouth, I cringe at how they sound. Frazzled and desperate and panicked. All things I feel but nothing that Maximus deserves to be on the receiving end of.

He halts, seemingly frozen in the doorway despite the late-afternoon sun beaming in from behind him. His eyes are tired and his hair is wild and windblown. He smells like the ocean, ramping my curiosity higher. At the moment, it's a welcome break from my worry, allowing me to indulge the gratitude that he's finally here.

He finally steps inside fully, shutting the front door behind him. "I was with Z. You knew that."

He comes a few steps closer, and I can feel his exhaustion. It brushes against my own weariness, making it heavier. Making this whole day feel like it's already been a week. I twist a lock of my hair tightly around my finger, wishing I could roll things back thirty seconds and give him a better hello than this. Except it's too late.

"You were gone a long time. I was worried, and—"

Before I can explain the nonstop commotion that began the moment my mother started to commandeer our lives this morning, one of her assistants, Natalie, appears from the guest bedroom. Her eyes light up when she spots Maximus.

"Oh, great. You're here. Perfect timing. The stylist just finished steaming all the new wardrobe pieces."

Maximus answers with a slow blink. "Stylist . . . for what?"

"It's just for dinner tonight," I rush to explain. "And a few other events that Mom wants us to show up to this week."

"Okay." His acquiescence is slow, still unveiling his confusion. "So where are we going for dinner? Is it like black tie or something?"

"No, it's nothing like that. It's just . . . "

"Then what's wrong with this?" He waves a hand over his current attire—though my hungry gaze hardly needs the prompt to go wandering.

Kell wasn't wrong. Not by a single syllable. Maximus Kane, my devastating demigod, looks incredible in anything. His department-store T-shirt and well-worn jeans show off his stunning V of a torso and long, chiseled legs. But his seashore-messy allure is definitely not the accidentally-on-purpose, casual-but-expensive look Mom wants. I can already hear her snipping about it in my head, a preview of what she'll be dishing out tomorrow morning if we step out in the wrong look tonight.

"Nothing." My voice is high and taut, exposing the little lie. "Just humor me, okay?"

I take his hand and lead him to the other room. Before I can explain any more, Natalie tugs him toward the stylist who's already sliding garments back and forth along a hanging rack.

I check my watch. "We have ten minutes before the car gets here."

Maximus pivots toward me with a wide-eyed look. "The car?"

"I figured we'd get a driver for tonight." I force a smile, hoping it looks genuine.

"I can take us in my truck—"

"No, that's okay. It'll be easier this way."

"Why?"

His voice carries a slight bite. The man isn't slow. It's one of the reasons I've fallen so fast for him. But it's also why tension creeps deeper through my veins, rising along with his. He's starting to get it. "Just dinner" isn't going to be *just* dinner.

But there's no time to give him a full primer. Natalie and the stylist are already buzzing around him, plucking at his hair and *thwick*ing measuring tapes along his body. For the first time today, I have a welcome distraction from my anxiety. But I also know I've been saved from further inquisition, so I wave off his query and take the opportunity to escape.

I find my purse in the kitchen and am in the middle of texting the driver when Kell saunters by in her favorite stilettos. She's dressed to kill in a skintight cream bandage dress. My jaw falls.

"You're meeting Arden in *that*?"

She smirks. "I can't have him thinking he got stuck with the ugly duckling, can I?"

I get her point, but I'm not reassured. Not by a long shot. "You're sure this is the right strategy? After everything I've told you about him?"

"No, but you said he'll see right through my tricks. So I figured why not turn the volume up instead?"

I answer with a half shrug, half nod, wondering how much extra volume Kell will have to deliver to throw Arden off and give her some power to manage this new relationship with him.

Who knows? Maybe she's onto something.

She leans her hip against the counter and looks me over. "How about you? You sure the professor is ready for the real storm?"

I shake my head. "Not even sure I am. But it's only a week, right? We can survive a week."

Her stare is flat. Her normally expressive nose gives nothing away. "A week, huh?"

"Sure. That should be enough time . . . "

Unless it's not. Unless this turns into our new reality. Our *normal*.

The sound of shoes scuffing across the floor pulls me from that particularly worrisome thought. When I turn,

Maximus appears—six feet, seven inches of dangerously good-looking demigod in crisp new threads. Slacks that hug every important part of his legs. A heather-gray long-sleeved tee that looks spun just for him out of angel sighs.

I know how they feel.

I mean, I would sigh . . . if there was any air left in my lungs. Or oxygen in my blood. Or awareness in my senses . . . beyond acknowledging the sensory miracle of him.

"What?" he says, responding to my plummeting jaw as if sound has emerged. Remarkably, it does. At least one word.

"Wow," I stammer.

"Oooh," Kell coos, crossing the room and then circling him. "Don't you look the part?" She trails her finger over the shoulders of the blond wool topcoat he's now sporting atop the T-shirt.

He shifts restlessly, his anxiety radiating through the room in hot, angry pulses. The subtle twitch of Kell's nostrils tells me she knows it too.

"Kell," I warn.

She answers with a short hum and says, "Have a good night, lovebirds." Then she removes her touch and saunters out of sight toward her room.

Maximus fixes his gaze on me. His jaw is tight, like maybe he's keeping all his present thoughts strapped down for the moment. I should ask him if he's all right or how his day with Z was, but I worry if I do, we might never get out of here.

The doorbell chimes, saving me just in time. I force

another smile. "That's the driver. Time to go."

Seconds later, we're ushered into the back of a black SUV and on our way. With the privacy divider raised, it's already the most calm I've had all day. I rest back against the headrest and release a weighty sigh.

As we head up Mulholland Drive and through the hills toward Hollywood Heights, Maximus mutters a curse while wrestling his coat off. He tosses it into the row of seats behind us. As he twists back around, our gazes tangle again. His is surprisingly apologetic, as if he's been caught in an honest moment.

"I run hot," he says, pushing up the sleeves of his shirt. "Not to mention, this is LA. Who the hell needs a wool coat?"

I can't help the smile that forms or the laugh that bubbles up from my chest. A much-needed break in the tension of the day. He returns the smile, also seeming to relax as he does.

"Sorry," he says, collecting my hand tenderly in the warmth of his. "I'm not trying to be difficult. I just wasn't expecting half of this."

"Believe me, neither was I. And I'm sorry too. I didn't mean to snap the second you got back. My head's been spinning all day."

"Something tells me when Veronica Valari lands on your doorstep at sunrise, that's to be expected."

I sigh again, relieved that he's being as understanding as he is. "It is, but you're not used to all this yet."

"Not exactly, but I'll do whatever I need to do." He

turns my hand over and presses a gentle kiss to my knuckles. "You're beyond worth it."

My pulse races. Or skips a bunch of beats. I'm not sure which, and I don't care. It's not the first time he's whispered the promise, so heartfelt and soul-deep. Though, in this moment, it's a stab. Not so much a comfort to me as a glaring reminder that he doesn't really get what he's signed up for with all this.

I just need to prepare him for the rest. No better time than with him captive in the car.

"You should know that tonight is a little more than dinner."

I carefully study him for a reaction. He's nothing but quiet calm, waiting for me to go on.

"This is about being seen in public."

"I know that already, beautiful," he assures me.

"It won't be like at the bookstore. Things are probably going to be a little more up close and personal, especially since being photographed is the point. Otherwise there'd be ways to get inside unnoticed."

He threads our fingers fully together now and draws his thumb back and forth over the top of my hand. "All right. I can handle that."

I hope he can. I hope the second he steps out of the car in front of Yamashiro, he doesn't regret this whole plan. I hope he doesn't regret me and the chaos that being with me has brought into his world.

He draws his brows together tightly, as if he can read the worry running endless loops through my brain.

"Kara, listen to me. I don't care what kind of circus your mother has planned. I'm sure it's going to test me in ways I can't even imagine, and that's fine. I just need to know it's still us under it all, no matter what kind of show we're putting on for the cameras."

"It will be, I promise. You don't have to act any differently around me. The whole point really is for the world to know we're—" I stop myself from finishing that thought, pretending to readjust my balance as the driver turns the car onto the steep hill up to the restaurant. The world needs to believe we're in love, but I'm not brave enough to voice those words yet. I take a deep breath, collecting myself. "We're telling the world that we're in a relationship now. We're still us, just in different clothes, showing up at strategic places in a very public fashion, with a driver who will be able to help us part the sea of photographers everywhere we go. But under all that"—I take another deep breath, partly to reassure myself—"it's still just you and me, Maximus."

"And the coat." He winks my way, clearly proud of his droll charm, while swooping the jacket back into his lap. "We *can't* forget our stylish third wheel, can we?"

I break into a giggle as the driver slows the car and takes the turn up the steep hill that leads to the restaurant. My laughter's short-lived, because I am *not* missing the chance to watch this beautiful man slipping back into the luxurious, if sweltering, garment.

The car slows as we near the final, sharp right that'll bring us to Yamashiro's ornate front gate. Straight ahead, the city is a glamorous array of bright buildings against a movie-worthy sunset. I hear the snaps and rush of voices before I glimpse the swarm of photographers through the tinted windows. Mother came through on her promise to tip them off, that's for certain. As if I had any doubt.

As we roll to a full stop on the painfully narrow drive, I tighten my grasp on Maximus's hand. Ready or not, it's time to introduce him to the world. At least we have the advantage of knowing when and how, which gives me the smallest comfort.

The driver steps out and opens my door, removing the only barrier between us and the shutters and shouts, not to mention the full sensory assault of the throng's frenzy. I tense and turn my body to step out, bracing myself for the impact of the crowd. When I do, Maximus uses our connection to reel me back the small distance. The resistance throws more panic into the tornado of my senses.

I whip my stare back, preparing to convince Maximus that venturing into the crowd under these circumstances isn't total insanity. But who am I trying to kid? It definitely is.

But it's what we have to do. And somehow, I've got to let him know that I'm here. That I won't let go. That we're in this together.

My train of thought derails when Maximus shocks me with a soft smile. With one hand on my cheek, he draws me close, suspending time and drowning out the chaos outside with his proximity. Then his lips are on mine, his fingertips twisting in my hair, holding me in the moment. As if I'd ever want to escape his embrace, unexpected as it may be.

When he swipes his tongue into my mouth, a fervent heat skitters across my skin, making me feel wild enough to forget the audience impatiently waiting a few feet away. I twist my hand into his shirt, holding on to him as tightly as he is to me. I don't know how long we stay that way, sharing breath and essence and a sliver of peace in the contact. But it's long enough to calm me down and wind me up all at once.

He's the one to pull away first, giving me a moment to catch my breath. Rapid flashes reflect in his gorgeous blues.

I smile. "You sure know how to put on a show," I whisper so only he can hear.

He touches his nose to mine, gifting me with a sexy smile that melts the last of whatever was stressing me out moments ago. "That wasn't a show. That was me kissing the hell out of you because I needed to."

The bustle outside seems to grow the longer we delay, probably caused by all the people who *aren't* getting the shot. Maximus doesn't seem to care.

After another unhurried brush of his lips across mine, he nods toward the door. "Now let me take you to dinner."

CHAPTER 7

Maximus

OUR SERVER, WHO'S CHECKED in at least a hundred times during the meal, now appears at the table with dessert menus and a sugary smile to match. If there was anything normal about this dinner out, I wouldn't mind extending the evening. But Veronica's been texting Kara nonstop, and the two paparazzi who sneaked into Yamashiro's bar are about as subtle as the table of women beside us who have been snapping enough selfies-that-aren't-selfies with Kara and me in the background.

"Hmm, what looks good?" She leans into me.

I take a quick glance at the fancy parchment. "Apple tart," I supply quickly.

She lifts her smile to the server. "Make it two."

I lift my finger before he darts off. "To go."

She lifts a brow and reaches for my hand. "In a hurry, are we?"

My attention snags back to the bar as I let her fingers

curl against mine. "How'd they get in?" I mutter. "There's a security gauntlet outside."

"All hail the mighty hand of Veronica Valari. Where there's the will of a demon, there's a way."

I pull her fingertips to my lips. I'm not oblivious to the flurry of activity that causes. The swift whip of cell phones around the room.

But none of it really matters. None of it comes close to the real focal point of my attention. The exquisite expressiveness of this woman's face. The way her eyes get smoky as I linger my mouth over the sweet curves of her knuckles.

"Don't I know it." I thread the sentiment with a low growl against her cinnamon-scented skin.

Kara responds with a stare that nearly melts the world away.

I lean in, drawn even closer when she adds some sexy tinder of her own, biting the inside of her lip so only I can see. But the next moment, she's stretching out her arms and pulling away with elusive grace, providing an even better shot for every camera lens in this place. I grit through a smile. She looks like we're at home and getting ready to cuddle on the couch.

The image makes me chuckle.

"What?" She returns a smile.

"Nothing. You just amaze me, is all. How have you had a lifetime of nights like this, yet have managed to stay so . . . " I'm at a loss for words now. I finally surrender to the first thing that jumps to mind. "So *you*," I finally blurt, inserting an awkward laugh. "I mean, your fortitude is already something else—but there are more depths to it than I ever imagined."

Luckily, Kara seems to grasp my message, vague half poetry and all. "First of all, I'll tell you that I've never had a night quite like *this*. And as for being 'me'... Well, I don't even know what that is yet." As she confesses that part, she looks away. Teethes her lip more fully. "But I do know that more of me feels right when you're near and touching me like this."

And just like that, my heart is too big for my chest. The globe's whole atmosphere isn't enough to contain my feelings. "*Only* like this?"

She lifts her head back up. Our gazes entwine, full of too many meanings. I need hours to unravel her. A lifetime. Even then, it might not be enough. She's like Dante's layered inferno, only inverted. Every new circle I reveal of her is another step toward heaven.

I like that thought. A lot. While I know she can't decipher it word for word with her abilities, she seems to pick up enough of it to like it too. But we're torn from basking in it for too long. The waiter is back, bearing our dessert in to-go boxes. He pops them open long enough to show off the decadent tarts, each drizzled with sauces that promise perfect taste explosions.

"Oh, wow," Kara exclaims. "Those look amazing."

"And wait until you see where we're going to enjoy them." Her ogling of the desserts gives me space to scheme in the form of a fast text to Regina. She's not surprised to hear from me. This date is already a social media conversation, one she and Sarah have been following with rapt interest since the moment Kara and I got here.

It's an odd revelation, but their excitement is a welcome shift from Veronica's intensity. Somehow I can feel her presence here, even though she's nowhere in sight.

While I relax in the reprieve, I also respect its brevity. In the course of today alone, the woman has earned equal parts of my appreciation, irritation, admiration, and ire. Veronica absolutely lives up to her force-of-nature reputation. But with Kara looking so much better than dessert, I'm more eager to defy the queen mother—at least for another hour or two.

It's time to get my sweet little demon alone.

"Hmm," Kara coos in response to my playful smirk. "Somebody's concocting a plan."

"Yes, but I want it to be a surprise."

She answers with an adorable smirk. "You know how to keep a girl in suspense."

Fifteen minutes later, as I tug at Kara with one hand while balancing the dessert boxes with the other, we walk to the back of the restaurant, through the kitchen, and past the copse of thick trees that protect the place's back entrance. I'm thankful not to spot any more photographers, because under those trees, Reg has parked her vintage burgundy Mustang.

With perfect timing, Sarah climbs out from the passenger seat just as Kara and I emerge from inside. The dyed streak in Sarah's hair this week matches the car's color, and she's also dolled up in matching eyeshadow and lipstick.

"All right then, lovers," she calls out. "In you go now, before the rabble out front gets wise to us."

As she motions to Kara with her sweeping arm, Reg rises gracefully from the driver's side.

"Left it idling for you," she tells me before lifting her chin toward Kara in a silent but stiff greeting.

She's either still getting used to seeing a Valari at my side, or Reg actually knows the Valaris' deepest secret. Hell, it's a possibility. One I can't quite wrap my mind or feelings around. The whirlwind of the last twenty-four hours hasn't opened a second for me to find out, and nothing's going to change about that right now. In this moment, I have to settle for more surface-level communication, such as circling around the car to give Reg a tight hug.

Once we're doing that, I murmur, "Thanks for getting here so fast. I appreciate it. Honestly."

She thumps affectionately at the backs of my shoulders. "You call, I answer. That's how it's always worked, remember?"

"Getting a chauffeured car in return isn't a hardship either," Sarah adds and pulls Reg away by cinching an arm around her waist. "Now I can get you sloshed and take advantage of you, love."

"Yes, please." Reg pecks her wife on the cheek.

During their exchange, Kara's wide-eyed curiosity settles into a glittering smile. "We're really sneaking out?"

"Only if you're okay with it," I say.

"If *they* are, I definitely am." She turns giddily toward Reg and Sarah. "You both realize your date night is about to get hijacked, right? To the tune of about four dozen reporters and photographers?"

Sarah shrugs. "Just a handful more than the mob we've been dealing with at the store."

"It'll be fun," Reg adds with the swagger that's like home to me. "Messing with them is better than a trip to Disneyland."

Kara gifts them with her musical laugh along with two fervent hugs before climbing into the passenger seat beside me.

"I'll return this beast tomorrow." I peek up at Reg, past the rolled-down window.

"Of course you will."

Kara's warm charm seems to have relaxed Reg's stance, though I can't tell if the change will take for good.

"Just take good care of her," Reg says. "And I'm not just talking about the car."

"Always," I vow as Kara and I buckle up.

Just as I turn to take the car back down the hill and then out toward Mulholland, a surge of outcries hits the air. But by the time the reporters get to their cars, there'll be nothing for them to track but dark back roads and empty pavement.

Another fifteen minutes later, as I veer off the road and stop the car at one of the city's most perfect scenic pull-outs, it's evident I wasn't the only one with this brilliant thought tonight. Cars line the ledge, filled with couples either enjoying each other or the free philharmonic concert from the famous Bowl located in the ravine below.

Determined to find us privacy, I crank the wheel farther right and guide the car down a smaller side road. It leads to a wider spot where we'll have the ledge to ourselves.

The moment I turn off the engine, live classical music flows in, creating a peaceful soundtrack to the night. I rest my head back, relieved and oddly satisfied. Maybe this is how my students feel after exams, about to embark on a summer of freedom.

My students . . .

I've only missed a day of work, but it already feels like a year. I admit to a sense of daunting worry, though it's more about the administrative politics I'm likely returning to than functional makeup work.

"Hey. You okay?" Kara's soft voice carries over the lush instrumental playing down below.

I look over, as in awe of her as ever. Here in this time and place, next to this breathtaking woman, my emotions are an impossibly huge universe. A starscape of such fire and light, every inch of my physical form is tiny in comparison.

"Never been better," I say, a hundred percent sincere.

She lifts a smile to me before gazing out across the view, her eyes alive with wonder. I try to think of a proper comparison but can only think of those summers at the Observatory with Jesse, when we spent our snack money on the planetarium show instead. Feeling small had never felt so good.

"Maximus . . . This . . . It's so incredible."

"You like it?" I'm worried again, but this time for a better reason. Maybe she's just being polite to salvage my ego.

"Like it?" she rebuts. "No. I *love* it. I mean that. I love it." She presses her hand to the base of her throat. "I've never seen the city like this."

"From up here?" I pause. "You're serious, aren't you?"

She sends back a look matching the perplexity of mine. "And you're surprised. Why?"

For a second, my mouth works on nothing but air. "I just thought that . . ." I rest an elbow on the wheel. "You grew up here, Kara, same as I did. And you're completely irresistible. I'm having trouble believing any guy in his right mind didn't at least try for an end-of-date detour up here with you."

Through every word of that, I stare straight out the front window. It's been a long damn time since I was the most experienced person about this sort of subject. The recognition has me weirdly discomfited. But at least I'm not alone. A quick glance over reveals Kara's newly furrowed frown.

"You sure you're not confusing me with someone else, Professor? Like someone who's been on normal dates instead of synchronized productions?"

"Are you confusing me with someone who's going to believe that?"

"Demon's truth." She restacks the dessert boxes in her lap, then places a hand on top of one. "I solemnly swear, on both apple tarts."

I chuckle. "All right, all right. I believed you before."

"I know. But tarts make everything better."

"No." I lean over. Kara's face lights up, her eyes bright with invitation, her mouth a lushly bitten rose of welcome.

"*You* make everything better," I rumble before lowering all the way in to fully claim her.

It's so damn good.

So tender and soft and delicious.

So much of what I've craved the whole night.

The balm for my reeling mind. The completion for my careening soul. But now, best of all, the fire that feeds the force of my desire. As she lets my hungry tongue in all the way into her mouth, those surreal flames in my veins start to jump. Their heat ignites torches through my bloodstream like flares along a river. But I'm not afraid of those fires anymore.

Even with Kara so sultry-eyed and limp-limbed in my hold, the thought beats through my brain. I have to pull back to fully acknowledge it.

Kara's eyelashes flutter. She wobbles her head as if I've snapped her out of a hypnotic trance. "What is it?"

I force myself back by another couple of inches. But it's impossible not to keep touching her, at least a little. With one hand, I brush back stray strands of lush mahogany from her cheeks. I trace the bold angles of her expressive eyebrows. I spread my fingers along the proud angle of her jaw.

"You're breathtaking. My perfect little demon."

She lifts a dreamy smile, so I continue my exploration of her face. I don't slide south of her chin, even though everything inside me wants to devour every inch of her. Her cinnamon scent fills my next breath. The scent is even better when mixed with the spicy apple delights resting in her lap.

I force myself back, leaving her craning her body toward

me for more. I suppress a groan because all I want to give her is more. And I want to take too… I tamp down the ravenous beast in me when I remember this is possibly the first real date she's ever been on, and I'm not about to be the guy who ruins that for her.

"Come on." I take the two dessert boxes before getting out of the Mustang. I slide them onto the hood while sprinting to her side of the car. On the way, I shed my jacket and spread it onto the hood. Maybe the damn thing will serve a practical purpose after all.

She pouts as I help her out of the Mustang with both hands. Yet I don't hear her complaining as she uses the hold to her advantage, leveraging my grip to mold her sweet little curves flush against my frame. Before I can utter a gentlemanly protest, she wraps her gorgeous legs around my waist.

Then her lips are crushed against me. Her tongue tangles with mine again. And damn, it's nice. Really nice. I'm already wondering if the rest of her is so delicious when mixed with night wind and canyon sage and apple tart.

I groan, barely recognizing the dark and primal sound as me. The same inner caveman dictates my moves and has me cupping her ass to keep her from toppling back across the car's hood. But maybe that wouldn't be a horrible thing. She'd have broken apple dessert all over her, and then I'd have no choice but to try to clean it all off…

I moan again, deep and guttural, but this repetition has been force-fed to my lips. "You know that if this were the film reel of my fantasies, you'd be naked under me in this dirt, right?"

"Funny coincidence. The film room in *my* mind is playing the same feature."

Kara gives back as good as she gets, and then some, with a laugh that blends perfectly into the next song that flows out from the iconic theater shell below. I don't recognize the melody, which sounds more contemporary, but everything's more perfect because of that. It's so much like the woman sitting here beneath the stars with me. Soft but strong. Pure but passionate. Honest but layered.

So many incredible layers . . .

God help me, she's worth so much more than what my fantasy reel has to offer at the moment. At *any* moment.

I stumble back a step, gaining a necessary gap from the primal surge of our connection. I might as well be walking with a sword through my groin, though.

"Kara . . ."

I stab both hands through my hair, struggling for the right words. We stay that way, in sobered silence, for an agonizing moment. I close my eyes, then open them again. She's no less breathtaking, even in the outer frame of my vision. No less willpower-shattering perched on the hood of the car and looking like a wet dream.

I blow out a breath, determined to do this. To get the syllables out.

"I may be half god, but I'm still a man, and that means I can't help the places my thoughts go when we're this close. Call me crazy, but I want to do this right. You need to let me, okay? This is your real first date, after all."

She looks thoughtful for a moment. Then tilts her head

to the side. "If you insist."

My willpower is so threadbare at this point, she could do nearly anything to change my mind. But I do my best to hold my ground. "Yeah, I do."

She twists her lips into a coy smile. "Does that mean I have to keep my hands to myself, then?"

I laugh because it keeps me from doing other things, like kissing the tease—and the breath—right out of her. Or risking a bigger scene than the one in front of the restaurant if anyone were to notice our little hideaway here. That's the most sobering thought of all. The reality is that cameras are damn near everywhere, whether I realize it or not.

I clear my throat and shove my hands into my jean pockets.

"How about we keep our hands and mouths occupied with those delicious tarts, and you tell me about your day?"

Instead of tempting my resolve further—for which I nearly thank her out loud—she turns and pops open the two containers.

"Actually, I was hoping to ask you about yours." She breaks off a piece of the treat and brings it to her rosy lips. "What did Z have to say? Anything promising?"

I force myself to concentrate on her questions, not the way she broke them up by sucking the extra sugar off her fingertips. There's nothing flirty about her actions or a shred of boredom about her inquiry. I can clearly sense her genuine hopefulness. She's not alone in the nagging uncertainty about whether my father can really ensure her mortal safety.

I hop up beside her on the hood and welcome the distraction of digging into the dessert too. Savoring the apples and sugar affords a much-needed moment to think back over the day. I've hardly had a moment to process all of it. I'm certain we'll have many more days like these, though. Fast and overwhelming. Not all bad. Not all good. But they'll all be with her, so that'll be okay.

"He told me a little about how he met my mother. It helped a little, I think . . . having some of those blank spaces finally filled in, you know?"

Her lips quirk. Her gaze is soft. "I hope it was a little romantic."

I return her smile. "Actually, it was a lot romantic. I wouldn't be surprised if he wasn't still holding a torch for her, to be honest."

Her lips drop into a perfect *O*. She blinks up at me. "Seriously?"

"Seriously."

"Do you think he really wants to see her?"

"I get the strong feeling that he does. As weirdly intriguing as that is, I'm not sure he needs the distraction. Today, he got the father-and-son time I promised him. Maybe he'll want more, but I don't know. I sure could use some more answers, but not before he sorts things out with his brothers."

As she nods, her brows draw together pensively. I yearn to kiss away those troubled furrows but know my words will be more helpful right now.

"He said he'd be back in a few days. We'll know more

soon," I add, hoping to offer her more reassurance.

I feel a billion feet tall as soon as her smile returns. She comes in a little closer, pressing her cheek to my bicep. "What else did you talk about? I want to hear everything."

"Well, if what he says is true, there's a pretty good reason why I can't remember much of my childhood." I swallow down some more tart, working up the courage to even say the next words. To believe them. "According to Z, I spent the first eight years of my life in Olympus. He thinks something happened to my memories after my mother and I left."

She yanks back, eyes wide. "Something like what?"

"Something like . . . they were somehow tampered with."

"Wow. Really?"

I shrug. I'm still having a hard time owning any of it.

"That's . . . That's fascinating," she goes on, the awe in every syllable giving away her intense curiosity.

I wish I could share in it more. All of this feels like a strange dream that I can't reconcile with reality. A harsh, confusing reality I've lived for so long. I keep thinking that at any moment, a popular reality star will pop out of the bushes with a camera crew and announce that the joke's on me.

"Anyway . . ." I turn my attention to the horizon of glowing lights. "Fill me in, little demon. What else does Veronica have on our agenda this week?"

Suddenly Kara looks as wary about the future as I do about my past. "A few things."

"I'm afraid to ask." Truly, I am.

She sighs. "First, she wants us to hit up the farmer's market near your place Wednesday."

"That's easy enough. Maybe we could stay at my place for a little while. Jesse said the camera crews have thinned out considerably."

"That's actually what my mother had in mind."

I lift a brow—and my full grin. "Really?"

"She wants me to be seen there." She tenses her jaw but doesn't say more.

"Okay." I draw out the word, inviting her to elaborate. Actually, needing her to. Why does she still look like Veronica has mandated us to go get root canals instead of fresh-picked fruit? "What else?"

"Then Piper has a movie premiere on Friday, which I'm hoping we can get out of since this is all last minute. But knowing my mother, she'll make it happen."

"Wow. Red carpet. That would be my first."

"Thus the wardrobe assault."

I give in to a full laugh. "Makes sense now. I guess it could be worse."

"And Saturday, there's a private dinner for the university." She casts her gaze off to the skyline, spiking my curiosity in an inexplicable way.

"The Gold Circle Dinner that the president hosts?"

She nods and nibbles her lower lip even harder. After a few anxious beats, she settles her stare back on me. "You need to know . . . Arden will be there."

I pause, making sure I heard her right.

"We'll be there together, of course, but I figured I'd warn you now." Her gaze darts nervously across my face. "In case, you know . . . "

"In case what?"

"Well, if there's . . . friction."

My frown deepens. "In what world does your mother think there won't be?"

"Maximus." She takes my hand with beseeching desperation. "I understand your tension. And yes, maybe the event is tempting fate, but it—and all of this—is meant to legitimize us. Being taken seriously by the university is as important as the Hollywood elite." She swallows hard. "Beyond that, Kell is my sister, which means Arden's going to be in our lives whether we like it or not."

"I don't like it at all," I grumble.

"I know." Her eyes grow sad. "And I don't either. But more than that, I hate what this means for Kell. Tolerating him socially is a small price to pay when I think about what she's sacrificing. For us."

I thread my fingers into hers, sobered by the truth in those last words. If Arden had gotten to Kara before she came to me, there would be no *us*. Then again, she wouldn't be worrying for her safety at every turn either.

I accept those facts with resigned silence and a brooding acceptance of the inevitable. In a few days' time, I'll be face-to-face with Arden Prieto again. The demon who wanted Kara for his own.

I only pray, for everyone's sake, that he's worked on changing his mind.

CHAPTER 8

"COME IN!"

I step through the front door of the guest house at the sound of Gramps's muffled call. I don't have to venture far to find him. He's sitting at the built-in writing desk in the kitchen, crouched over an electric typewriter, dozens of half-filled sheets littered around him. His thin hair is a mess. His cardigan is wrinkled.

He keeps typing after I close the door behind me, shutting out most of the bright afternoon sunshine. The air is dank, like he hasn't opened a window in days.

"Hey, Gramps," I say, reminding him I'm here.

He answers with an absent grunt that I doubt has much to do with me. He reaches up to crank out another piece of paper and toss it away with the rest. Finally he turns. Through his thick glasses, his blue eyes seem to brighten. He smiles. Then all too quickly, it falls away.

"Is everything okay?" I ask, worry needling me instantly.

He rises from the desk. "Fine and dandy," he mutters on his way to the stove. He fills the tea kettle and sets the burner on high. "Tea?"

"That'd be great. Thanks."

Another grunt, but that's it. I'm not sure whether to be alarmed or confused.

"Are you writing again?" I haven't seen the dusty typewriter in years, but I can't deny it's a welcome sight. So maybe I should just be happy that he's into something else besides sitting in his chair and wrapping his mind in old movies.

"Wasting paper is more like it. I don't know why I bother." He squeezes the back of his neck.

I'm officially back to confused. "Is everything okay? You seem upset."

"Upset?" He lifts his eyebrows and draws his lips so tight I can scarcely see them. For a split second, he doesn't look so different than my mother when she's winding up for a fit of her own.

The resemblance doubles the knot of concern I've been nursing since I walked in.

"I've got eyes, haven't I?" He whips off his glasses and gestures toward the nearby living room, where a flatscreen hangs on the wall. "You're all over the news, ladybug. I haven't stepped foot in your mother's house in years, and let me tell you, I've been tempted today just to see what the hell is going on. Does she know?"

"Of course she knows. It was her idea." I can't help the

defensiveness in my tone. I wasn't sure what to expect from our visit today, but I didn't think my grandfather would be so upset the moment I walked through the door.

His jaw unlocks enough to betray his shock. "Her idea? So she knows about this young man you can't leave alone, even though—"

"Even though I was destined for someone else. Yes, she knows. She knows everything. And believe it or not, she's trying to help us make it work."

A shocked laugh escapes him, followed by a sudden weariness. A soft hunch of his shoulders. The unfurling of his angry fists. I twist a few fingers together, racked by regret. He's a drastic pendulum of emotions, and it's because of me. I was right to come today, but it's not going to be the kind of visit we're used to enjoying.

"Gramps, why don't you sit down? I can try to explain."

Wordlessly, we each take a chair at the little kitchen table where we'd visited not so long ago. Life had been different then. So very different.

I fold my hands in front of me, preparing to launch into the most important details. "You remember me saying that Maximus was different, right? And possibly not even mortal."

He nods, his brow furrowed in concentration. "Has something come of it? Have you found out more?"

"We both have. And it explains everything. His physical strength, his intellectual speed, his ability to heal, and even our connection."

He waves his hand between us rapidly. "Out with it,

Kara. I'm not getting any younger here, and you're worrying me into my grave."

"He's the son of Zeus."

He blinks once. Twice. Then leans back in his chair with a fierce shake of his head. "That's nearly unbelievable."

"*Nearly*. But not impossible. His mother is mortal. She's always been elusive about his paternity, and now we know why."

"So you're sure?"

"My mother is sure."

If Zeus passed my mother's appraisal, I have no doubt he is who he says he is. Plus, Kell would sniff out a fraud in our midst in no time.

Gramps acknowledges that with a tilt of his head. "All right. So you've been out on the town with a demigod." He pauses a beat. "Veronica must think this quite a coup. Her entire existence revolves around moving up in the world. This moves her up in nearly every realm. She couldn't have planned this better."

I wince at my grandfather's quick assumptions, partly because none of that ever occurred to me. My mother's meddling and superficiality have always been so transparent. Or so I've thought.

"She's never said that," I add quietly, unwilling to completely submit to his theory. "She seemed upset because the underworld had already sent someone for me. That obviously created a few wrinkles in her grand plan." I pause, remembering how smoothly she transitioned into her new agenda for me. "She's definitely approached this mission of launching Maximus into the public eye with typical Veronica Valari vigor, though. Maybe even a little extra punch of enthusiasm, but that's how she is sometimes. I'm her new project. She lives for this kind of thing."

Like Kell's social following. Like Jaden's film career. She finally gets to mold me and my life the way she's been dying to for years. More, she's trying to keep me safe. Alive. Above the surface. I want to believe that's higher on her priority list than moving herself further up in the world.

Gramps doesn't appear moved. He drags his hand over his salt-and-pepper-stubbled cheek. "Yes, well, it's always been about the family. Turning the Valaris into a Hollywood dynasty. She's taken the whole matter of breeding out your humanity to a different level. I can't imagine any demon has ever participated in a human's punishment with such self-serving bravado as she has. Even your grandmother couldn't be bothered with the human world for very long."

"Maybe because that's all Grandmother was—a pureblood demon. Sometimes I forget that Mom is more human than I am. I don't think that necessarily makes her more compassionate or kind-spirited than the rest of us, but perhaps she feels more connected to earthly things because of it. Or maybe she's trying to make up for the fact that . . ."

I let the words die on my lips. Even if my siblings and I have thought it, we've never dared bring it up. Not out loud.

Gramps frowns. "What?"

I glance around, paranoid my mother will suddenly appear through one of the windows, even though she rarely, if ever, ventures to this part of the estate's grounds.

"Unless you consider concocting an international media spectacle a special gift, Mom doesn't have any extra abilities. Not like us, I mean. I can pick up on how she's feeling before she even knows. Kell can sniff the truth out of anyone. And Jaden can catch a conversation the neighbors are having two doors down."

He nods in quiet agreement.

"Maybe that's why she's so determined to make a mark *here*. On earth. Doing what she does best."

"If that's the case, she's being incredibly short-sighted. She'll get a few hits of splashy news, but she'll lose far more." He swallows hard, his expression growing tight. New tension radiates off him. "She's not protecting you with any of this, Kara. If anything, you're in more danger than you were before."

Pricklings of fear race down my spine with his words, uttered so solemnly that I'm almost compelled to believe him without further explanation.

"Zeus is trying to work something out," I offer, hoping to reassure him and slow my sprinting heart rate. "With Maximus being his son, he thinks we can strike some sort of agreement. Until then, they shouldn't come for me if I'm in plain sight."

"If you're talking about Hades's minions, then you may be right. But there are others who have a far less diplomatic approach to vengeance."

"I don't think this is about vengeance, Gramps. We both know they've been making an example of you—"

He laughs roughly. It's enough to cut me short.

"You don't think Zeus fathering *another* illegitimate son would spark vengeance in anyone?"

My thoughts fly and tumble with this new rationale. I give up on smoothing out my pulse.

Oh no.

All this time, I'd been worried for my own survival. I'd been focused on my willful transgressions and atoning in whatever way could keep Maximus and me together.

More, I'd been completely wrapped up in Maximus. In all the fire and magic of our romantic relationship, falling for him in every wonderful way. Taking for granted that he could keep me safe until all this was sorted out.

It never occurred to me that he could be in danger too.

"Hera." I whisper the name, for fear that saying it any louder might somehow draw her into our presence.

Gramps's answering grimace tells me I've hit on the truth. Some unbelievable but equally frightening truth.

"But Zeus knows about Mother's plan," I argue. "He agreed to it. I'm pretty sure he helped craft it, in fact. It's buying him time to work things out with Hades . . . "

"Are you certain Hades is the only one who needs appeasing?"

I shake my head because I'm not certain of anything. Z is an enigma. Charismatic and powerful. Calculating and evasive. Pretending I know his true motives would only further prove my own foolish ignorance. I'm more perceptive than any human I've ever known, but I have nothing on the gods.

"Past that, Zeus—myth or man—is the poster child

for irrational confidence and blind ego," Gramps continues. "How many times do you think he's had to cover up his indiscretions over the eons?"

"Likely more than I can count, but why act on it now? Maximus is grown. And he's not a threat to Hera."

"He doesn't have to be a threat. He exists, which means Zeus was unfaithful. *Again*. That's enough for her to want to destroy all evidence of the affair or, at the very least, make Maximus suffer dearly for it."

I shake my head frantically. "Why would Z put his own child in that kind of danger? It doesn't make sense. He told us he's been searching for Maximus for years, and I believe him. Why track his son down only to risk losing him?"

"I don't know. But I suggest you find out what's really going on here before Hera does." He scrubs his hand down his face again. "Meeting you is either the best or the worst thing that could have possibly happened to Maximus Kane. Only time will tell."

I brace my elbows to the table as the weight of his words clamps over my shoulders. Horror and hope clang through my thoughts, and I let the noise take over—until Gramps rises with a frustrated groan. He flips off the burner under the tea kettle. Then he opens a cabinet and yanks out a small tumbler before disappearing into the living room. When he returns, the glass is half full of amber liquor, but not for long. He shoots most of it down in a big gulp, wincing as he swallows.

"Gramps… Don't you think it's a little early for that?"

I've seen him pour a drink from time to time, but never

while he's been so distressed. In fact, I don't think I've ever seen him quite like this. His gestures are jerky and impulsive, every movement loud for the way he makes contact with everything around him. At once, the din in my head is nothing but a dull roar.

"It's a little late for it, if you ask me." He tosses back the last of the liquor.

"Which means what?" I ask, not hiding my apprehension.

"It's been years since I spoke to your mother. *Really* spoke to her."

All my rattling anxiety heightens for a painful moment as I absorb what he's saying... what he's *implying*.

"Wait. What? You're going to talk to her?"

"Hell yes, I am. I've let her run the show around here for years. I've been obedient, I've been quiet, and I've stayed out of her way, but this is where I draw the line. She *will* listen to what I have to say." He illustrates that last point by jabbing his index finger in the direction of the main house.

Before I can talk him out of whatever he's planning, he's marching out the door. I'm tempted to tell him Mom's not home, but I know she is. When I arrived, she was mercifully closed up behind her office doors, allowing me to sneak out to the guest house unnoticed.

Once inside, Gramps and I intercept her just as she throws the doors wide, her three black-eyed Chihuahuas and her assistant flanking her. My mother's nostrils flare broadly the moment she notices us.

"Giovani—"

"Dad," he corrects sharply.

She scoffs out a laugh, stepping out as she waves dismissively behind her. The gesture has Natalie drawing the doors closed again, taking the yapping canines with her. The three of us have a much-needed moment of privacy.

My mother saunters toward one of the brassy vases holding a fresh arrangement of flowers in the center of the room. "Gio," she coos with that saccharine tone I know too well. "What brings you across the lawn today? Are you out of rations? Can I have something delivered to you?"

"No, Veronica. We're going to have a serious talk about Kara and this mess she's in."

My mother folds her arms across her chest, turning toward us as she does. "Oh? And what would you know about this *mess* anyway?" She arrows an accusing glare in my direction.

Gramps follows it. "You should go, Kara. Your mother and I need to speak alone."

My mother's lips thin. Her posture becomes as rigid as a bow. I take it as their silent votes of agreement. For all the times I've tried to protect my grandfather and advocate for him, I recognize now that his acquiescence to my mother's will has been at least partially his choice. While my fate may lie at the center of it, this fight isn't all mine. And while the recognition is an epiphany, it also eases some of the anxiety in my veins. I can take a full breath without pain again.

I turn to leave, but my mother's voice lances through the silence, stopping me.

"Kara."

Turning back, I curse inwardly. How bad is this going

to be if she insists that I stay?

"Yes, Mother?"

"Arden is looking forward to your next meeting. I expect you to reach out to him at your soonest convenience."

My breath catches. The uncomfortable pressure slams my chest again, joined by stabs that might as well be the thorns from every rose she's rearranging. "Next . . . meeting?"

She tilts her head, gifting me with her best condescending smirk. "Oh, *Kara*. You didn't think you could neglect *all* your commitments, did you? I've hired the man for our antiquities project and paid a sizable retainer. I expect him to see the project through. That means you will see it through, as well."

I manage an uneven exhale. "You expect me to work side-by-side with him?"

She widens the smile, sleek and sure as a Siamese that's just swallowed a mouse. "That's exactly what I expect."

"Are you sure that's a good idea?"

"I've already told you, Arden and I have come to terms. You're perfectly safe with him. Besides . . . " She glances at her father briefly before returning her incisive stare on me. "I believe you owe me a favor."

CHAPTER 9

MAXIMUS

IT'S MY FIRST FULL day back at Alameda, and my office entrance seems to have grown an invisible revolving door. If the visitors were all just students seeking answers to their wonderings about divine authority, moral justice, and the true definition of hell, I'm sure I'd be pumping my fist in triumph instead of grinding enamel off my teeth—especially as another knock at the doorjamb cracks the air.

"Yes?"

I don't hide the asshole-level growl from my voice. Already I wonder what new emissary has been sent down to me from Veronica Valari's hill. So far today, I've had stop-ins from the woman's social media manager, press adviser, legal team lead, brand endorsement specialist—and yes, even a coiffure consultant, who tried coming at me with trimming shears.

I was kind about my hard *no* to that. I'm not feeling so kind anymore. How many more can there be?

I'm done stressing about the answer, so I keep my head down and my fingers going on my laptop, eager to finish commenting on the essay filling the screen—the same essay I've been grading for the last two hours.

"Weird flex from the guy with the little miss hottie walking out of his office, muttering nonstop about his goldilocks."

I look up and laugh. "I don't think I've ever been happier to see your face, Mr. North."

"Good thing I like yours too, sweetheart," he quips. "Because I'm seeing it a lot lately. By the way, I think your right side is your best. At least from what I could see during the 'Juicy Scoop' segment on the monitor over the gas pump this morning."

"Jesus." I drop my nose into my fingers.

"So, back to the cute little number dedicated to your luscious locks. You got her number, right? Asking for a friend."

"Married," I supply while pushing my laptop aside. "With one kid. Trying for another."

Jesse mutters a curse beneath his breath.

"Yeah, yeah," I say, unwilling to surrender my grin. "Just get in here and flip the sign on your way." If any more members of the Valari optics squad swarm in, they'll have to wait.

After fulfilling the request, Jesse pins me with an impressive version of his scientist's scrutiny. His eyes are steely as scalpels, his jaw's set like a canyon wall, and his shoulders are the cliffs to go along with that chiseled rock.

It's all enhanced more because his hair isn't in the way. The unruly waves have been wrestled back, leaving some dancing room for his impressively wicked brows. Alameda should hire every member of the science department by auditioning them on *that* look.

"Has the student tidal wave been that bad already?" he questions. "It's still October, right? Too late for adds or drops, and too early for semester-finals stress. Maybe they're all just interested in Alameda's newest pop culture *it* dude." He snickers but cuts in on himself with a grimace. "Or has it been more drama with the board? You were vague about it in your messages."

"I was vague because the board was too. I was advised to take a few days off, but then I wasn't."

He frowns. "Just like that?"

I refrain from mirroring his look. It *wasn't* just like that, thanks to Veronica pulling magic strings behind the Alameda curtain in order to reopen the university's gates for me. But no way am I ready to hit him with all that. I give Jesse complete credit for how his scientist's imagination can stretch, but there are limits to the realm of scientific possibility—even his.

Besides, there's another reality I've got to bring him up to speed about. One that's more urgent than craziness like my king-of-gods father and my eight forgotten years in the land of myths and immortals.

"Just like that," I finally say. "Maybe the board finally gathered their collective shit and realized that in the grand scheme of campus scandals, Kara and I are a blip on the radar."

Jesse settles his elbows on his wheelchair arms. Then narrows *that* stare again. "Just a blip," he repeats. "To the tune of hair stylists making office calls and—"

A knock on the door cuts him off. "Professor Kane? It's Natalie, from Ms. Valari's office. I need to know how much longer you'll be, please. I have to take a picture of your ID so they can expedite your security clearance for the red carpet on Friday night. I also have Veronica's preliminary talking points for the Gold Circle Dinner. You have to review them as soon as possible so the research team can have them done by Saturday. All of this is time sensitive, so—"

"Natalie?" I hate answering her interruption with the same, but there's no other choice.

"Yes?" The young woman is softer, responding to the authority in my tone.

"There's a café in the courtyard in front of the library. I'll meet you down there in thirty minutes."

Already I feel her hesitancy. In Mama Valari time, that's *a lot* of minutes. In my world, where I've got to explain the last forty-eight hours to Jesse with clarity and diplomacy, it's a hiccup. But not in any funny sense of the word. Already his face reflects stunned creases at the mention of the Gold Circle Dinner. The annual event at President McCarthy's home is so swanky, most of the Alameda professors aren't invited.

"Very well, Professor," she finally says.

My relief is palpable. So is the low hum of frustration I've been battling to subdue all day.

"And that officially hit my saturation point on the

day for hearing Veronica's name," I grumble, half to myself, half to my audience of one.

"Red carpet clearance, eh? *And* the Gold Circle Dinner?" Jesse works his jaw back and forth while studying the mesh of his fingers at the center of his lap. "I guess the board really did come to their senses about welcoming you back to the fold."

I pull in a harsh breath. "Jesse . . . "

"Hey. It's cool, man."

"I can assure you, it's not."

"Oh, come on." He drops his hands. "You know me better than that, sugar Kane. Am I pissed because you're going to the Alameda University version of the VIP backstage party? Of course. But will I hold it against you?" He spews some gruff air. "Fuck that."

"Want to swap places?" I'm half-serious and tell him so with a deliberate stamp of my gaze. "You know that just thinking of this stuff gives me hives."

"Hell yeah, I know. Which, of course, only firms up my overriding conclusion about all of this."

"Which is?"

"That you must have it bad for that woman." He brings his hands together again. "Clearly you've been holding back a few details since we last spoke—all of them beginning with *Kara* and ending in *Valari*."

"And you can dream on about getting any more details than that," I jibe in response to his waggling brows.

He shrugs. "A best friend since childhood can only hope."

Though his banter is obvious, it gives me pause for thought—and inspiration. I fix a tighter regard on him, rubbing at my bottom lip. "Would a best friend since childhood consider a Gold Circle invite as an acceptable olive branch?"

"Whoa. You're serious?"

"As much as I can be." I lower my finger and rest my chin on my knuckles. "I have no idea how much sway I have with the venerable Veronica, but it's worth an ask."

He looks equal parts gobsmacked and humbled. "All right, but an 'olive branch' isn't necessary, man. We're good. You don't have to do anything to prove that."

"Maybe I want to. And maybe . . . "

"What?" he pushes after my significant pause.

I spin my chair around and then rise to look out the window before answering. "Maybe it's a selfish move on my part."

I'm grateful when Jesse backs off on the pressure. Hopefully he gets it with those simple words and won't get nosy on me for the rest. Normally he can read enough of me to know which end of my mind is up and which is down. And there's a damn good possibility those poles won't be correctly balanced come this Saturday night.

"Well, if that's the case, you know I've got your back, buddy. Even if we're barreling headfirst into the Valari family fray."

"Thanks. Though I'm pretty sure it's not my head leading the way this time."

"You won't be the first in history to say that, my friend.

Nor the last."

"True," I mutter. *Just maybe the most screwed.*

Especially once I'm in the same room as Arden Prieto. Maybe even forced to interact with him.

Even if Veronica is flexing her full PR muscle to enforce the new order of things here, Kara can barely stand to say his name.

I'll just have to stick to the facts and trust that Prieto feels the same and will act accordingly. That he yearns to please his underworld overlords more than he wants to throw down with a son of fucking Zeus.

I force myself to kill the budding fantasy of all the ways it could go down. Because that party *has* to go right. Everything this week has to.

If Kara and I fail to win massive social clout...

If Z goes bust at making nice with his brothers...

If Arden decides he doesn't want to place nice...

I can't begin to consider the very real consequences. A life without Kara.

The truth is as biting and brutal as the chilled wind that beats at the window and visibly slices across the courtyard below. It tears dried leaves and twigs off the trees, making people huddle into scarves and light jackets. Overnight, Southern California has decided to become Upstate New York. A different landscape.

Just like me. Suddenly changed. Confronting a new, uncontrollable normal. And trying to prevent the useless leaves from clogging up my mind.

In the days, weeks, and even months to come, keeping

my head screwed on straight—and my self-control tethered—is going to be more crucial than ever.

CHAPTER 10

"WHAT EXACTLY DO YOU plan to do with all that forbidden fruit, Miss Valari?"

I smirk and ignore Maximus's teasing question as I hand over some cash to the young woman working one of the food stands at the farmer's market.

"Thanks so much," the worker murmurs, her hands shaking as she returns my change along with a bulging sack of ripe GoldRush apples. "Have a great day."

Her nervousness, which I try to soothe with a kind smile, gives her away. She's one of a dozen people who've already recognized me here. Plenty of photos have been snapped. I've noticed a few familiar faces from the Yamashiro swarm lurking in the periphery, but luckily we've managed to miss the full onslaught of media attention this afternoon. It's a welcome and wonderful change from the horde who've been tagging along on our public outings the last few days.

I take one of the golden apples for myself before

Maximus collects the bag from my hand, adding it to the others lining his arm.

"Not to mention the lifetime supply of fresh produce you've amassed here," he adds.

I take a second to just bask in his gorgeous glory. Between the wind in his hair, his tight black T-shirt, and the jeans hugging his stunning legs, I almost forget where I am. What day it is. My own name.

"The apple is just a metaphor, you know," I manage to get out. "Most likely not the actual forbidden fruit that got poor Eve into so much trouble."

He cuts in on my verbal apple essay by swiping it from my grasp and taking a bite, his eyes alight with mischief.

"*Malus*," I continue, "is Latin for both apple and evil. Wordplay is all. I'm surprised you didn't know that, Professor Kane."

"What makes you think I didn't?"

I snatch the apple back. "Because you're just the type to interject when you know the right answer. But all I heard was you chomping on my apple."

He chuckles softly. "Sounds like you're projecting a little bit, sweetheart. Missing your classes much?"

"Mostly just yours," I say with a listless sigh.

The truth is, I miss more than his lectures about sin and morality, along with all the wicked thoughts I get from his poetic baritone and graceful hand motions. I miss the peace that always comes with just being on campus and focusing on my academic work in general, but with the new agenda in full swing, it's been impossible to get back to the routine I love so much.

So maybe I was premature in my gratitude for my mother's benevolence. Maybe she knew exactly what she was doing—giving me permission to go back to school, knowing full well it'd be impossible while juggling her packed schedule for us.

Even so, we have bigger problems to face. Threats that were never on my radar. Another layer of worry that I don't know how to tell Maximus about—or even if I should.

I haven't been able to get my talk with Gramps out of my head. And in the hours since I left my mother and him to talk it through, I've been waiting for any sign that she's changing course. I'm still waiting… Waiting and worrying.

Maximus's playful expression sobers when our gazes meet, as if he's somehow picked up on my mood shift. "How about tomorrow, then? We can drive to campus together."

I avoid his gaze as we cross the street on the walk back to his place. "Maybe. I can't promise anything right now."

"Why not?"

"Getting ready for a movie premiere is a little like prom. It's an all-day affair." I try to hide the dread in my tone and push on. "To answer your earlier question, I was thinking that since we're *looking* domestic today, maybe we could *be* domestic and I could try my hand at apple tarts. I'm not much of a baker, and they won't be nearly as good as the Yamashiro ones, but…oh…" I glance down at my watch, my thoughts suddenly derailed. "Shit."

"What is it?"

"Nothing. I guess I lost track of time." Which is not a good thing. At all.

He frowns. "Do we have to be somewhere?"

We? *No.*

Me? *Unfortunately, yes.*

"Just a quick thing I have to take care of," I offer, hiding a wince. Maximus is the most vital person in my world, which means he should be getting the least lies. Instead, I keep being forced to hide things from him. I hate the situation and myself for it.

Thankfully we come upon the entrance to his building, which provides a couple of minutes of distraction getting inside and bringing all the bags upstairs. I find a wooden bowl in a high cabinet of his kitchen and arrange some of the fruit artfully in it, creating a colorful centerpiece in the tiny space.

After a few silent minutes, his wordlessness has me lifting my head. I catch him staring at me, his blues as brilliant as the sky outside. Just as openly, I stare back. He's leaning against the counter, one hand tucked casually into his jeans, now shamelessly dragging his gaze over me.

"I like seeing you at home here," he says quietly.

Warmth rushes to my cheeks because I like *being* at home here. Modest as his condo is next to my place, it's still cozy. And quiet. And, most importantly, private. So blessedly, wonderfully *ours*.

Granted, I'm not ungrateful for the house up in the hills. It's better than living at the Valari complex, which has every amenity but comes with dangerous proximity to my mother's controlling vortex.

But between Kell running in and out of our place and

my mother's support staff bothering us at nearly all hours, it's been a revolving door since she and Z showed up.

Hardly romantic . . .

But the way Maximus looks at me now feels decidedly more than romantic. The heat in his gaze, with the outer rings of his irises augmented to pure cobalt, hints at a cascade of longing waiting to be set free. It heightens my own pent-up desire. I'd love nothing more than to see it free.

Instead, I swallow over the rush of need coursing through me and refocus on rearranging the fruit bowl. No point starting something we can't finish.

"Well, Mom actually wants me to stay here for a couple of days. She says the optics are priceless. So if it's okay with you, I was thinking after the premiere—"

"If it were up to me, Kara, you'd never leave." The words are low and swift, removing any doubt as to his genuineness—as well as every hot, needy thing it does to my bloodstream.

I close my eyes with a sigh, savoring his adoration more than my aching senses. "And if it were up to me, I don't think I would either. I just wish it could be that simple."

He takes one long stride toward me. Inside another second, he's cradling my hip in one of his large hands as he spins me to face him.

I gaze up, my lips parted as I'm knocked breathless from his speed and his strength. Not to mention the sheer force of his appetite for our closeness. For *me*. Every molecule between us is weighted with that beautiful, inexorable truth.

"We could make it simple," Maximus murmurs.

"What?" I force out. "Make what simple?"

"Us. All of it. To hell with the movie premiere. To hell with class this week and photo ops and anything else that puts distance between us. The way my phone has been blowing up every hour of the day, I can assure you, everything we've been doing has been sufficiently high profile. Jesus, they're even calling us 'Maxkara.'"

I spurt out a soft laugh. "That's almost catchy."

"Can't that be enough publicity to buy us a few days? Just you and me?" He touches his forehead to mine, his eyes searching, passionate and vulnerable all at once. "With nothing between us," he whispers against my lips.

My breath rushes out, but he doesn't give me a second to recover. To argue . . .

With the urgent press of his kiss and the way he pins himself against me, I'm swept away in him. In the heady way he makes me feel and the beautiful fantasy he's painting of us. Just us. Just this fire and falling and connection. Our bodies reunited. Our souls fully soldered. Our hearts beating as one. Losing track of the days in his bed.

Overwhelmed with that possibility, I moan against his mouth. I can't reel it back, even knowing how it's greenlighting his next motions. He begins working the buttons down the front of my dress, carefully enough not to tear the threads keeping them attached to the fragile vintage garment.

He makes enough progress to push a sleeve over my shoulder, dragging his teeth across the firm ball of muscle. Then his tongue. I arch and sigh. Tunnel my fingers into the long luxury of his hair. Groan with relief when he hoists me up and against him and carries me to his bed.

We tumble down together in a flurry of urgent breaths, rough kisses, and desperate touches. I drag my hands up his muscled abdomen, taking his T-shirt along the way. He rips it off, returning to the more important task of kissing me into wild oblivion.

Having seemingly given up on the tedious buttons of the dress, he hikes the skirt's hem up to my hips. I'm blind to everything but the sensation of his fingers slipping under my panties, over my most sensitive flesh, then teasing my opening.

I draw in a ragged breath, taking the scent of him into me. Apples and rain, flesh and muscle, heat and desire. Maximus . . . this man I've fallen so deeply for in so many ways. In every way . . .

A groan vibrates from my lips, echoing from him as he pushes inside, penetrating me with fast, firm strokes.

"I . . . Kara, I—" He closes his eyes, wincing with emotion.

My eyes flutter closed too. The sharp rise of my orgasm blocks everything out—everything but the perfect pressure of his palm against my clit, his dedicated ministrations sending electric pleasure through every cell. A beautiful delirium.

I tremble against him as his movements slow.

"More," I whimper, even as the pulses in my core persist. I need to feel him losing control too, taking his pleasure from my body the way I've taken from his.

In this very bed. On these sheets.

How can he do that to me? Satisfy me and make me crave more still...

I don't have a moment to rationalize how, because the promise of more is shattered with the shrill ring of my phone.

Maximus drops his head into the bedspread beside me. "Fuck... Please tell me that's not your mother."

Boneless, my brain cells still scattered, all I can do is sigh.

And then remember.

He pulls gently from me. The absence of contact is made even more miserable with the sudden realization that now I won't be enjoying more of him in *any* form.

I groan, this time with angry frustration.

He rolls to his back with his own sigh. I rise and surge toward my phone but end the call. It doesn't matter. Veronica will call back in a few seconds. She'll call until she hears a voice, a surefire guarantee that she connects with whoever she pleases, whenever she damn well wants to.

I set the phone back on the counter and button up my dress.

"What are you doing?" Maximus sits on the edge of the bed. His hair is mussed from my eager fingers pawing him like a wild animal. His cheeks are flushed, which makes his eyes even more intensely blue.

What I wouldn't give to shut my phone off and crawl back into those sheets with him right now. For hours. For *days*.

"I have an appointment," I say instead, hoping my hurried preparations will excuse me from the lack of detail.

But he's not letting me get away with it. My luck runs out as soon as he pushes up to stand.

"With who?"

I swallow and focus on my buttons. "Fine," I finally say. "You deserve to know. I'm meeting Arden. At his office near Rodeo. Mom wants us to wrap up this project we started. She's adamant about it."

Max's reply takes several seconds to come. Some of the longest ticks of my life.

"*Arden.*"

I don't have to look up to pick up on his outrage.

"I'm sorry. But this isn't a permanent situation. Even so, if I never had to see him again, I'd be truly happy. But she's forcing the issue—"

"No." He growls the word like it's law.

I finally risk a look in his direction. The second I do, I'm pulled more fully into the sudden shift in his intensity . . . from raw and sexual to possessive and pissed.

"You're not seeing him alone. Is Veronica insane?"

"Likely. But she's also confident I'll be safe with him."

I utter the reassurance with a little more fervency than I feel. Arden's never made me feel especially safe. And at his worst, he's made me feel very *unsafe*. I haven't nearly forgotten. But worrying Maximus needlessly isn't the answer either. He's holding up under the stress of this new life, but for how long? He already looks like he's ready to snap. Now more than ever.

He shakes his head. "I don't trust it. I don't trust her. And I sure as hell don't trust *him*."

"She's my mother, Maximus. If I can't trust her—"

"But *can* you?"

I pause, because the vehemence of his question forces me to dig deeper for my own truth. *Do* I trust her? Implicitly? I take a deep breath, buying more time to question everything.

"I trust you, Maximus, and I haven't known you that long. I trust Z because he might be the only one who can save me now. And . . . yes, I trust my mother because she's my mother. She's difficult, I know."

His jaw tightens with that.

"Okay, she can be downright vicious. And love isn't exactly an emotion she's well-versed in. We might not have mutual affection in abundance, but I believe she's invested in my safety. In, you know, keeping me alive."

For a minute, I think he'll keep pushing me. But he simply stares, his breathing evening out, like maybe he's beginning to understand the insanity of it all. The illogical but inescapable contradiction that is my mother. My family. My life as a demon who's done everything to be someone different.

"Fine," he finally says, throwing his shirt back on.

I blink back my shock at his sudden acquiescence. "Okay."

"But I'm coming with you."

CHAPTER 11

MAXIMUS

SHE'S NOT COMFORTABLE WITH my ultimatum. But as I lift her into my truck, I linger my hands on her waist to convey my gratitude for her reluctant acceptance of it.

I hope she picks up on the rest of my feelings too. How I hate unsettling her like this. How I desperately wish I could change my mind, but that's not possible. Not right now. I don't trust Arden and Veronica by a fucking inch. Even a fraction of one. Arden's a snake. An ambassador of hell itself.

So like it or not, she's stuck with me. And everyone will just have to deal with it.

"Maximus."

"Hmm?"

"Maybe you should stop and think about this."

I start the engine. "I appreciate that, beautiful—especially because I know the place in your heart that it's coming from."

"If you really knew that, you'd be stopping and thinking." Her tone points to her persistent worry.

I turn my focus back to the GPS screen in place of kissing away the little V between her eyebrows. Damn, the woman is hot when she's fretting. "Done all the thinking I want or need to." Like the engine warming to a roar beneath the truck's hood, my blood heats with the heritage that it's been too long denied. The legacy from Olympus. The spirit of a king. It feels good to let that pedigree flow a little more freely. "Who knows? I might even prove useful on your grand treasure hunt."

"You mean by being the best treasure in the room?"

Her flattery doesn't fall on deaf ears. I swoop toward her with a fast but passionate dip of my lips. I don't even mind that a persistent pap has found his way into my complex's garage to snap us in the clinch—until a separate flash joins the first.

I snap my head around. Once I spy the two men there, the electrocution takes over every hair on the back of my neck—just like it threatened to do over the weekend when I saw the same pair in the bar at Yamashiro.

But in the two seconds I take to glance back at Kara, the photographers have rushed away, probably to the garage's deeper level. "Did you see those guys?" A useless query and I already know it, which doesn't stop me from going on. "One of them had a beach bum smirk and a glitchy walk. The other stared at me like a goddamned wolf."

Kara releases half a laugh. "That's a pretty specific observation, even for you."

"That's because I've seen them before."

"Very likely," she says. "Lots of the guys cover the same beats. Some of them have been snapping Jaden, Kell, and me for years."

"Any of those guys stare at you like you just fell from heaven?"

Her smile fades. "That's not funny."

"I'm not trying to be funny."

She settles back into her seat with a heavy sigh. "I also don't think we should try to be late," she mutters with gentle firmness.

I roll my shoulders to shake off the paranoia—which is all it is, damn it. Instead of looking for false monsters around every corner, I've got to support Kara in facing the real one a few miles away. As I head toward Wilshire on our journey toward Beverly Hills, I use stoplight pauses to sneak glances across the truck's cab. Kara's expression is stoic. She taps a finger on the armrest in time to the song on the radio. This clearly isn't her ideal way to spend the afternoon either, but she's being brave about all of it. Admirably so.

Despite my frustration with the situation, I'm proud as hell to be by her side. She inspires me. I tell her so by reaching a steadfast hand to her knee. I back up the action with a determined murmur. "You're the most courageous person I know, Kara."

She molds her hand across the top of mine. "Except I'm not wholly a person, Maximus."

"By that definition, neither am I. But here I am, wondering how I'm going to keep my hands to myself for the next few hours."

Her answering grin matches my heated energy. "Why don't you just use them in some fantasies instead?"

"Now there's an idea."

"But if you do, you have to promise me one thing," she murmurs.

"Just one?"

"You have to pay careful attention, because there'll be a quiz later."

I answer with a low chuckle. "On my fantasies?"

"Maybe not a quiz," she amends. "I'd call it more of a . . . long-form exam. Really long. It'll probably require us pulling an all-nighter."

I kick up one side of my mouth. "So you'll need to stay over. Maybe for quite a while."

"Well, that's a given."

"And what kind of special notes are you allowing for this test?"

"Notes?" She lets out a cute *psssh*. "Who said anything about notes?"

I flick over a playful glare. "Is that fair?"

As soon as she turns in her seat, the intensity of her stare scorches my whole profile. "You know what's *not* fair?"

"Hmm?"

"Having to wait so long to have you inside me again." She practically whispers it, which only adds to her gorgeous irresistibility. She's so small, inviting, and entrancing against the expanse of the truck's passenger seat. "Last time I checked, I was a demon, not a nun."

I drag in a breath, patching up my willpower for what

feels like the hundredth time since those blessed moments when I *was* inside her. "A fact that my own body won't let me forget," I assure, turning a tender glance toward her. I want to caress her with much more than my gaze but don't dare trust myself right now. But the temptation lingers, especially as she crosses her arms, turning her breasts into pert plumps.

"At the risk of stating the obvious, Professor, you have a funny way of showing it."

"Not 'funny,' Kara." My voice is a soothe now because I need the calm as much as she does. "I just want to make sure . . . "

"Of what?" she demands when I pause too long.

Screw it. I take the risk of scooping her hand into mine. As always, that incredible energy flares between us, but I breathe deeply before it can ignite the rest of my blood.

"Being with you, in that way—I feel like one of those beams of light on the ocean, right as the sun is setting. You know what I'm talking about?" I feel corny as hell, but I'm committed to the subject now. Time to see this through. "They're tiny specks but part of something so much bigger . . . greater. And while the ocean goes on, those lights are only there for moments each day. But when you're looking at them, those are the very best moments of the day."

Her small fingers tighten around mine. There's a sweet, sublime smile on her lips. "Yeah," she murmurs. "I do know what you're talking about."

"Then you understand why I'm not going to simply dive between the sheets and just fuck you again, Kara." I pull her knuckles to my lips. "Not with all this insanity going on around us." I turn her hand over and capture her palm with a gentle kiss. "You're the fire on my ocean. The sunset that's worth waiting for."

Her breath audibly snags. I savor the sound and the fusion of our heartbeats via the press of our palms.

Until I notice we're on final approach to Prieto's office. The blaze in my blood is instantly iced down. Not even Wilshire Boulevard's high-end bustle, with edgy sculptures and cycling studios and exotic car dealerships, takes me from the freeze.

By the time I toss the truck's keys to the valet at Arden's office, I've extended that chill to my basic self-control. For Kara's sake, I promise to keep it that way. I offer her my elbow as we walk across the lushly landscaped inner courtyard and then board the elevator for the third floor. By the time we disembark, I've actually managed to school my features into a semblance of calm neutrality. It stays put until we head toward a set of ornate double doors that look like they belong in the Palais Versailles instead of a chic Beverly Hills complex with a relaxed Moroccan vibe.

The doors swing open suddenly, revealing a smiling Arden Prieto. The guy is decked out like he's been practicing his Humphrey Bogart impression all morning.

"Darling Kara," he croons, drawing out every vowel. "Don't you look like a delicious dream today?" He hums seductively, licking his gaze shamelessly over her.

I'm conscious of the figurative smoke between my coiling fingers.

The moment stretches on until he seems to finally notice me, if the downward dip of his glance can be clearly deciphered. The distraction of Kara's beauty aside, he undoubtedly can't miss the stiff loom of my posture and balls of my hands. While taking on this kind of tension serves me well with college clowns and standard-issue assholes, it only makes Arden's eyes alight with humor.

"Professor Kane. I wasn't expecting you." His smug smile melts into a grimace. "But of course, none of us were."

"*Arden*," Kara all but hisses.

"It's okay, sweetheart," I mutter, not really meaning it.

"No. It's not." She nails Prieto with a matching glower. "I'm here to honor my mother's request about this project, okay? Out of respect to her and my sister, I'm willing to be nice about it if you are. Completely your call."

"My call." Prieto strikes another practiced stance, cocking his head. "You're absolutely certain about that? Because if it was actually *my* call . . ."

She wilts a little, as if Arden's sarcastic banter is already starting to wear her down.

I want to flatten his face like molding clay.

Instead, I stretch out my fingers for the sake of grasping Kara's hand. "Come on, Arden. Surprise us all. Become the gentleman you keep hinting at instead of acting like a teenager who got turned down for prom."

"Says the guy who's already screwed the prom queen?" He punctuates the verbal jab with a silky smirk, brandished with the glee of an evil prince.

I freeze every muscle, recognizing his game. He's still

openly baiting me, which means he's either fearless, stupid, or tempting me into a display of jealousy that will serve his own interests.

My money's on the latter, so I fight down the rage. *Again.* It's not easy. I focus on deep, cool breaths through my chest while ignoring the violent viscosity of my blood. Prieto won't own any part of me like this—just like he'll never possess any part of Kara.

"Some things just aren't worth it," I say, glancing quickly to Kara. The determination in her eyes is like the end of a smoky sunset, nearly knocking me down. *So worth waiting for.*

"But some things are," she says, "like taking care of all this so we can go home." A faint smirk curves the edge of her lips. "And bake apple tarts."

This time, I'm ready for Prieto's nasty comeback, whatever it may be—only it never materializes. Though I don't bother with even looking at him now, his stare is a palpable witness to my lingering look with Kara.

He clears his throat loudly. It's a victory bell to my ears.

"In any case, Veronica has asked me to update you on the latest procurement opportunities for the collection."

One day, hopefully soon, baking and making out *will* be our sole priorities in life. But for now, my stunning little demon has to wear a congenial smile.

With an arch of his eyebrow and a sweep of his hand, Arden gestures us into his office. He wastes no time ushering Kara toward his desk with a hand along the base of her spine. I hang back but ensure I'm in his periphery with my best thundercloud glare. I'm not at the point of openly threatening... but if he inches that hand any lower...

"Now this piece here..." he begins. "This is a listing I found just yesterday. It's *very* interesting."

"Beautiful," Kara concurs, peering longer at the image of a circular object crafted in detailed silver and gold and dominated by two figures, a man and a woman. "Is it a plate? Oh, no. There's a shallow lip along the edge and a center indentation. It's a phiale."

Arden's approving hum sets my teeth on edge, but I keep my face set in careful neutrality.

"You're absolutely right. The Greeks used these shallow bowls for libations. But you probably already knew that." He grins shamelessly. "Are you sure you're simply majoring in classics and not pulling a minor in Art History or Archaeology?"

She laughs, but it's a courtesy. I saw her pull this too many times at the restaurant the other night, with those shallow brackets at the corners of her mouth, to conclude anything else.

"I only know the kind of artifact this is," Kara protests. "Not who made it, or when, or even what this couple is supposed to represent."

Arden pulls back and braces a hip on the edge of the desk. He finishes with a confident cross of arms, and I'm so relieved he's not touching Kara anymore that I don't mind the cutting glance he spares for me.

"The artist is unknown," he says. "Likely because it's been dated to the fourth or fifth century BC. They were also able to narrow down the age due to the piece's subject matter."

He takes another defined pause and swings his renewed focus on me.

"They're definitely a couple, right?" Kara queries. "Either that, or those fourth-century heathens knew how to stare each other down."

Arden pulls in air through his nose and juts up his Armani model chin. "They represent Heracles and Megara."

"Heracles." The name is instantly familiar, of course. At least once a week since hitting puberty, I've been compared to the Greek version of Hercules. "A half-mortal son of Zeus."

"Very good, Professor," he says, calmly dropping his hands between his outstretched legs. "Are you familiar with their story?"

And *here* we are, at last. To the heart of the point he's been deftly angling for. The plot point that should have Kara's ears perked, but nothing about my little demon is close to perky. Anxious is a better word, based on how she tosses the photo down as if it's caught fire.

"Arden." She shakily clears her throat. "An essay about every single one of these pieces isn't urgent."

"Or necessary." My voice verges on a growl as I watch her tension spiral. I want to punch the wall, but flexing my intellectual might is clearly the better choice for helping her right now. That, and I'm curious about where he's going with all this. "Megara was Creon's daughter," I push on. "A princess of Thebes. She was given to Heracles as a prize of war and then bore him several sons."

"Bravo, Professor." Prieto smacks his hands together—

applause that sounds more like he's hailing a dog. "And now for the bonus-round points. What eventually happened to the happy couple?"

"I can assure you, it doesn't have *anything* to do with this piece of art and what we want to bid for it." Despite her adamant claim, Kara fidgets through every word.

I abhor how her unease seems to feed Arden's arrogance, represented by his new preen. "Oh, come now. Every story matters. Certainly you know it, yes?"

"Heracles was struck with madness, killing Megara and their children," Kara finally says. "Happy now? Can we finally move on?"

He pushes buoyantly back to his feet. "Call me cruel, but that's actually my favorite part."

"But it wasn't Heracles's fault," I argue.

"No. You're right, of course. It's deliciously tragic. With Hera being so overcome with jealousy and so dedicated to destroying his happiness at its pinnacle, he simply had no chance." He pivots and regards me with a bold stare. "Wouldn't you agree?"

I shrug. He's just messing with our heads for his sick sport. I'm sure of it, even as new concern fires through my thoughts. Sport or not, the game is still on, and he seems determined to make it as ugly as possible as fast as possible.

Kara claps her own hands together. "Okay, gentlemen. Story time is over. I think everyone in this room is too overeducated to waste any more time on these pointless retellings."

"I must humbly disagree." Arden circles around and

resettles onto both feet with confidence. "You gave me a theme, and by the fires of hell, I'm committed to it. Besides, you *are* the one who brought such an interesting plus-one to the party." He uses the notation as an excuse to again examine me. His concentration is no less cutting and calculating as before. "You have such heroic possibility, Professor. I shall be watching and waiting with rapt interest to see how it all plays out. In all its tragic glory."

With those words, Arden's revealed more than an ancient threat. As if there were any doubt, he's revealed who—or what—he's really rooting for. My failure. My imminent doom. Despite the new sprint of my heart, I pretend that his story is just that. An ancient tale that couldn't possibly touch our lives here and now.

"You know what, sweetheart?" I murmur, tugging her back to my side. Just the cinnamon scent of her hair brings an invigorated smile back to my lips. "I think you're onto something. This meeting really is going nowhere."

I raise my gaze back up and over to Prieto, positive I don't have the slick smirk as mastered as he does. But I'm also the one leaving with the woman he still clearly craves and will never have. It's more than a fair trade.

"Maybe it's a better idea for us to go through this batch by email," Kara offers gently to Arden. "You have my address. I can respond right away."

"Of course." But his pupils remain razor-sharp, and his smile gives way to a terse line. "But I'll have to copy Veronica. The general who signs the checks is allowed to inspect the troops, after all."

Kara releases a resigned sigh. "If that's what she wants, that's not a problem."

The journey out of Arden's office has my head nearly buzzing with relief. But Kara's demeanor stays locked in that pensive space as we ride the elevator back down and walk across the tropical courtyard toward the valet stand. Right after we enter the long exit archway, she twists her head up and around, peering back at his office like a heroine in a gothic Victorian novel.

Then, even in the shadowed light of the tunnel, I watch her go totally pale.

"Hera," she mutters almost too softly to hear.

I pause our retreat, turning her to face me. I respond to her shivery whisper in one of my own. "Kara? What is it?"

She lifts her face toward me. Her gaze frantically searches mine. "What if he's right?"

I wince at the thought of giving Arden credit for anything. "Right about what?"

"About Hera. About the story," she adds. "What if—"

I cut in with a soft laugh to lighten her growing anxiety and to hide the fact that I'm now nursing some of my own. "It's just a story, Kara. He's trying to get under your skin just like he did mine. He's bitter and looking to piss us off any way he can, but we can't give him that satisfaction."

I'm not sure how thoroughly I believe that, but it feels good to state it.

Still, Kara shakes her head fervently. "I don't know. Remember the first time we met Z? He said his wife kept him on a tight leash. Who else could he be talking about?"

"We're talking about myths and legends here—"

"*Maximus*. Don't you get it yet? We're *living* the myths and the legends." Her voice shoots up an octave, echoing through the tunnel. "Everything we discount as too unbelievable to fear could kill us." She swallows hard. "Arden might be onto something with Hera or maybe knows something we don't. I saw my grandfather the other day, and he thinks we should be worried about her too. Everything you and I have done in the spotlight could backfire if it draws attention to you. If the story is true… Hera's merciless. She'll try to find you, and… and…"

The wobble of her words cuts into me, right past my own worry. "*Breathe*, Kara." I match my tone with a soothing glide down her arm.

She works her lips together and then complies with an inhalation through her nose. I'm suddenly driven to allay these new fears and save the rest of our day without Arden's words haunting her. I can't do it with total confidence until I know more, though, and that won't happen until Z resurfaces. For now, I'm in a holding pattern about discrediting Arden's threat.

But I can take full advantage of the small informational opening she's given me, and that may be just as well. Perhaps even better.

"All right. If your grandfather's onto something with this Hera business, then maybe we should lie low for a while."

She swallows roughly. "We probably should. But the premiere… My mother—"

I lean in and cut her off with a soft kiss. "I'm not letting her ruin another minute with you," I whisper against her perfect lips. "Not today. Not tomorrow. Until I talk to Z, we do what we want. And that starts now."

She gazes up at me, her eyes glittering with enough emotion and surrender to give me hope.

"My place." I brush my thumb over her bottom lip.

Visions of possibility cause me to bite down on my own to keep the growl in my chest from tearing free. She releases a long and heavy breath, letting me collect her against my chest.

"Your place," she murmurs softly.

Those two little words send an avalanche of celebration and relief through me as we head back to the truck. And as I catch a glimpse of Arden's shadowed figure peering down at us through the glass wall of his office, I don't bother denying myself the satisfaction of that small win.

CHAPTER 12

I'M OBSESSED WITH THE feel of Maximus. The sheer force of him. The intoxicating contradiction of his strength and the care he takes when he's making love to me. I melt into every blissed-out second of it, not taking anything for granted.

I revel in the brush of his lips along my neck, soft and rough at once. His sexy whispers in my ear. His strong hands on my hips, controlling the angle and pace of my motions as I'm straddled above him, taking him deeper and deeper into me.

The sheets have long been torn off the bed. The air smells like sex. Like *us*. And my cries of pleasure have turned into raspy whimpers.

We've passed the frenzy. This is delirium. Slow and decadent stokes of the flame that's been burning all night. We've discovered and rediscovered each other in a thousand electrifying ways. I should be exhausted. But hours of being brought over the edge haven't made me want him any less. The rising sun spears through the hazy, early morning rain clouds and filters in through the little apartment's picture window. Still, I refuse to give up these last moments. Like a true addict, I cling to every charged slide of skin against skin. Every meaningful drive of his body into mine. Every precious second of this closeness between us.

"One more," he whispers as he reaches between us to stroke his fingertips against my clit.

I gasp and brace my hands on his broad shoulders, feeling too sensitive to come that way again. "I can't . . . "

"Yes, you can." He pairs the low command with a wicked smile. Then he wraps his other arm around my waist possessively, shifts his hips higher, and deepens our connection, stealing my breath.

I gasp and press my nails into his flesh. I don't know if I can, but oh, do I want to. My eyes flutter closed as I lose myself to the sensations once more.

"That's it," he murmurs, taking total control over my body, moving me exactly how he wants. "Love it when you get tight on me."

As if on command, I clench at his depth and the change in our lazy rhythm. I'm chasing my next breath. Colors snap vividly behind my eyelids. I let my head fall back, trusting his hold on me. He takes advantage of the arch, sucking my nipples into his mouth, teasing the tips with the edge of his teeth, all the while fucking me like the ragdoll I've become in his powerful arms.

One more . . . One more . . .

My tired brain latches on to the plea. Reaches for it. Craves it just as badly as I've craved all the others.

The soft rain hitting the streets creates white noise in the background of our heavy breaths. Hardly a distraction from the orgasm thundering down on me. I tense and bow, bracing myself for all the beautiful waves of it. The sharp hit of release cascades over me as hints of tears collect in the corners of my eyes. I don't know why they're there all of a sudden. I can't sort it out when I'm flying this high.

All I know is that my throat is even tighter from the words I can't force out but desperately want to in this heightened moment. Not for the first time since last night either. Everything in me wants to tell Maximus that I'm in love with him. That I'm wildly, madly, and deeply consumed with an emotion I've never experienced before. But that doesn't mean I'm not sure of it. I know what this is as well as I know my own breath and blood. It can have no other word but love.

But as he grates my name into the air again and again and fills me with his release, I keep the sentiment tucked away. The effort causes me to deepen my clench on his shoulders, drawing crescents of blood to the surface. If he feels it, he doesn't let on. They'll heal before we catch our breath anyway, as I've learned more than once tonight. His physical regeneration is not unlike the fires in my eyes that dim once my desire cools.

We're inseparable for a long time as more sunshine breaks through the gray storm and fills the room. Our chests are molded warmly together. We're damp with sweat and shaking from yet another explosive climax—one that I'm certain will haunt my thoughts all day.

I've never had a lover before Maximus, but somehow I know he isn't like anyone else would be. Maybe it's the fact that we're not entirely human that creates this off-the-charts energy between us. I only know it's not like anything I've ever experienced. And doubt I ever will again. As if I even want to.

My soul supplies that answer just before we collapse onto the bed together once more. I don't want anyone else in my body, especially in my heart.

I've never wanted to tell him more . . . or been more afraid to.

I'm vaguely aware of the time now. The clock ticks quietly on his nightstand. It's the dawning of a new day. I haven't broken the news to my mother yet that we won't be going along with her plans for the night, but I've resolved to endure whatever verbal wrath may come from it.

Maximus is right. We've jumped through enough media hoops for a week to have satisfied my mother's PR plan. Besides, I'm more than ready to get back to campus. Back to something that feels a little more . . . normal. Less for show and more for my soul.

And listening to my favorite professor wax poetic about Dante is just the salve I need.

I turn into Maximus's chest and peer up at him. "I can't wait for your lecture this afternoon. I have a feeling the sixth circle will be one of my favorites."

He doesn't open his eyes but answers with a smirk.

"You expect me to lecture intelligently now that you've completely wasted me? I've hardly slept."

I hoist myself higher and press sweet kisses across his chest. "I suspect I have not wasted you *completely* yet."

He laughs. "I hope you're joking. Seriously, Kara."

"You seemed pretty intent to test the limits of what *I* could do earlier, so it seems only fair to test you."

"You've tested me. Trust me."

I smile broadly. "A plus," I murmur against the warm skin of his neck, breathing him as I do. He smells like a summer storm. Heat and lightning. He feels like home.

He trails his fingertips along my arm with a satisfied sigh. "I guess you weren't wrong about the all-nighter. Thank God we're bailing on tonight's plans."

He finally opens his eyes and studies me when I don't respond.

"We *are* bailing on them, right?"

I nod tightly. "I'll work it out with my mother."

He furrows his brow slightly, then turns his body so we're lying facing each other. "Good," he answers quietly. "Because after we get home from class, I want you again."

I giggle and let my head fall against the rumpled sheets. "I thought I wasted you."

"I heal quickly," he shoots back. "And don't you know it."

"Sorry." My cheeks heat with a flush of embarrassment. "I hope I didn't hurt you."

He kisses my forehead. "I like it. Every second of it. I like feeling how this affects you."

"I never... I never knew anything could be this intense."

He feathers his fingers across my cheek before tunneling them into my hair. "Me neither."

He looks like he might kiss me again, which brings all sorts of other possibilities to mind. But if we keep this up, we'll be more than exhausted. We'll be late.

I lean in and kiss him before rising swiftly from the bed. I grab my dress from the floor and peek over my shoulder at him. His jaw is slack, and his eyes have a familiar lusty glaze.

"Get up, Professor, or we'll be late for class."

The whispers are worse than they've ever been when I walk into class hours later. Maximus appears oddly immune, maybe because now he knows there's merit to them. I'm not just the famous girl with rumors swirling like wildfire around her. He *is* the rumor, and we've spent a lot of time spreading the news. Having a hand in our own narrative, despite Mom's heavy sway on the pen, has given us back a little control. Not a lot, but enough.

The palpable new energy skittering over the class is almost enough to distract me from the way Maximus runs his tongue over his bottom lip as he flips through his worn copy of the *Comedy*. Or the way his forearms look like they're going to split his rolled-up sleeves. Or his fingers, long and commanding, finding his way to the page with knowing strokes. Every inch of my visual journey is a heart-halting flashback to the many hours we spent in his bed last night.

I'm the only one in the room who's seen him stripped bare. I've seen him overwhelmed. Past reason. Vulnerable. And in this strange moment, it feels like the greatest gift to know him in ways no one else has. To have shown him pieces of me too that only he's been able to uncover.

He clears his throat and peers out across the crowded room, his expression stern. I can't help but smirk. Thankfully he spares me his direct scrutiny, and I wonder if he'll manage to avoid it all class. At least this time I won't blame him for it.

"Apologies for the last-minute cancellation of our Monday and Wednesday classes. In the interest of staying on pace, I'll cover both cantos today. I trust you've all done the scheduled reading. To ensure you have, I'll expect full summaries on both for Friday."

Gasps and a few groans. I bite my lip at my classmates' bemoaning the extra work he's just tacked on to the weekly assignment. He's such a hard-ass, but I completely love it. Yes, even as I struggle to figure out when I'll actually meet the demand as one of his students, my schedule being what it's been.

Maybe I can give him my summary orally. Later.

Maybe if I do it naked, he'll give me some extra insights too.

I bite my lip harder and struggle to untangle my thoughts from memories of our more intimate moments as he kicks off the lecture. But within minutes, I'm lost to the literary themes instead and this man's obvious, addicting passion for the material—from the wasters to the wrathful, carrying Dante further along his journey. Maximus lingers on Dante's shift in tone, the gradual hardening of the heart and lack of pity for the fallen. Though Maximus observes the shifts without his own judgment, I still feel strangely saddened.

I take notes dutifully, looking forward to sharing all my thoughts with him later. Dante's lapses in compassion strike harder than they should. Then again, I'm not like everyone else. I'm not a distracted undergrad. I'm more fallen angel than human. And I'll never be able to walk away from this heritage.

I'm thankful when Maximus doesn't meet my gaze for most of the class. If our interactions in here were weighty with double meanings before, it's so much worse now. Because as he talks about the flaming red towers and iron walls of hell's capital and its swarming crowds kept behind guarded gates, it sounds more real than ever. As daunting as it could very possibly be.

What if the city of Dis is more than one man's dream of hell? What if the gates closed to Dante had opened for me days ago, to punish me for my own rebellions? I wonder if that's what Maximus is thinking too. If he is, he doesn't show it.

I'm not taking such avid notes anymore.

Instead, I sketch nervously in the margins of my notebook, wondering whether coming today was the best idea after all. Perhaps further rumination on the subject of hell isn't the best thing for me right now, at least until my future is less uncertain.

The artful cadence of my professor's voice pulls me

from the worry and back into the lecture though. I try to concentrate on the words and the strength of hearing them in his beautiful baritone. The poetry instead of the literal threat.

I notice where Maximus pauses and the small moments where his own thoughts seem to wander before he begins reading a new passage of note.

"*Take heart. Nothing can take our passage from us*
when such a power has given us warrant for it.
Wait here and feed your soul while I am gone
on comfort and good hope; I will not leave you
to wander in this underworld alone."

Maximus gently closes his book. He's ominously quiet for a long moment, though his pace is casual along the front row of students.

"This feels like a big moment, doesn't it? They've finally arrived at death's kingdom. The place where all the fires of hell burn. But they're met with rebellious angels who will give only Virgil passage. Not Dante. Yet Virgil gives Dante these words of comfort. Why?"

A long silence ends with someone calling out from the class. "Faith?"

Maximus purses his lips with a nod. "All right. Why?"

Another long silence. He finally meets my eyes, the question beaming silently between us. I smile softly and lift my hand.

"Kara?" My name is a mere murmur on his lips, lacking the sharpness of his typical professorial tone.

It's not personal, but it's intimate enough to make my

heart knock a little harder against my ribs.

The curious energy spiking in the room is matched with the noisy twists of bodies in seats to stare up at me. Of course sitting in the back again would do little good. Not when I'm so much more than Kara Valari these days. I'm half of one of the most talked-about couples in LA. And my other half is a six-foot, seven-inch golden god walking among men. If they only knew . . .

"Well," I start, "God has given them warrant for their journey, which means that divine aid should allow them passage. '*At his touch all gates must spring aside.*'"

I know Maximus's face well enough to recognize his fight to smile. Instead, he pinches his brows together and adjusts his glasses, quickly hiding the other tells that he's satisfied with my response.

"Miss Valari has made a good point," he finally says. "Which also brings us perfectly to next week's reading. Will the Great One arrive and save our poetic duo?" He drops his book on the table like a judge adjourning the court. "Summaries due in my office by Friday. Late delivery is an automatic incomplete. You know the drill."

The room breaks into a rush of movement and chatter as everyone files out. I'm in no hurry to follow them. Instead, I wait for the curious lingerers to give up and leave too before walking down the stairs toward Maximus.

As I get to the main floor, he's packing his laptop and paperwork into his messenger bag.

"Thank you for another intellectually thrilling lecture, Professor Kane," I tease.

He traces his tongue along his lower lip the second his eyes meet mine. "Thrilling, eh?"

"Positively stimulating, if you ask me."

He laughs. "Really? You are by far my most appreciative student. I'm afraid everyone knows it now too."

I shrug and stop in front of him. "Well, I'm not afraid. We're definitely not a secret anymore."

"Honestly, that part is almost a relief." He takes his glasses off and slides them into a side pocket in his bag.

"Why does a man who heals in seconds wear reading glasses?"

His expression freezes a moment as he contemplates my question. Then he breaks with an awkward laugh. "All right... You've got me."

I lift a brow. "Busted?"

"Completely busted." He softly laughs again. "I started wearing them at interviews when I was trying to get a teaching position. I was younger than most of the other candidates and didn't really look the part. Still don't, so I guess I just stuck with it."

I hum quietly and draw my fingertips down the front of his shirt, my nails ticking along the buttons. "So you think if you wear them, people will be able to concentrate on what you're actually saying and forget you're only twenty-seven and built like an immortal god?"

His eyelids get heavy. His breathing quickens. "Something like that."

"It's very Clark Kent. I like it," I murmur, lifting on my toes to kiss the corner of his mouth.

He turns enough to capture my lips and make it a full kiss, inciting his own breathy hum when we part. "What were you saying again, about that stimulating lecture?"

"Just quietly admiring your intellect. And figuring out how I'm going to make time for all the extra work you piled on us this week."

"We have all night."

I draw in a deep breath through my nose and step back on my heel to create a few inches of space between us. "About that."

He sets his jaw. "Let me guess . . . Veronica is dead set on us going to this damn premiere."

"No. She's dead set on *me* going."

He frowns. "Without me?"

"She thinks it'll give people even more reason to talk. We've been inseparable all week. Stepping out to a major event like that without you will be fresh news. Everyone knows we're together now, so pretending like maybe we're not is even juicier."

He works his jaw harder. "Will Arden be there?"

"I don't think so. I didn't ask, but it's not really his scene."

"It's Kell's scene, though. Piper Blue is the star of the film. She's one of Kell's best friends, right?"

"She is. But this is a lot different than a meeting alone at his office. Red carpets are chaos. No one gets a chance to socialize until the after-party, and I'll be on my way home to you by then. It'll be safe, I promise."

Even safer without Maximus being there, I silently

remind myself. When my mother posed the compromise, I didn't balk for that very reason. Mainly because she never extends trade-offs like this, so appeasing her and keeping Maximus out of the limelight is a win-win.

Except that now he doesn't seem overly thrilled. Still, I recognize a glimmer of acceptance in his eyes.

He tugs me close again, lowering his mouth to mine. "I just hate being away from you."

"Ah, parting is *such* sweet sorrow."

We pull apart as a voice from the back of the hall cuts into our romantic haze. We look up together in time to watch as Z saunters in, his voice as unhurried as his footfalls down the stairs.

Maximus joins me in shifting back by a step. His father's dressed in beige linen pants and a short-sleeved white button-down today. His fedora is back and tilted on his head, matching his crooked grin.

"What are you doing here?" Maximus's tone isn't as cold as it's been toward Z in the past, but it's not exactly warm either. "Do you have news?"

Z doesn't speak until he's joined us on the lowest level of the lecture hall. "Some," he answers lightly, shifting his focus to me. "Hello, Kara."

I offer an awkward wave because Maximus is even more intense now.

"What news?" he presses.

"Just a meeting. One that might go a lot smoother if you joined," Z replies coolly.

My breath catches. "With who?"

"My brothers happen to be in town. Figured they might want to meet their long-lost nephew." Z grins then and slaps Maximus affectionately on the arm. "What do you think? Up for a little family time? Get your mind off missing your beloved for a few hours?"

Maximus and I share a knowing look. A meeting including Hades means Z will be negotiating for my safety. For my freedom. And that's exactly what we need to happen. But it doesn't mean I need to feel comfortable about it.

"Should I be there too?" I ask.

Z clucks his tongue a couple times. "I think not. Let's see how this goes, and we can see about introducing you to the in-laws a little later. Sound good?"

"He's right," Maximus says to me, skipping clear over Z's innuendo. "I don't want you near them until we hear what they have to say. The safest place you can probably be is at the premiere with your mother." He looks back to Z. "When?"

Z turns his palms up. "Ready when you are."

CHAPTER 13

MAXIMUS

WE DON'T TAKE MY truck to Labyrinth this time. After Z pries me away from a final kiss with Kara, he snaps his fingers, and we're standing in the vestibule of the Olympian watering hole. Outside, there's still a beach and waves and a cloudless sky. But this time, the surroundings don't vaguely resemble Ventura. I'm not even sure we're still in America.

I *am* sure that I don't really care. It's time to focus on the business at hand. No matter what story Z is trying to sell me here, this isn't a family reunion. It's a negotiation. That simple. That vital.

Do I wish things were different? Of course. For so long, I've begged Mom for the keys to my past. Now they're just steps away. As easy as sitting down with my father and my uncles, ordering some nectar from the back, and listening as they tell me stories from my childhood. Memories that have been taken from me.

Except even that's not the important point right now. I'm here to fight for Kara, no matter what it takes.

"Son."

Instinctively I bristle at the word until better sense takes over. The fortitude in Z's undertone is exactly what I need right now. I heed him with a silent glance.

"Are you ready?" he asks.

"Does it matter if I'm not?"

He nods, but it's just the top of his head. His stubbled jaw is already firmed. "Said the wise kid to his proud dad."

It's the boost I need to keep moving forward. By his side, I move through the mullioned glass doors that slide apart on our approach. Beneath the wide, arched doorway and into the main room of the bar, I'm slammed by perception-pounding shock, along with the most unsettling realization.

Walking into the Labyrinth before earned us a few stares, but none like the two men pinning their otherworldly gazes on us. The seasoned surfer and the brooding hellhound, obdurately serene.

And obscenely familiar.

Z and I come upon their slick mahogany bar table.

I stop a couple of paces behind Z like I've just run into a cement slab. That fast, my recognition has morphed from shock to outrage.

"You've been following me," I blurt.

Z looks over his shoulder, an eyebrow arched in question.

I jab my chin at the pair before us. "You got past the security gauntlet at Yamashiro. Then the parking garage at my apartment building. Now, here you are."

Only this place can't be found with a GPS and doesn't seem to have bribable doormen. I don't see the men's cameras anywhere, which solidifies what I fear to be the truth. They're not paparazzi working the celebrity beat. They're my fucking uncles.

"Do I get an answer?" I bite out.

The surfer has a walking cane, its grip carved out between two tines of an ornate trident. He nods toward an open chair. "Why don't you relax and have a seat?"

My feet refuse to move me an inch closer. "Why don't you tell me why you've been following me for nearly a week?"

"Why the hell do you think? Sit down and quit your posturing." The hellhound growls it with a sinister energy that matches his crimson three-piece suit. He drums the table, making the blood-colored gems decorating his fingers glimmer in the dim light. I don't miss the pin on his silk tie either. It looks like a snake wrapped in a cypress leaf. Even in the human realm, nobody could mistake his king-of-hell vibe.

My blood is pounding. My pores are on fire. But there's nothing in my mind to anchor these feelings to. There's no validation for this. There's no memory for this. Nothing except an eerie whisper at the back of my senses. Like it or not, despite the men's obvious deceit, they are my blood. Outside of Mom, that's never meant much to me. But as I stand here now, it means more than I ever expected.

Z, pretending not to notice the friction between us,

waves to where Honey's drying off glasses behind the bar. "A round of the good stuff from the back."

"I'm fine," I mutter, circling the table to take a seat between the two strangers.

"You will be. Soon." Z lowers into one of the plush chairs like it's become his personal throne. "Po. Hades. This is your nephew, Maximus. Maximus—"

"I think we're fine with skipping the introductions," Poseidon cuts in, though I suspect more to get to the meat of things than to rebuff his brother. He strokes his silvering blond beard, exposing some smaller braids twisted around seashells, before sweeping out his free hand. "Like the boy said, we've been keeping an eye on him already. His existence wasn't exactly a secret."

"Was news to me, actually," Hades adds. "Not that I would have cared one way or the other."

"Now there's a charming first impression," Po mutters.

Honey breaks the tension by distributing a small tumbler of dark-brown liquid to each of us. "On the house, fellas."

Hades snickers. "They always are."

Honey shrugs. "What can I say? I like to stay in business."

Po and Z toss half theirs back in single gulps.

Hades takes a more conservative swallow, all the while peering at me over the glass. "You're not drinking."

I push the glass away. "I'm not here to drink."

"No?" He kicks up his brows, black as raven wings, which frame his equally dark eyes. "Then you must be here to discuss the disobedience of one of my subjects."

"Her name is Kara," I reply through tight teeth.

Z clears this throat loudly. "Brother, I think you may be overlooking a detail there."

"I don't think I am. She belongs to me, and you're all here to talk me out of taking what is rightfully mine. It's boring, gentlemen—and frankly a little pathetic. I have better things to do."

I ball my fists, the rest of my body tensing as I ready myself to rise and correct him, no matter what it takes.

Kara is *mine.*

But Z beats me to the argument. "Technically, Kara is only a little more than *half* your subject," he offers matter-of-factly. "Human blood runs through her veins too, which means she's my subject as well."

Not an inch of my tension relaxes until I finally catch where he's going with all this. I finally see his very interesting—and hopefully useful—point. At last, I get down a couple of calming breaths.

In the meantime, Hades is impaling my father with a dark glare. "The Valaris are mine," he utters with lethal seriousness. "Giovani Valari may be human, but he became *my* subject the moment he crossed the threshold of *my* kingdom." He pauses before his tone goes even lower. "I don't get in the way of justice in your world, Z. Don't get in the way of it in mine."

"You misunderstand me," Z counters. "We're here, after all, in the middle ground. Everyone wants to sort it out."

"There's bound to be gray area from time to time," Po chimes in. "That's obviously why Z's brought us here.

I'm sure it's not for the pleasure of your sunny company, brother."

Hades snarls and leans forward. Po doesn't flinch, only anxiously twists the trident in his grasp.

"This isn't a gray area," Hades goes on. "The word is disobedience. Lest you've forgotten, it means refusing to honor the rules. Neglecting authority. Disregarding your betters."

Z releases an exasperated sigh. "Fellow deities, it seems you've both forgotten an important detail here." He looks to me, but I'm unclear why. My confusion doesn't waver his definition. "We *make* the rules."

Hades shifts his scrutiny to Z. "And we've had thousands of years to make them. If we're constantly challenging expectations to suit our whims, what is the point of having rules at all?"

"Tell me, then, what are the rules on sending your minions across the river to deflower half-blood demons on earth? I must have missed that in the fine print."

Hades tightens his jaw. "Maybe you missed it while you were deflowering humans all over creation."

Z laughs halfheartedly, avoiding my eyes. "My dear black-hearted brother, you've spent too much time keeping your subjects' endless sorrow on a steady churn. You have no appreciation for spontaneity. You need to live a little. Is Persephone out of town again? Is that why you're so sour over this?" Z uses that moment to loudly hail another round from Honey.

"You'd be very wise to leave Persephone out of this,"

Hades levels. "And for the record, your *spontaneity* has caused you nothing but trouble for eons." His stare is fixed on me then, the obvious result of one of Z's many indiscretions. "Does Hera know about him?"

Z chokes awkwardly on his last swallow of mead. "Of course not. You know she'd lose her lid if she—"

"She knows."

All eyes shift to Po and the threat he's just knelled in the tense air. I swallow hard because being on Hera's radar is pretty high on the list of things I don't want or need in my life right now.

"She knows about me?" I challenge, my posture clenching. "How?"

Z's shoulders are equally stiff angles now. "They were hidden. Nancy was safe. I made sure of it."

"How could you be sure? Even you can't be everywhere at once." Po starts twisting his trident again. "And when you were away, threats were made on their lives."

"Why didn't you tell me?" Z's loud challenge marks a rare break in his composure. "Hera is *my* problem, not yours."

"Some would even call her your wife," Hades mutters.

Z ignores the comment and rises to his feet, his breezy exterior decidedly shed. "You should have come to me, Po. I knew you were involved. I *knew* it."

"Enough!" Po bangs down the base of his cane, and the sea beyond the patio responds with twenty-foot breakers. "Just take a breath and *listen*, Z." Just as swiftly, the waves mellow out. "I did what I felt was best under the circumstances. And the circumstances were such that it was better for you not to know where they went."

"He's my *son*." Z stabs a finger at him, the tip alive with small but angry blue sparks. "You had *no* right."

Po swings the trident forward, tilting its gilded tines toward Z. "And *you* were idiotically in love with his human mother who had absolutely no place anywhere near Olympus. To think you could keep them truly hidden from anyone, let alone your *wife* and *queen*, only proves how blinded you were—and frankly still are—to the dangers of keeping the mortal in your life."

Z openly seethes. "They were my responsibility!"

"And they'd be dead if you'd kept on assuming that responsibility. Even her keeper didn't think you were up to the task. She reached out to me because she felt it was a matter of life and death. What was I supposed to do?"

While Po speaks, a strange instinct fires in the depths of my brain. Something here is feeling familiar, but my mind won't zoom the memory into focus.

"Keeper?" I latch on to the word that first fires the sensation.

Everyone looks to me, their expressions suddenly full of chilling gravity, as if they've just remembered that I'm here. The silence becomes heavier than all their heated words combined. It's not comfortable. I still don't care.

Po pulls the trident back in, along with a deep and measured breath. "I believe, my boy, that you know her as Regina Nikian."

"Reg?" My shock-struck throat practically chokes it

out. "What the hell does she have to do with—"

"She's a soldier of Olympus." Po ignores Z's censuring glare. "Was, anyway. Even though you were kept out of sight of the gods, she was the one tasked with your and your mother's safety when Z decided to raise you in his world. The choice wasn't Nancy's, of course, so Regina was in part hired to *keep* you and your mother in Olympus, as well." He finally acknowledges Z by raising an accusing brow. "He needed the assistance, since he was often gone, taking care of other . . . affairs."

"Fuck you, Po." Z drops down angrily in his chair when Honey brings the second round.

Po shrugs. "The boy has a right to know."

"Say whatever you'd like. I was faithful to Nancy."

Hades hums playfully. "No wonder Hera was in such a fury."

My father rears up with a curled fist but falls back just as fast with a taut glower. I'm certain my features are arranged similarly.

Out of all the revelations I've had, this new truth is the most astounding. But the deeper I consider it, the more it all makes sense. Reg's steadfast protectiveness. How she often knows me better than I know myself. How she's always been there for Mom and me.

But with the tidal wave of astonishment, there's anger too. And confusion. More of that than anything—which comes as a blessing at the moment, helping me focus on forming new words.

I exhale a breath that's felt clamped in my chest for

too long. "Why can't I remember anything?" I claw a hand through my hair. "None of this . . ."

Po settles a thoughtful gaze on me. The dark-blue monsoons in his eyes sock me square in the chest. Something else is stirred now, whipped into life by this intense contact with my uncle. But again, it's maddening and elusive. I know it's something that's part of me but buried deep. So goddamned deep . . .

"Because we knew you were never going back," he answers calmly. "And if you were permitted to remember more, you'd likely push for deeper answers and risk being discovered on earth. Perhaps not just by the gods, either. It was all for your own safety."

There's another long moment of silence, weighted and thick, in which Z and Po study me with different degrees of intensity. I have no idea what they're thinking. I have no idea what *I* should think right now.

Po draws his lips into a regretful line. "I am sorry to have done it. I hope you know that. I believe your childhood was a happy one."

"It was," Z adds, slamming his emptied glass onto the table. "Some of the most joyous days of my existence." Z's comment is hoarse yet tender. He points to Po again. "You and me. We need to talk."

Po's nostrils flare. "I suppose I deserve that much. Let's try to keep our elements to ourselves, though. Earth has enough to face right now without two gods at war, breaking all the china in the house."

Z mutters something I don't catch on his dash to the

door. Po rises too. His huge shoulders strain at the confines of his jacket as he leans hard on his staff and limps unhurriedly after Z.

I look to Hades. "What's with the limp? He's a god."

Hades doesn't lift his attention from studying his tidy fingernails and positioning his rings. "A fish out of water, so to speak. We're all a little out of sorts outside of our own realms, which is another reason I'd love to get back to mine. My brother gets rather chatty after the mead, though, so I'm afraid we'll be here a while." He tips his chin toward the still full glass before me. "Try some."

"I'm all set." I keep my tone and my posture guarded. The fewer flanks I expose, the better.

"No memories of Olympus and you're turning away the magic mead?" He *tsks*. "You're just missing out on the best of everything."

I push out a hard huff and mutter a soft curse. Something about the god's good-natured challenge needles me now—to the point that I give in. I take a short sniff of the rich, dark liquid in my tumbler. It's got to be one-eighty proof, maybe more. I toss back a swallow of it. The alcohol is pungent, piercing, but delicious. Yeah, I'll have to go slow on this. As in, not any more at all.

I try to parse out the flavors and compare it to something I've had before, but before anything clicks, I'm hit with the one thing that has always evaded me. A buzz. An instant blanket of warmth and...happiness? The heaviness of my own body is just a little lighter. Hell, I almost feel like laughing, until I suddenly catch Hades boring a hole in me with his stare.

A cloak of dark energy takes over the air. It reminds me of stepping into an air-conditioned building. It smells like humid dirt, and it's accompanied by a mocking sigh.

"Shall you and I have a chat, then?"

The question mark at the end is the most unnecessary punctuation since we got here. This face-to-face with the demon is exactly what I've come here to accomplish. All the rest of this crazy shit—Mom, Reg, my past, my memories—can wait.

For now, I hope Z and Po take their time so I can get this right, even if my brain is swimming a little more than I'd like. This could be the only chance I have to convince the brooding god to spare the life of the woman I love.

But I don't dare give the thought another second to gather steam, especially when Hades speaks up again.

"Let's go see what Honey has on special, hm?"

He grabs my shoulder and guides me toward the bar. And I let him.

Is it because my body feels a hundred pounds lighter? Or because I'm starting to latch on to the twisted truth that we're *related*? Worse, that I'm already feeling more connected to him and Po than I ever expected to?

But *is* that the absolute worst?

I've been seeking this my whole life. The revelation of my roots. The knowledge of my family. Maybe I'm just uncomfortable with having to actually accept those concepts now. Maybe, with time, some of this will feel a little less crazy.

Says the demigod strolling up to the fire bar with the king of hell . . .

We take two stools at the back end of the O-shaped bar. The only light source continues to be the tower of endless flames at the core of the area. They're not contained behind any glass or barriers, yet their heat is still subliminal at best. It's not so gaudy and bold back here, where the fire cone drenches everything in an amber and orange glow.

"What can I get you?" Honey's not mirroring Hades's slanted smile. He looks like he'd rather be drowning in the waves past the windows instead of waiting on our drink orders. Back here, his hair and tats seem to gleam brighter. But that doesn't mitigate the darker, more disquieted side of his demeanor.

"You have any more of the Ninth Circle Rye?"

Hades's blunt query has Honey responding like an on-duty sentry. "Yes, sir. Two glasses?"

Hades looks to me.

I shake my head. "Water for me."

Another drink of anything else in here will put me soundly on my ass. Not acceptable. Not right now.

The dimmed light should help hide my discomfort from Hades's long scrutiny. It doesn't. I continue feeling like a science experiment as he stares his fill of me. But I let him take all the time he needs. I hate it, but I do it.

Thankfully, Honey is speedy about delivering the drinks. Clearly the guy wants to drop the booze and move on from our atmosphere completely.

I lift my glass. "Cheers, I guess."

Hades collects his own tumbler without ceremony. "Toasts are for the hopeful." He slugs back a swallow. "Which probably brings us to why you're here. Z must have thought meeting you would soften my position about my little rebel."

I hesitate. "Has it?"

"Not sure if you've noticed, but I'm not that sentimental. Not even about family."

"You seem pretty interested in what *I've* been up to."

An appraising smirk breaks across the god's angular face. "Oh, you still think all that's about you?"

I frown. "Why else would you and Po be following me around LA? Certainly wasn't a coincidence."

"It wasn't."

I take a guarded gulp of my water. "All right. Enlighten me, then."

"Po's eagerness to see you in the flesh dovetailed nicely with my interest in seeing *her* in the flesh."

I'm certain the fire has swallowed all the oxygen in the room, because I can't breathe right for a few counts.

Shit.

"Kara," is all I can manage, though the sound is a little broken past my lips.

He was watching her, not me. Not even us. Because who cares about *us* when he's already convinced she belongs to him?

"Why do you want her?" I finally get out from between my teeth. "Why is she so important?"

"I could ask you the same thing, Maximus. Why do *you*

want her? Why would you defy me, and the very edicts of hell, to keep her?"

I tilt the glass back and forth between my hands, frowning. *Want* has never been a word I've associated with Kara. Does a tree ever just want sunshine? Does a page simply want for words? Is a fire okay with merely wanting kindling?

The metaphor knocks me back to what's in front of me. The play of the fire cone's glow on the water in my glass. The mix of liquid and light is mesmerizing. I'm thankful for the modicum of mellow it lends. I'm everything but mellow right now.

Hades taps his fingernails against the bar. "You're fully aware of what she is and what she's done, yes?"

"I am."

He swallows down more of his rye, which sends a waft of it in my direction when he exhales again. "She's defied the decrees and requirements of her ancestry."

"Yes. I know."

"Risked her entire family's standing in both of their worlds."

"*Yes*, damn it. I get it. And I don't care."

He pauses, studying me with a hard coal squint. "That's what I'm trying to figure out. Why?"

"If you're looking for me to convince you of all the ways she's stitched into me now, I won't. I just . . . can't. Some things are beyond words. Words are what I'm good at, and I have none that come close to describing what exists between us."

He hums softly. "Words fail the poet. How romantic, I think."

"I'm no poet."

He pauses thoughtfully again. "And she must share this inexplicable attraction as well. Since she's done all of this for you."

"For me," I return, too torturously. "I'm aware of everything she's done and every rule she's violated, *for me*. Now that we've beat those facts to a pulp, let's cut to the main point here." My knuckles are still white against the bar's edge. "You haven't tried to take Kara yet. That means you want something else."

"Perhaps." Hades motions to Honey for another hit of the alcohol. "Perhaps not."

I don't buy it, but I wait until Honey's finished with pouring him some more Ninth Circle and walks away.

"What. Do. You. Want?"

"To be honest, I wasn't sure when all this started to unfold, but now I'm beginning to want what you want." When he grins, his canines show. "Greed and envy and complicated sibling rivalry playing no small part, I'm sure."

I grab the bar's ledge and twist hard. The gold lip gives up a noisy creak beneath my grip but nothing else. Great. I finally find a place that can take the abuse of my strength and I can't wait to get out of it. And what I'm feeling in it.

"Name your price. Anything."

He answers with a mild chuckle that perplexes and enrages me in equal measures. He's laughing at my agony. At my desperation.

What else should I expect, though?

"How can I put a price on something so fascinating?" He tilts his head one way and his smirk the other.

I scrutinize him harder. "And that's a reason to laugh?"

As quickly as it's hit, his humor fades. "To be honest, I haven't been fascinated in a while."

A while. I hear it for the understatement that it is, though I'm nervous about fathoming the extent of it. Does he mean a couple of years? A hundred? A thousand? And what does that mean for Kara and me?

After another refill, he gulps down his third glass as swiftly as the first two. Though his eyes glass over, none of his discomfort disappears. He's allowed me to step behind his magic curtain, seeing the maudlin truth beneath his surly shell. He's the ruler of the most frightening empire there is, the overseer of every sin committed. He's seen it all, from the mild infractions to the truly evil—and now, nothing is new anymore. In any other circumstances, the revelation might have me pitying him.

But being the center of his new puppet show is worse than adhering to Veronica's Tinseltown merry-go-round. Worse, because Hades is more opaque about his end game. There's no itinerary, flow chart, or wardrobe stylists here. When I'm longing for Mama Valari's control factory, something is definitely wrong.

"So what does that mean, exactly? You're fascinated. Where does that get us now? You want a medal? A statue out in front of the bar?"

I'm playing with fire again. Literally. Tiny, raging

hurricanes of it whorl from the ruthless centers of his eyes. But there are new quirks along the ridges of his jaw too. Maybe some levity before he tries to kill me. I can't tell, and I'm not sure if I want to.

He cuts into the thick pause with a determined murmur. "I just want . . . "

He falters.

"You want *what*?" I press.

He stares at me even harder. Deeper. "I want . . . to understand."

I'm tempted to try bending the bar again. This time, aided by wrath and confusion, I'd probably succeed. *To understand what?* I've never been further from the verb in my life. My senses are all over the map. My thoughts are a million live wires, neurons yanked from their ground wires.

Until he reaches out, molding his hot palm over my shoulder as he did before. This time, his clutch keeps me motionless—or maybe it's the deep burn in his eyes that's stunning me into this unexpected paralysis.

What. The . . . ?

His grip tightens and he closes his eyes. Like he's concentrating. Like he's searching for something in the darkness behind his eyelids. Then suddenly every synapse in my brain comes back online. But I'm in no more control than I was before. Before the mead. Before this strange and terrifying contact.

Contact that's bringing a rush of Kara into my thoughts. Not like they're normally hard to summon, but this is different. Very different. It feels . . . *forced*.

Memories surge to the forefront of my psyche, plucked like chosen scenes at stop points in a movie. Only the movie is my life and the moments are specific to Kara.

That first electric touch in the lecture hall at Alameda.

Our first kiss in my apartment.

Touching her beneath the constellations at the observatory.

Watching her wonderment in the hills above the city.

Getting lost in her body between the sheets of my bed.

It's more than the rush of visuals. It's a concentration of the sensations and emotions attached with each one of them, supercharging this single moment that I'm certain I'm sharing with a stranger—this powerful, fascinated stranger who seems to have no intentions of stopping the show. But it has to stop. *I* have to stop it.

With a gut-deep roar, I summon a cruel, primal rage at the violation. I tap a part of myself so deep, it feels wrong but very right. An instinct that was buried in me, so long ago. Calling it up pulls apart all the thoughts he just put back together. Splinters them so violently that all my senses go black for a long moment.

When I can blink myself back to clear vision, I'm a full ten feet away from the bar, damp with sweat and vibrating with the aftershocks of whatever just happened. Hades is still at the bar, though it's gratifying to see him leaning against it, bracing himself through a lot of harsh breaths. Honey is nowhere to be seen, not that he'd volunteer his account of things if he were here.

"What . . . " I swallow hard. "What the fuck just happened?"

Hades leans back on the bar with both elbows, shaking his head, speechless.

"Got what you wanted?" I straighten fully, though every muscle and bone protests getting into my menacing stance. "We solid now?"

He laughs and pushes back to his full posture too. There's not a wrinkle in his suit or his composure as he rakes a fresh smirk over to me. "Oh, Maximus," he chides. "We're just getting started."

I hate him. It's official now. I hope he receives *that* message, loud and clear.

I no longer want to beat up the bar. My mind has a new target. But I'm far too stunned to act on any of those budding fantasies. Besides, I don't imagine giving the god of the underworld a beating is going to resolve a damn thing. I'll only be adding his wrath to his newfound preoccupation—a preoccupation, I sense, that has landed Kara solidly in his crosshairs. And now, for entirely different reasons than before.

I can't even issue the warning for him to forget she exists. It's impossible. Hades makes it so, as his physical body fades away where he stands. In his wake, there's only a residue of morbid energy—and the billion questions in my baffled mind.

Honey's amused expression materializes through the thinning smoke where Hades once was. "You need another round?" His gruff hest is like a miracle angel choir right now.

I shake my head. "Bring me the bottle."

If I can even put a dent in my consciousness right now, I'll count it as a win.

CHAPTER 14

"GRAMPS," I GASP.

The woman applying my lipstick pauses long enough to sigh but doesn't bother to see who's joined the chaos of the premiere prep squad gathered in the hotel's penthouse.

The door swings shut with a quiet click, and Gramps hits me with a dashing grin as he walks closer. I'm grateful when the woman finally steps away so I can smile fully at our unexpected guest. Gramps is nearly unrecognizable in his tuxedo. He's groomed and tall and stunning. I've seen him this way plenty of times, but only in old photos. From another, happier time . . .

I slip off the makeup stool and walk toward him, gathering up the tulle skirts of my dress as I go. His eyes glimmer with emotion.

"Ladybug. Look at you in all that pink."

I shrug, warmed but a little embarrassed by his praise,

and look down at my designer gown. The bodice is fashioned like a corset, seductive but elegant, and I'm sad I'll have to wait for Maximus to see me in it. I have a feeling he'll like the look too. A lot . . .

Have we really been apart just a few hours? I truly hope the movie is riveting, because I'll need the distraction. I ache with missing him already, but I'm anxious too for whatever Z has planned for their meeting.

I flatten my hands over the fluffy layers of tulle. "Thanks . . . It's just another dress. Another event."

"I know, but I only ever see you like this when they're talking about you on the news, if you can even call those shows news. It's different in person seeing you all dolled up."

Smiling, I reach up to straighten his bowtie. "And I only see you like this in pictures. So handsome. You know, you waited so long, your old-school tux is back in fashion again. You'll fit right in."

His eyes dim a little. "Fitting in isn't my main concern tonight."

"Oh?" I try to give it a breezy casualness. "So what actually brought you out?"

His warmth recedes a little more. His attention shifts to the other people rushing around the room, packing up their kits. I take his hand and lead him to the hallway, where we can have more privacy.

"Gramps?" I press. "What is it? Is everything okay? What did you and Mom talk about the other day?"

He clears his throat. "First and foremost, we discussed your safety."

"Okay." I draw the word out a little. "That's a good thing, right?"

His features are more formidable as they tighten in a frown. "I'm still not convinced her head is in the right place with all this."

I swallow hard. "You don't?"

"Kara. I don't doubt your mother cares for you. I just worry some pieces of this have more to do with her ego than what's truly best for you." He pauses. "And I decided it was time to stop hiding."

I shake my head, unsure what he means.

He finally laughs then, but it's underlined by sadness. "You don't think I stay holed up in the guest house all day because she keeps me prisoner there, do you?"

"Well . . ." That is sort of how I've thought about it. It's never seemed fair that he couldn't join us for events. But here he is, as if he's always been with us.

"I haven't just been staying away from you or from my family. I've stayed away from everyone. Don't let this monkey suit fool you. I'm terrified to go down there and be recognized. I'm not flattering myself that someone will—"

"Of course they will, Gramps. You're a legend. Everyone who's anyone in this town knows Giovani Valari. That will never change."

His lips pull into another rueful smile. "Yes, well, that sort of attention isn't always good. You know how that goes."

I rest my hand on his shoulder. "People are going to be thrilled you're here. Piper and the movie's team, especially. They'll be honored to have you."

"Maybe." He's still terse. "If I can just get through the night without someone asking me about what happened all those years ago, it'll be a miracle."

Suddenly I understand what his apprehension is made of, at least in part. I tell him so with a firmer hold. "It'll be fine," I assert, but I don't kid myself. It's for my benefit as much as his. "You don't need any miracles."

But he has a bloody past, rife with questions that were never answered. And people in this town will make up the truth if they don't get their greedy hands on the real deal. That's exactly what they've done to him for years. Made up reasons why he was caught between one of the most notorious couples of his time and why they both ended up dead after a night of suspicious circumstances. He was the only one who pulled through that violent drama, so he's the only one who can set the record straight. I just don't think he wants to.

But I don't tell him that. Now's not the time nor the place.

The show must go on. Which means it's time for a subject change.

"Mom was really okay with this?" I ask. "She was a bit bent a while ago. Tonight was supposed to be Maximus's big debut to the industry's elite."

"At first? No. But you know her. She soon realized having me here would be even bigger buzz for her. I haven't walked a red carpet in . . ." He runs a hand through his silvery hair, which is also on-trend in its unkempt glory. "Hell, it's been a long time."

"Is that why you came? For her?"

He winces. "No, ladybug. I'm here because if someone has any designs about taking you from us, in any realm, you can be damn sure I won't let that happen."

I smile once more and fight the emotion welling up inside. This side of him, fierce and firm, is new—and I like it. Not that I haven't felt his protectiveness over the years, but it's always been subdued by the circumstances of our family. The required distance between us.

Now he's here, and I don't have to pretend that the affection between us doesn't exist. There's actually no one, short of Maximus, I'd rather be my date tonight. I smile wide and give him a hard hug, internally demanding that I keep my tears at bay lest I ruin the work of art my face has become after two hours in the makeup chair.

"I'm so glad you're here. It'll be okay, Gramps, I promise."

When we pull away, he slips his arm through mine with a little flourish. "As long as I know you're safe, it will be. And that's all that matters to me."

As the clock creeps toward midnight and my shoes are killing me, Kell sidles up to me at the after-party.

"So what did you think?" Her gaze floats across the crowd.

"I think I'm ready to be home."

The night feels like it started three weeks ago. An hour working the step-and-repeat out front and another round of hug-and-pecks in the lobby before two hours of struggling to stay still during the film. Layers of tulle aren't forgiving in a quiet movie theater.

"About the movie," she clarifies with a soft laugh.

"It was decent, actually. I think it lived up to the book. Piper did really well."

Kell grins and takes a sip of her champagne. She looks sleek as ever in a one-armed Armani gown with provocative angles of sheer fabric over parts of the bust. We've been schmoozing with people for hours, but she's still flawless and radiant.

"Wow," she says with a perky smirk. "A five-star review from one of the biggest literary snobs I know. Color me shocked."

I wave my hand at her. "Just because I'm serious about school doesn't make me a snob."

"We're all snobs, Kara. That's the allure of the Valaris. We just have our own specialities. Jaden's the adrenaline guy—anything that goes fast is right up his alley. And you have the market cornered when it comes to books and art."

I slant my head. "Fine, I'll play. What is your *speciality*?"

She looks away into the bustling party, her lips curved into a broader grin. "Men, I think."

I laugh. "Can you be a snob in an area where you're forbidden?"

She glances back to me, her dark brows drawn together. She doesn't offer anything else, so I decide to change the subject.

"Have you talked to Gramps?"

She follows my gaze to where he's chatting animatedly

with a couple of other gentlemen in tuxedos. Maybe old friends, or perhaps he's making new ones. But he seems happier than I've seen him in ages, an observation that has my heart swelling with pure joy for him.

"Hmm. Looks like Gio has plenty of people to talk to." Kell's voice is cold and clipped. "Plus, we all stood for the photo opp. Treasured family memories, right?"

As she punctuates it with a fake smile, my senses shiver. Despite my mental push at her rain on my parade, this is no sprinkle of snark anymore. She's a storm front of antagonism.

"Standing next to each other for a tabloid photo isn't a family memory." I narrow my gaze as she wrinkles her nose. "Why are you being so cold? What did he ever do to you?"

"I'm not interested in pissing Mom off. That's all you, Kara."

Her steady sarcasm does nothing to quell my rising surge of righteous anger. "Gio—our *grandfather*—is a good man. He took care of us when we were little—"

"You mean he took care of *you*."

"Excuse me?"

"Oh, Jaden and I always got fed, cleaned, and walked. But you were always his favorite. We were young, but I still remember."

My jaw falls open. "Are you kidding me?"

She finishes off her glass of champagne and hands it to one of the servers without a word or a look. Her energy, still radiating like lightning jolts from a roiling cloud, confirms what her body language is already saying. She's upset about something, but I can't believe it's because Gramps is here, especially with our mother's blessing.

"You've never said anything about this before," I press.

"It never mattered. It still doesn't matter."

"Still . . . maybe we should talk about this."

She cuts in with a laugh. "Right."

I hesitate, my head suddenly spinning over her mood shift. Kell can be haughty and indifferent at times, but this is more than a fleeting feeling. A black cloud she's been toting around for years . . . decades? No. This seems hooked in even deeper than that, and I need to know why.

"Is this really about Gramps?"

She shakes her head, avoiding my eyes.

"Kell—" But my determination is for naught. I hesitate, afraid to say what's in my mind and heart. But I have to, otherwise we may not get to the other side of whatever this strange new tension is.

"Is this about Arden?" My tone is softer because I don't want it to sound like an accusation.

Her silence confirms, though, that it's likely the truth.

"Where is he?" I ask. "I thought he might be here with you tonight."

"No." Her pretty red lips remain pursed and pissed. "He has other matters to attend to."

I don't linger long on the thought. But those two seconds lend ample opportunity to picture Arden's "other matters" involving a certain meeting that Hades is taking right now. What will Maximus do if Arden is a leering fly on the wall during Z's negotiations?

I can't let it be my concern right now. I have to trust

Maximus and the self-control that's like second nature to him. I have to stay sane right now—to help my sister as much as myself.

"You should be happy you didn't have to spend all night with him."

She grabs a newly filled flute off a passing tray but only grimaces at the bubbles. "So I should be happy that he doesn't want to be seen with me in public because he still thinks he has a chance with you?"

Only then does she meet my gaze. My jaw unhinges again, as I process the scalding lash of her jealousy—followed by a terrible new concern.

Arden really hasn't given up on having me.

"He didn't say that." It's a hopeful affirmation but also a desperate question. I pray she's just jumping to conclusions. That he hasn't actually said this . . .

"No." She purses her lips again. "But you know, I could smell it. Disappointment has a very distinct odor."

I exhale a harsh breath. "Kell. I'm so sorry. I did this to us . . . I did this to you, and I can't undo any of it."

"And even if you had another chance, you'd choose the same way." She levels a hard stare at me because she already knows it's the truth.

And so do I. Maybe it's the demon in me, but I know deep in my selfish heart that I would choose Maximus again and again, even understanding that I'd be damning Kell. Maybe it's because I know he'd choose me too. Likelier, it's because I knew that she was as damned as me all along, no matter what. Could Arden be better than the incubus she was destined for? Could he be worse?

We'll never know. And that's entirely my fault. And my soul is an aching, exposed wound because of it.

"Kell, I don't know the right words to say..." I gulp back a sob, and it feels like a million razor blades in my throat. "I fell in love, and no one expected it less than me. But love can make people selfish, and I admit that I have been."

She nods and pretends to be studying her nails. "Maybe one day I'll know what that feels like."

Her lips soften, and she lets go of a breath. Those little shifts take some sting out of her words.

"Will you ever forgive me?"

She laughs quietly. "A demon asking for forgiveness. That's funny."

"I don't know about you, but I think we're more than what's in our blood."

She looks up at me again. "Says the girl who's breaking all the rules and apologizing for it later."

I sigh. "Kell..."

She shakes her head. "It's fine, Kara. Just... It's fine."

It's not fine, but I have no way to make things right, so I let it go just like my daunting vision of Arden and Maximus.

Damn it. Every passing moment feels like a slog right now. A mire of meanings deeper than the *Inferno*'s nine levels, filled with just as many spirits to hurt for... and sins to atone for. But I have to just accept it as the place we're in. For now, but hopefully not forever...

Every minute of the party seems to drag after that, and

I'm relieved when Gramps is ready to go. He's tired and a little buzzed, and his happiness manages to eat away at my own melancholy, which I try hard to hide during the drive home.

When the limo driver drops him off at the Valari estate, we part ways with a hug and a promise to visit soon. I laugh when he slaps Dalton on the arm, coaxing a curious smile out of the butler as he saunters into the house.

The drive home is too long. I'm a tangle of emotions. Nervous and hopeful and then terrified all over again that there may be no good way out of this mess we've made. My only comfort will be the shelter of Maximus's arms again. I grow needier for him with every mile we cover and stoplight we clear. Soon . . . soon . . .

But when I return, the house is eerily quiet and entirely too dark.

"Maximus?" My voice bounces off the high ceilings.

"He's asleep."

I whip my stare toward the sound. Small sparks of light crackle off Z's fingers, illuminating his face in the darkened sitting area. I move farther into the room and switch on a table lamp.

He looks me over with an appreciative gaze.

"My my my. If Maximus saw you in that dress, I'm not sure I could have dragged him away from you."

I drop onto the couch adjacent to him and fold my arms across my bodice defensively. I'm not in the mood for diplomacy or for his frivolous flattery. "What happened?"

He lifts his brows. "A few things. Some good. Some not

so good. And your beloved may have a bit of a headache come morning..."

"What?" I stiffen and jolt, moving to perch on the cushion's edge. All too quickly, my vision from earlier bombards my brain. If Maximus and Arden really did lock horns...and then trade blows...

"He's fine," Z reassures as if reading my mind. "He just had a little more of the devil's poison than he probably should have. Then again, I wasn't too far behind him in that department."

The devil's poison. I frown. Then his meaning clicks. "He's...drunk?"

"Very."

I'm a little annoyed and worried over this news, but my curiosity about the meeting itself wins out. "What good came of the meeting, then?" The next question, what *not* good came of it, is there too, but I don't voice it aloud. I trust—and dread—he'll get there, whether I like it or not.

"Well...the meeting itself, I suppose," he finally says.

I grip the cushion's edge to avoid overtly clenching my teeth. "Excuse me?"

"Getting three conceited bastards such as ourselves to sit down and have a conversation without starting a war is always a win."

Outwardly, I deflate a little. Inwardly, I'm ready to toss the whole coffee table through the window. I truly hope—and damn near pray—there's more good news than that.

"But what about Maximus and me? What did Hades say...about us?"

Z curls his bottom lip between his teeth, a gesture that makes him look either torn or confused.

"We didn't get as far with that as I would have liked," he finally confesses.

I slap my hands on the cushions now. "Are you serious? You didn't even discuss it?"

"No, we did. But we're of two minds when it comes to this dilemma, and it will likely take more than one meeting to sway him. Hades... He's very..."

"What?" I demand when he tries to buy time with the lip-gnashing move again.

He frowns. "He's very interested in you, I'm afraid. Specifically."

I push together my own brows. "Which means what? Are you sure?"

"I am. Maximus couldn't talk about anything else once we left the Labyrinth. After he and Hades spoke in private, he seemed convinced that this is about more than my brother keeping all his subjects in the right place."

Nothing about his countenance gives me a glimmer of hope. In fact, I'm washed over with fresh dread.

"But you said Maximus was drunk."

He lifts his brows. "Oh, yes. Definitely."

"And you still believed him?"

Z shrugs. "Gods are unpredictable. Much like the weather. But if Maximus's instincts are correct, you being the object of Hades's fascination... Well, it could be an interesting development."

My eyes bulge. "Interesting? Nothing about this is

interesting, Z. This is terrible and terrifying. My fate is hanging in the balance here, and you're both out getting drunk!"

I shoot to my feet, enjoying the brief advantage of height over him, which is ridiculous because he's a god and I'm just wearing stilettos. The inequity between us is staggering, but I'm not deterred. I'm furious to the point of fires igniting in my eyes, enough that I see the little bursts reflecting in his.

"You should be fixing this, damn it, not sitting around drinking and bickering and bantering."

He sighs and rests his cheek against his propped-up fist. "But Kara, that's how politics works. If all we did was remove the hindrances and fix our problems without delay, eternity would be so incredibly dull."

I give in to gnashing my teeth, internally biting on the verbal lashing I want to dole out right now. Because as pissed off as I am, Z is still my best bet. I can afford just about anything I could ever want, but I can't afford to lose him as a resource right now. I force myself to take a deep breath, a concerted effort to calm my nerves.

"So what now?" I finally bite out. "Another night at the bar?"

"Perhaps. Po and I have had it out, so it's time to wait. The ball is in Hades's court. I've staked a claim, if you will, and he knows now that there won't be peace between us if it isn't settled properly. But it could take time. Try to be patient."

My breathing is labored, despite all my efforts to calm

myself. I'm not patient, and I'm not empathetic whatsoever to his deity boredom. I take a step closer to him. I feel strong, but not from my height now. From the fire roaring inside me.

"If you can't fix this… If Maximus loses me, he will never forgive you. *Never.* I hope you realize that."

He has the decency to look solemn in that moment, and with a small nod, he says, "I know."

CHAPTER 15

MAXIMUS

AN OX WITH THE flu is tromping through my head. I clutch my stomach, ordering him to back the hell off. That's before realizing the dumbshit animal is me.

"Fuuuck . . ."

Never has such a tormented sound erupted from me. It comes hot on the heels of feeling like I've licked a summer sidewalk after a fighter jet joyride. I've never done either but am sure I don't want to after this.

And the kids run out of class, excited to do this every weekend at their dorms and frat houses, *why*?

At least I know where I am and how I got here, which is nothing short of a miracle. After Hades poofed out of Labyrinth last night, I'd finished his bottle of the good stuff, hoping it'd soothe the chaos in my thoughts. Huge mistake—one I acknowledged in that moment but traded for the hope of erasing what had gone down minutes before. To forget, if only for a little while, how it had felt to be the psychological filing cabinet for the greedy demon king.

It hadn't worked.

Even an hour later, when I'd forgotten my birthday, my address, and damn near my name, every moment of the ordeal haunted me. The protest of my nerve endings. The scream from my blood. The schism of horror, up and down my spine, as he invaded any thought he desired and looked at every vital intimacy...

A new groan erupts from me. This time, it has little to do with my hangover. The pounding at my temples is smothered by the protest march in my heart. The roil of my gut has nothing on the bile in my throat.

The symptoms only worsen when I realize Kara isn't sleeping next to me. She isn't in the room at all. And the air in the spacious hillside house...

Too damn still.

"Shit." I vault out of bed. The downy sheets tangle around my legs, hindered even more by my jeans-clad legs, but I finally leave them behind and sprint for the door. I don't skip a beat before hauling it open.

As light blasts my eyes, I throw a hand over my face and snarl. Just as quickly, I lower my hand. It's only sunlight. The full, midmorning version of the stuff. And in the middle of that white-gold blast from the heavens is an angel—in the form of my gorgeous demon sitting on the couch.

The new air in my lungs is warm and welcome, especially as she lifts a curious gaze toward me. She's beyond beautiful. Her casual little dress, with its short hem and suspender-style bodice, is a shade between red and purple.

She's still barefoot, meaning I get the chance to appreciate her sparkly gold toe polish, as well.

Headache or not, I want to run over and flatten her into those cushions—in all the torrid senses of the phrase. Kara flares her gaze, obviously picking up the force of my craving. But she only gets two seconds' worth before other thoughts rush to the surface.

"Hi." Her tone is cooler than I'm expecting.

"Hi." I scrape my hand through my hair, gripping it at my nape before adding, "You're here."

Kara drops her brows. "Where else would I be?"

"You're right," I concede. "I just thought—well, I was afraid that . . . "

"What?"

I drop my hand, thrumming it a few times against my thigh. It's better than continuing to stand here, suppressing my immediate answer. It's one thing to be dealing with a new strain of terror courtesy of Hades. It's another to add all that anxiety onto Kara's plate.

Though to some degree, it looks like I already did.

"Maximus?" She sets aside her laptop and the textbook from which she's working. "Talk to me, please. What's going on? What happened last night?"

I lean against the wall, resigned to the pointlessness of offering lame excuses for my apprehension. She already knows it's gut-deep and real. From there, she can—and probably has—skipped to its correlation to last night. She deserves to know it all, but only after I straighten it all out enough to talk about it.

"Poseidon... Po... He was there too. He told me some things I'd never known. He and Z also had some time to hash things out."

"Z told me that."

I push off the wall, giving away my surprise. "When?"

"Last night. He was here when I got back from the premiere. You'd already passed out."

I give my head a small, fast shake. Why did my father stick around after the ordeal at Labyrinth? I won't waste time considering any noble motives. He isn't exactly a nighttime story and lullaby kind of guy, though I remember him walking me into the bedroom, making me drink some water, and watching me collapse into bed. "You talked?"

"Yes."

I nod. "How did the event go?" I try to make it sincere and conversational. Not easy when all I want to know is one thing. Was Arden there? If so, did he dare put his hands on her? "Who was there?"

Kara scoots to her feet and folds her arms. "Uh-uh, Professor. No side hustles on the main subject. Your evening fun report is far more vital than mine."

It sucks to concede how right she is. As strongly as I want her to climb back into the dress with the innocent color and the sexy neckline and then reenact her red carpet game just for me, what happened at Labyrinth can't just be washed out to sea.

"Well, what did Z tell you?"

She twists her lips. "Not enough."

"But he said some things." I persist. "Like what?"

A sharp huff tumbles from her. "Isn't this the part *you're* supposed to be filling in? Or did you get so obliterated that you really don't remember?"

I pivot hard, tilting my head. "Is that what you think? That I finally got a chance to meet with the people deciding our fate, and I hit the sauce first?"

She looks away, uncomfortable. She drums her fingers against her elbows.

"Kara. Look at me." Thankfully, she does. "I was coherent for every second of what went down with Hades."

Her shoulders sag. Her eyes are tender. "I believe you."

I release a big breath. "Thank you."

"So what did happen?"

Her plea is so desperate, it edges on a sob. My gut responds by contorting into a new pretzel. I don't even try to loosen the mangle of my heart. But if I want to salvage either of them—and save the life of the woman I'm brutally in love with—I've got to start putting my *head* to work again. Which means I have to hit her with my next miserable words.

"I can't talk about it yet. I'm sorry."

I don't blame her for flinging up a hand, blocking my sincere approach.

"*Kara*. I have to get some distance from it, okay?" To wrap my head around how to tell her that the king of hell has now seen her naked. And aroused. And . . . more.

And that I let it all happen.

"To put it together properly, I have to pull it apart first."

She lifts her head, showing me the smoke in her eyes.

As always, she's as magnificent in her indignation as her passion, and for a moment, I'm stunned into silence. But then I remember that this memory might not always be mine alone. That one day, maybe even soon, Hades will be back to "borrow" it for a few minutes.

No.

Just. Fucking. No.

I've got to get some answers about this. And right now, there's only one person I know to get them from.

The determination becomes motivation. I push closer to Kara, relieved when she stands and lets me pull her in and nestle her close. "Thank you for understanding," I murmur into her adorable top knot, which still smells like a whole salon's worth of pricey products.

"Who says I understand?" she mutters into the dip at the center of my chest. "I trust you, though," she goes on, wrapping her arms all the way around my waist. "So grab some coffee and get to work on . . . whatever you have to do. Patience isn't exactly my strongest virtue."

I drop my head down as she pops hers up. Our lips meet in a sweet but sizzling kiss. It's over all too soon. "Ah, but you have so many other virtues that are better."

She smirks. "Says the demigod who took the obvious one?"

"A gift I treasure every day," I whisper.

She presses a kiss directly over my heart. "For that, Mr. Kane, I'll even get your coffee for you."

"Oh, baby." I sniff her lingering curls again. "I'd seriously love to take you up on that and more. But I was thinking I would head over to Recto Verso. I can grab a coffee there."

She flashes a new frown. "Do you need to grab something from your place for tonight? Mom had your suit and shoes delivered straight from the tailor. And the Gold Circle Dinner is at the Huntington Gardens, out in Pasadena. You'd be going way out of the way."

"No. I'm good for tonight." I gently kiss her forehead. "Thank Veronica for me. She's been generous in handling all that stuff." For once, I'm actually grateful for it too. I now have time to do something more important than worrying about looking the part. "I have to go to Recto Verso."

"Okay." Confusion knits her brow again, though she doesn't press for details this time. Not a shock, considering how my turmoil is probably hitting her like a wall of bricks. Soothing her is out of the question, though. If I comfort her, I'll want to do more. And *more* will have to wait until I get a handle on the possible depths of Hades's mental fuckery over me.

To do that, I've got to get a better handle on who I really am. I'm pitifully lost about the answer, which even Z couldn't supply after a few hours in a buzzed haze. All I got was a sheepish admission that, despite siring a staggering number of half-breeds, he's never taken much of an interest in demigod biology. The only factor he *can* confirm is Hades's inability to perform his nifty memory-harvesting thing on any full-blood deity.

While that revelation has me relieved for Z and Po, I'm back at a lot of square ones in my own bizarre journey. Is Hades capable of wreaking more kinds of cerebral chaos on my gray matter? If so, what's his play now? How far does the demon's spite go when Po's lies are added into the equation? How much flesh does he plan on taking out of my hide for Kara's offenses? Or Z's? Mistakes during years I don't even remember?

Right now, there's only one person I know who might have any of that information. The former Olympus security guard who's serving coffee in downtown LA right now.

I get to Recto Verso as the morning crowd is starting to thin. In the seating areas, there's only a small book club and a few students in Alameda sweatshirts. Outside, the air is edged with the salt from the new onshore flow. Inside, the rich caffeine scents are tinged with pumpkin and caramel.

As I hope—and in more than a few ways, dread—Regina is front and center behind the counter. Her braids are piled atop her head, intermixed with a long red scarf that compliments her faded T-shirt.

"Good day, superstar." She bids me to sit by thwacking a towel toward one of the stools at the counter.

I opt for standing, but that's not an alarm-dinger for her. I stand at the counter a lot.

"So sorry. If I'd known you were coming 'round, I would've ordered up the paps for a nice warm welcome."

I give her a half snort for that, more out of habit than anything else. It hits me then, a brand-new epiphany. *Habits*. How many do I have with her? Too many to track. So many that don't feel ingrained from that first day we met in the store. They've felt strangely . . . older. Easier. Like my whole relationship with Reg. An odd *deja-vu* I've always sensed but never questioned, figuring I owe the universe some gratitude for a friend who's always been so easy and knows me so well.

But now what do I feel? Knowing she's been part of the grand cover-up? Knowing she was the one who set it in motion?

To keep me safe.

From what? Or, if Po is to be believed, from whom?

I know so much more now—only to realize I know so little.

"'Course, you've probably had your fill of flashbulbs after last night," Reg goes on. "Though Sarah grumbled for the better part of the morning, looking for pictures of you at the premiere. Where were you? Ducking and hiding? Looked like a grand affair. We found plenty of shots of your pretty girl and her fam—" She cuts herself short after looking at me again. This time, *really* looking. "Ohh. You weren't even there, were you?"

I shoot her a dark look while taking a sip of the brew she's poured for me. "That's not exactly an awful thing."

"Says your *mouth*. But the rest of your face is giving me a different line, Maximus Kane."

I push away the coffee. My one sip sours in my stomach. "Imagine that."

She tosses down her cleaning rag and impales me with her full attention. "What happened? Did you two fight?"

"No."

"Then was it Veronica's meddling?"

"No."

"Then why do you look like you slept in those clothes after drinking a half gallon of kerosene?"

I work my lips together. My mouth is still a dry husk, and my mind is still a casserole of confusion. Now that I'm here, I have no idea how to plunge forward. Nothing's going to be the same with Reg after this. Inside, I cling to our normalcy for a few seconds longer.

"It wasn't kerosene," I finally force myself to say. "Something called Ninth Circle Rye. Or, as my father likes calling it, 'Honey's good stuff from the back.'"

Regina grips the bar before dropping her head between her shoulders. For a long moment, I wonder if she's preparing to be sick in the sink. Instead she rasps, "Bloody. Fucking. Hell."

"Not exactly." I use the weighted moment to finally slide onto a stool. It's less about my comfort and more about the proximity that now feels like a necessity. "Unless that's where they really park Labyrinth. I doubt Po would have much fun swimming in the Styx, though."

Through another long moment, she still says nothing. A louder laugh from someone in the book club crowd brings her head back up, but not swiftly. "You know, then? All of it?"

"All of it?" I echo. "Is that an accurate phrase for any of this, Ms. Nikian?"

It's a strange but pleasant experience to watch her bust out a soft laugh. "Fair question." She doesn't hang on long to the humor. "As fair as anything is in all this, I suppose."

"*Fair*." I engrave that one with harder sarcasm. "Now there's something the gods definitely don't recognize."

Her demeanor changes. Though she doesn't move from her forward hunch, there's new purpose in her face. "The gods haven't endured centuries by being fair, Max. What they've had to do to keep each of their realms whole . . . "

"Is that made up in *your* mind, then?" I meet her stare with just as much determination. "To serve the world of the gods instead of just—"

"We all serve the gods, Maximus." She pushes back to her full stance. "Some of us are just more aware of our function than others."

As she states it, she seems to roll her shoulders back even more. I blink, regarding the woman with new eyes, as hers fill with a specific sadness. I get it now. She's used to hefting weapons and a shield, not coffeepots and book boxes.

I have a hundred questions for her now, but ninety-nine of them have to wait. I have to get out the most important one. "So when you chose to hail Po . . . and secretly sought out his help, behind Hades's and Zeus's backs . . . who were you serving then?"

Regina doesn't hesitate a single second about her answer.

"You."

I take advantage of the chance to do my own leaning back. The outer action aside, I'm not taken aback. Like so many parts of my new normal, this revelation actually brings new light on so much of my history with the woman. A reality that feels so much more right—because now it's the truth.

Right . . . but not complete.

There's still something missing.

Some*one* who should be here and deserves to be here as much as Reg, if not more. Someone who might be able to help, even more than Reg.

I pull my phone out and push the speed dial button for Mom.

CHAPTER 16

PAST THE KITCHEN TABLE, which is presently littered with notebooks and homework papers, the dusty hills glow amber in the afternoon light. Our multimillion-dollar view hasn't changed since Kell and I picked out this house years ago, but so much about our lives has. Very little looks the same these days. And it sure as hell doesn't feel the same.

Maximus hasn't been gone long, but I'm distracted by his absence. Strange, since I normally revel in this kind of silence, which was always a rarity in a Beverly Hills compound crowded by siblings, stylists, assistants, and housekeeping staff. But my thoughts are hopelessly muddled, my mind swimming toward some unknown point.

Only one thought bangs at me with aggravating clarity. I should have pressed Z more on details about last night's meeting instead of assuming Maximus would fill in all the blanks. Because right now, there are *a lot* of blanks. The cryptic way Maximus left this morning, his brain a very different kind of muddled, makes me think there's something he's not telling me.

But I have to trust he will. It's just that trust, in any of its variations, has never been a favorite concept of mine. When I was little, perhaps, and the word meant taking my first steps to Gramps or sharing silly secrets with Kell and Jaden. But as the years went on, trust became a stand-in for much different things. Like *risk*. And *exposure*. And *vulnerability*. And *weakness*. Concepts I couldn't afford to indulge. Humanity I couldn't admit to having.

I shake my head, banishing those moping musings before refocusing to my laptop and typing out the closing paragraph on the cantos summary that was due yesterday. I date the assignment for Friday, smirking as I do because I am more than willing to accept favoritism when it comes to this seminar. Of course I'm sleeping with the professor, but that's not my justification. If sex and steam were the only things happening here, I'd have turned in the paper yesterday or accepted the consequences for my tardiness today. But Maximus knows, more than anyone, how taxing it's been to keep up with anything school-related. I've scarcely had time for any of it until now.

I try to concentrate on the assignments for next week but end up staring out the window instead. Once more, my brain cells seem to drift like the motes on the canyon breeze across the patio. Nothing's secure or solid. I need something to ground me.

I need some*one*.

But he's not here.

My eyes land on the thick tome at the edge of the table. With a lack of anything better to do, I pick it up and flip through the *Comedy* until I get to the next reading assignment. It's silly and I shouldn't be in the mood to read about hell, of all things, but I convince myself that somewhere in these pages I'll find some truth. Even better, some connection with my beloved's mind in the absence of his body.

I let myself get lost in the poetry. In the strange budding friendship between Dante and his guide. In their faith and protectiveness and determination. Somewhere there's hope, even as they take their first steps into the deepest recesses of the underworld.

"*Rarely do any of us enter here,*" I murmur, tracing my fingertip along the lines as I speed through the stanzas. "*Take heart, that is the last depth and the darkest lair and the farthest from Heaven which encircles all.*"

The front door slams closed, startling me away from the text. It can't be Maximus. He promised to text when he was heading back. And Kell left an hour ago, mumbling something about a spa appointment to prep for tonight.

"Jaden," I gasp with surprise.

My little brother saunters in like he owns the place, a sly grin painting his easy expression. He doesn't need to own the place, because for nearly as long as we've been grown, he's managed to get nearly everything he wants. The joys of being the baby demon in the Valari family, I suppose.

He strolls closer, his moves drenched in practiced grace.

He's dressed in dark jeans and a crisp white shirt unbuttoned enough to show a glimpse of the artwork tattooed on his chest. He's got the kind of look that sells millions of gossip magazines whenever he graces the cover. To me, he's just the kid who still steals my fries and coaches me about fidgeting too much. Jaden's never fidgeted a day in his life.

"What are you doing here? I haven't seen you in forever."

He slips his mirrored aviators up into his dark-brown hair, its waves overgrown but sleek and unruly in that bad-boy way that makes him "perfect for the big screen," according to our mother. His deep-amber irises swirl with mystery and mischief that perfectly match his playboy reputation.

"I was in Cabo with some friends. I needed a break."

I laugh. "A break? Jaden, you don't even work."

He takes a chair, slouching casually into it. "Oh yeah? What would *you* call getting taxied all over town, taking meetings that Mom's obsessed with setting up?"

He's got a solid point. Not that I'm going to say that out loud. "Some people might be grateful to have such a dedicated agent working on their behalf to achieve maximum fame and fortune."

He rolls his eyes. "Right. I forgot you're the expert in gratitude."

I wilt a little. It's not a secret that I've never embraced our lifestyle—at least not to the degree that Jaden and Kell have. Thankfully, he doesn't seem to notice the nerve he's hit with fighter-pilot precision. If he does, he pretends not to.

He nods toward the mess of schoolwork in front of me.

"What's all this?"

"Just catching up on some homework. Things have been busy, so I'm trying to catch up."

His gaze lands on the *Comedy* opened in front of me. He leans in, getting a glimpse of the text. "Dante, Kara? Really?"

I close the book with a clap. "Yes, really. Why do you care?"

He answers with a bored shrug. "For someone who hates being a demon, you're weirdly fascinated with it, big sister."

I pause. "That's not true."

"Isn't it? You've spent the past few years basically nerding out on our ancestry."

"Classics is much broader than that."

He lifts a brow in challenge.

I keep my lips pinched shut, but I've had the same internal discussion with myself more than once. Something drew me to the classics. The fairy tale histories. The actual histories. Like a strange puzzle of myth and truth that no one will ever be able to truly piece together. But trying to is half the allure. Maybe that's why I've been so dedicated these last four years. And now I have an even better reason than most.

"So," Jaden cuts in, interrupting my thoughts. "I stopped over at Mom's when I got back and heard a very interesting story from Gio."

I huff. "You *can* call him Grandfather, you know."

"Uh, right. Anyway, this obviously explains why you're

getting more Page Six real estate than I have lately."

"What?" I frown hard but finish with a huge eye roll. "That is so not true."

"Actually, it is," he replies. "But it's not a competition. I hate those guys. But still . . . "

"What?" I prod.

"Damn, Kara." His chuckle is dry and only half humorous. "What kind of mess are you in?"

A sigh pours out of me. "A pretty big one, I guess."

He nods, his expression a little more solemn. "A demigod, huh?"

I twist my lips. "That would seem to be the case."

"Are you crazy?"

"Are *you* implying I went out looking for this kind of trouble?"

"Of course not." He tackles the mess of his hair with one hand, scrubbing haphazardly through it. As the strands fall back into their same artful mess, he lifts his wrist to glance at his diamond-studded watch. "Anyway, I just thought I'd check in and see how you were doing, but I've got to run. I have plans tonight."

"So do I. And a ton more of this." I wave my hand over the mountain of reading I still need to catch up on.

Jaden's back on his feet and jabs his hands into his back pockets and shrugs with purpose. "So . . . are you going to be all right with all this? Can I help with anything?"

For a second, I'm not sure how to respond. His halfhearted query is more concern than he's probably ever shown me, but it's dripping with how much he doesn't want to have to offer up any actual help, which would interrupt his streak of carefree living.

"I'm good." I smile kindly, grateful that Jaden thought to stop by at all. Then I think of Kell . . . and last night's friction between us. "Hey, before you go, can I ask you something?"

He slips his phone out of his pocket with a small sound of acknowledgment.

"When we were little . . . Do you remember when Gramps would help take care of us?"

He nods slowly, clearly taking care not to make eye contact. "A little."

I pause, weighing my next words. Not for Jaden's sake but so I can get the answer I'm looking for. I already know Jaden doesn't care.

"Do you think that Gramps favored one of us?"

He snorts out a laugh, finally lifting his gaze all the way up to mine. "So now that he's escaped the backyard bungalow, you're getting insecure about who he likes best?"

I frown. "No."

He laughs again. This time, there's real humor in the sound. "Then what? I don't get it. Why do you care after all this time? If he *were* playing favorites, it's pretty obvious who would be at the top of that list."

I sigh and shake my head. "It's nothing. You're right. It was a stupid thing to ask."

He studies me for a long moment and seems to reach some inner resolution for his effort. "Listen, I don't remember much about him. By the time I could start latching on to memories, he was out of the picture for the most part."

He's right, of course. I have more memories of Gramps than the others, but even those early ones are few and sketchy. For the first time in my life, the realization has me asking myself *why*.

Why was Gramps entrusted with us as children and then suddenly exiled from our lives? Why were we threatened with my mother's wrath if we dared show him any kindness? Why weren't we ever given the causes for the threats?

What happened?

I ruminate on that as I walk Jaden to the door. His canary-yellow Lamborghini is parked in the drive. He jostles his keys in his hands a few times, pausing at the threshold before turning back to me.

"Okay, now I have a question for *you*," he ventures.

I fight to school my features. Knowing Jaden—though I really don't anymore—this might be anything. "Hmm?" I answer noncommittally.

"What are you doing tonight?"

"Oh." My surprise is evident as my brain scrambles through the agenda. "I'll be at the university's Gold Circle Dinner."

He clucks his tongue. "Right. Forgot about that. Thankfully I got out of that one."

"Lucky you," I tease, even though I have plenty of good reasons to suffer through it.

He chuckles. "I've got a callback for some angsty new show they're putting together at Fox, but afterward I'm headed to a little get-together at Rerek's place."

I stifle a groan. Barely. "You're still hanging out with Rerek? Does Mom know?"

"She knows what she needs to know," he replies while finger combing his hair via his reflection in the window. "Besides, Rerek's mellowed out a bit. I swear."

"Define 'a bit.' And define 'a little get-together.'" Because in Rerek's world, that means a head count anywhere between fifty and five hundred.

"It'll be fun." More of his calculated subject dodging. "And it's going to be a nice night. We're hoping to have a bonfire on the beach, since Rerek's place is right on the sand. You should stop by after the dinner if you want. Bring the new guy."

I find myself warming at the offer. More because I can feel him actually . . . trying. I'm not entirely sure why he is, but I'm happy that he is. Because only days ago I chose Maximus over a life that I would have shared with Arden but also with my family. Now it seems like maybe I can have Maximus and keep my family, strange as they all may be.

I smile and give Jaden a hug. He's tense for a second before returning the embrace.

"Thank you for the invite. I'll be there," I promise.

CHAPTER 17

Maximus

I NOD UP AT Reg in gratitude as she sets a second cup of coffee in front of me. Without words, she knows how much I need a liquid recharge of what she calls the "Sleepless in Maximus Special." It's appropriate on days after I've slept three hours and then gone to the gym just as long. This is the first time she's ever dosed me for the opposite. I'm learning, with fast and furious agony, that god-booze hangovers are *not* consequences to tempt.

Does Z feel this way too?

I don't want to know the answer to that. Not that I can spare an extra brain cell for the duty.

With the remaining three cells that are actually functioning, I focus on what to say next to Reg. We're settled on a couple of couches in the shop's back corner, the spot they cleared so Piper Blue could hold court with fans and press a few weeks ago. I can't believe it's really been less than a month since the night of that party. Those first moments I pressed in on Kara over in the classics section and realized that our chemistry was more than a fluke thing were undeniable—and incredible. At once, I saw that she recognized the same thing. That was the first night I felt her spirit tug on the middle of my soul, waking me up to how incomplete it really was.

Those memories are my strength now. Reminders of the destiny we've honored despite the costs are validation that we've embarked on the right climb together—and though the summit is still shrouded, it's there. And when we get there together, there'll be light. So much blinding, beautiful light.

I have to keep believing that...

"So the father god finally sussed it all out."

Though Reg's remark drips with dread that actually makes me feel a little defensive for Z, I'm thankful she's spoken first.

"I'd been afraid of that," she grumbles and downs a big chug from her own mug.

From here, I can smell the bourbon she's added to her tea, affirming how wise the woman really is.

"From the moment I saw how dotty you were for the demon... and then on Sunday night, when the freak storm hit..."

"You figured it out then?" I lean forward as she drops her head into a hand. "And you still decided not to talk to me about it?"

She straightens quickly. "What should I have said? 'I hope you're enjoying this fine weather, love. Oh, and PS:

You're a demigod who likely just screwed a demon.'"

I bristle. "I didn't *screw* her."

While Reg means no blatant disrespect, the verb still needles me that way. She might as well know, straight out of this metaphorical gate, that I'm a lot more than *dotty* for Kara Valari.

"Fine. Semantics," she snips before taking another long drag on her magic tea. "Carnal knowledge was had by all important parties. Why don't we establish that as a hard fact and move on to the part where you caused a god-summoning storm?"

For a moment, I'm caught between two extremes. The urge to laugh but also to cry. They tie back to the same revelation. Being seen for who I really am but still being treated like the next normal Joe on the street. It's like I'm a kid again and the woman's about to assign me latrine duty for toppling a bookcase while playing hide-and-seek in the store with Jesse.

How I wish those simpler rules applied now. But this mess can't be washed away with a few scrubbed toilets and some reshelved books.

Regina's demeanor already tells me so. Her posture's stiff. Her gaze is fierce with wordless entreaty. She doesn't want to be right about her allegation. She wants me to say I have no idea what she's talking about and that the storm was only some freaky barometric event. But I can't. We're past the point of covering the truth in the name of safety. I have to move forward now, and she has to help me.

During the pause I take for determining how to

best express that, the bell at the front door jingles. Before turning to look, I know who it is. Mom's presence already calms a lot of my soul, despite my brain warning me otherwise. But only now do I recognize how that protest has dimmed. Thanks to Po, I've finally been able to penetrate deeper levels here. Like Dante on his own journey, I understand more. I can forgive more.

"Hey there, buddy." Her slip with my childhood nickname betrays her exhaustion faster than her weary tone. After we hug, I get a glimpse of her sleepy but anxious gaze before she drops into the wingback chair next to the cup of chamomile Reg has set out.

"Sorry I had to wake you," I offer while she sips the fragrant brew.

"It's all right." My comment seems to have peeved her, and it probably has. Not because I woke her after a twelve-hour shift and approximately three hours of sleep but because I apologized for it. "It's always all right. You know that." She casts a furtive glance between Reg and me. "What's going on?"

Reg *whooshes* a rough breath. It sounds like a laugh that she's thought better of.

Mom frowns. "What's happened, for God's sake?"

"Now that one's funny," Reg says.

Mom clearly has no idea that I'm now in on the subtext. "Does this have to do with that young woman you've been seeing? The one you've been followed everywhere with? What has she done, honey?" She sets down her tea, concern stamped on her features.

"Mom."

"You can tell me. I can be discreet."

"*Mom.*"

"If she's hurt you, I swear to God, the little brat should be taught what a treasure she has."

"Her name is Kara," I growl. "And I care about her. Deeply."

"Shit." Regina slides her head back into her palm. "I was afraid of that."

"Afraid of what?" The edges of Mom's mouth tilt up. "That he likes a girl? Good Lord, loosen up, Reg. This is a good thing." She surges to her feet. She's dressed in her work shoes and sweats, and her steps make cute, rubbery squashes along the wood floor. When she reaches me, she hauls me into a hug. "No. This is a *wonderful* thing."

As Mom peeks around my bicep, Regina lifts only her eyes over the ledge of her fingers. "Wonderful. Sure." When she lowers her whole hand, her whole face is grim. "Except that he's already slept with her."

"Umm. All right." Mom attempts a deprecating laugh. "You're a grown-up. That's your choice."

Reg is fast with her interruptive trigger finger. "There's more to it." She shoots a meaningful glance my way. I nod in return.

"All right." Mom's less certain about her approval encore. While that's probably a good thing, my gut doesn't agree. How can this be the moment I've waited so long to get to but the scenario in which I never imagined it occurring? The fully crappy circumstances.

"Listen to me, Nancy. He's. Already. Slept. With. Her."

"Yes, Reg. You've already established that part," Mom says with an awkward laugh.

"And she's a Valari."

"Right, I've heard of the name. But if he loves her, why would that matter? She's famous. So what?"

Reg clears her throat. "They're the same Valaris I did some temp work for, back when we were first here in LA. Remember?"

Mom tenses a little, but it's obviously more from curiosity. "Okay, where exactly are you going with all this?"

Reg pulls herself up higher. Rubs her hands along the tops of her thighs. "I worked for them specifically because I was instructed to keep an eye on them for a while."

"What?" Mom is genuinely baffled. She really doesn't know this part.

Another glance Reg's way helps me confirm that. She was probably on the path toward telling me that, when Mom arrived in record time.

"Keep an eye on them . . . why?" Mom asks.

"Because they're demons."

Mom sags against me. "They're *what*?"

Though I support her weight with physical ease, her anguished stare rips apart my heart. "I didn't know either," I confess. "Until it was too late."

"Too . . . late?" She stammers it like the words are scrambled. Or perhaps as if she doesn't want to comprehend them.

"After he bedded the woman." Reg takes a deliberate

beat, then another, before she drops the bigger bomb. "And brought down a royal-class rainstorm last Saturday night."

"A royal—" As fast as Mom clenches her fingers into my arms, she shoves away. A manic sound spills from her quirking lips. I think she's trying to laugh again but miserably failing. "You know how ridiculous that sounds, right? All of it. *Both* of you," she adds when observing the somber calm I match to Regina's.

"I didn't believe it at first either, Mom." I brace my stance, sensing I'm going to need the new fortification. "Not until Zeus showed up and forced me to see the full reality."

My mother turns a terrifying shade of white. "No. No, that can't be. It . . . it just can't . . . "

Then she buckles at the knees.

"Shit!"

I'm close enough to break her fall. Regina is blessedly—or scarily—silent as I gather Mom up and lower her back into the wingback. "It's all right, Mom." I thunk to my knees beside her while Reg finally mutters something about fetching a glass of water.

"Maximus." Mom reaches out to touch my cheek with tender fingertips.

My relief at the contact is cut short by her anguished sob. But her real tears never come.

Finally she grates, "So you know."

I rise up, pushing some matted hair off her forehead. "Yeah. I do."

She's still pale and seems so frail. I'm struck by just how much this woman has done for me, for so long. She's given up her whole life. Her entire existence. Did she give up her identity too? Who is she, really? Does she—do *we*—have mortal family members somewhere who are wondering where she is and what she's doing? What life did she leave behind for all this? *For me?*

It slays my soul that I can't ask any of that right now. There's no time. Not if I want to get to the questions that matter most.

"How much?" Mom rasps, grabbing my forearm with open desperation. "How *much* do you know? What did he tell you, Maximus?"

My chest burns, drenched in its own acid spill. "I'm not sure." I let her see the remorse in my stare. "I don't know how much there is."

"But he came to you. Oh my God." She clamps her free hand across her eyes. "He found you. *Damn it.* I've been so careful!"

The new tears in her voice compel me to lean closer. "This was inevitable. He told me he's been searching for me. For a long time." I accept the damp cloth Regina brings and press it to my mother's forehead. "And the storm just sped things up a little." I shrug and manage half a smile. "Or maybe a lot. But Mom... I'm glad it did and that I finally know. You made some tough calls, all in the name of keeping me safe. Both of you did."

I circle my gaze out, including Regina as much as Mom. But while Reg answers with a respectful nod, Mom yanks the cloth away and sits up.

"Tough calls," she reiterates, doubling down on her

agitation. "Is that what Zeus told you too?" She swings her glare, full of bitterness, up at Reg. "Or was that the part *you* filled in?"

"I walked in less than fifteen minutes ago," I interject. "And since then, Reg has been making tea. What are you getting at?"

"There was nothing 'tough' about my decisions. Desperate? Yes. Terrifying? Oh hell, yes."

From the waist up, fury and mortification make me stiff as a statue. "Z told me we were living in a nice place. That he was keeping us comfortable and safe."

"Of course he was," she says. "It was all those things and more—but it was also surrounded by very high walls and very set perimeters." The faintest wisp of a smile breaks through before she reaches to me, rubbing my cheek with soft, adoring strokes. "But have you ever tried telling an eight-year-old boy that he *can't* go somewhere?"

Heat collects behind my eyes. I dismiss it, and the string of profanity it coaxes in my mind, with gritted teeth. "Yeah," I mumble. "I'm beginning to get it."

"One day, you finally outsmarted us all. You were only outside the estate for a few minutes . . . but that was long enough for several of Hera's maids to see."

I grind my teeth harder. "Hera," I echo. Of course. *Fuck.*

"I knew it that very moment," Mom whispers. She retracts her hand, guiding my gaze to the unmistakable sheen in her eyes. "The life that had been my semi-bearable quarantine would lead to *your* death by her hand."

"So we got out of there." Regina fills it in before I can.

"As fast as we possibly could."

I drag in a long breath, looking to both of them with the same somber purpose. "And now, I'm damn glad you did."

I hope that lends Mom some validation, yet she's just as jittery as before. "But how did Zeus ever find out? How did he know where to follow you? Where to come? We were so careful when we left. So thorough about making it look like—"

"We'd been killed already?"

Reg chuffs. "You were never a daft boy."

Instead of taking the bait to banter with her, I reach for Mom's hand again. "He found out how and why you left at the same time I did. Yesterday, at Labyrinth—when I met Po for the first time."

"Po?" She turns whiter than before as comprehension clearly strikes. "Poseidon?" Her fingers are icy and shivery against mine. "You met him too?" Before I'm done nodding, she blurts, "Was anyone else there?"

No sense lingering over a bandage that has to be ripped off. As my mother succumbs to heavy tears that might as well be that spilled blood, I force myself to push on. "He's the king of the underworld, Mom. And Kara is one of his subjects. At least partially. And we pissed him off."

"Royally," Regina puts in.

"Just...stop for a second. Both of you. Please." Mom pushes me away and lurches back up, framing her forehead with her hands. "I have to think. I have to *think*."

She starts circling the coffee table like an electron

around a neutron, propelled by an unseen but real—and powerful—force. Her apprehension is intense. Trouble is, I'm no better. I came here and then called her because I'm in equally crappy shape. With more questions than answers.

"Maybe we can all think together." It's my awkward form of assurance, for myself as well as her. A dialogue means I can work in some questions.

But not yet.

Mom's think-tank mode has an unmistakable look. I've seen it too many times to be mistaken. Though she doubles her pace, she scans her intended path like it's full of landmines. "This isn't good. Not at all." She takes several more laps before halting and pivoting toward Regina. "Have you maintained any of your connections to Olympus since we left?"

"Do centaurs cheat at poker?" Reg scoffs.

"Good." The smallest hint of relief crosses Mom's tired features. "We may need to call on them. Now that Hades is involved... Well, we have no idea what or who he'll be after."

"Actually...I might." I pause my interjection, waiting for them to snap stunned looks my way before going on. "I know exactly what he dragged into his skull last night, at least."

The admission spilled out a hell of a lot easier than I'd expected, but maybe that's because I filtered some things from last night's memories. Those factors flood in now. The stunned bewilderment. The loathing surrender. Finally, the impotent rage.

Mom's the first one to sense it all. That's obvious as soon as she sits back down and seizes my hand again. Her gaze darkens. Her nostrils pump in and out, betraying the force of her rampant emotions.

"Tell me what he said," she demands past trembling lips.

Air leaves me in a heavy rush, but it doesn't stop my chest from turning into a furious kiln. "It was more what he did than what he said."

A pair of tears escapes her restraint, one rolling down each cheek. Mom jabs a hand up and furiously palms them away. "Say whatever feels right, however you need to," she rasps. "We're going to figure this out together." She reaches up, and the familiar cherry-almond of her hand lotion mixes with the salt of her sorrow as she rubs my cheek. "I know you don't have a single reason to believe me anymore—"

I pull at her hand to wrap it in both of my own. "I believe you, Mom. I really do." A rough swallow thuds down my throat. "I'm beginning to understand. A lot more than you think."

She looks ready to lose control of more tears. A stuttering sob replaces them. "You do?"

"You fell in love. You weren't planning on it. You sure as hell weren't planning on the complications that came with it—not that they would've stopped you." A gruff laugh leaves me. "Gee, Mom," I add, extending my wry smile. "I don't know a damn thing about that."

Now her tears come, but they all melt my heart because she's smiling through them. "I love you so much."

"I love you too."

"I hate to be the one breaking up the family mush hour," Regina grouses. "But right now, what's most important is that you tell us everything about this triumvirate summit from last night." She leans forward, locking elbows on her knees. "We need all of it, Max. Any and every detail you can remember. You understand?"

"Yeah." I nod swiftly. "I get it. I do." *Know your enemy* has never seemed so damn relevant or accurate. But never has *enemy* been such a vivid reality for me.

"Good," Reg says. "And what would be even better is if you agreed to stay away from Kara too."

She extends the courtesy of at least turning and looking me in the eye while driving that dagger into my heart. Of course it doesn't matter.

"Not happening." I set my jaw to the point that it aches.

"Calm down. I don't mean for forever, okay? Just for now. Only until we can figure—"

"Not. Happening." With the first word, I fling the symbolic blade back at her. With the second, I make sure it sticks. "Not now. Not ever. If Hades wants to come find me again, he'll have to crawl off his turf and onto mine. We'll meet in *my* light, not *his* dark." I chuff out another bitter laugh. "Remarkably, Veronica Valari may just know what she's doing about this one. Hiding in plain sight. It's kept him from overtly messing with Kara so far, so we'll stay that course for now."

Reg mutters a curse beneath her breath. "Except that you do know Hades's definition of playing, yes?"

"I'm acquainted with the experience, Reg."

"Then I'd better get started on rounding up some adequate security."

I shake my head. "Wait. Reg. Hold up. Security? Are you serious?"

"As the blood oath I first made on the highest step of the palace in Olympus."

She stands, straightening her shoulders in a way that promises her next words will be final—or at least too difficult to argue with.

"Protecting you is what I've dedicated half my life to. If you think I'm stopping now, you're a fool, Maximus Kane."

I give her the courtesy of a nod, but I'm still unsure whether I've just gotten my best or worst news of the day. Patience will bear out that answer, along with the growing pile of my other unanswered questions, but the stuff is getting harder to come by every hour. I only hope I have enough to get me through the Gold Circle event tonight. With Kara on my arm, it'll definitely be easier.

With Kara in my world, *everything* is easier. Brighter. Better.

Always, *always* better.

CHAPTER 18

ANOTHER DAY, ANOTHER DRESS. Another mansion filled with servers passing out Moët in delicate champagne flutes. This time, it's Saturday night—at least the last time I checked—and I'm in a summery peach chiffon thing, given glam touches with über-bling jewelry and rhinestone-encrusted heels. The multimillion-dollar digs are impressive, even by Mom's standards. I can easily imagine the modern, airy rooms and sprawling pool deck being graced by a crowd of Hollywood's elite.

Except right now, the guests milling around on the cream and gray furniture aren't celebrities or aspiring VIPs. Apart from my mother and a handful of other notable donors, the guests are made up of distinguished Alameda staff. Some are familiar faces, like President McCarthy and Maximus's best friend, Professor North, who are chatting animatedly on the other side of the room. But many others are new, and despite the fact that we're mingling in a posh estate in one of LA's most prestigious zip codes, Maximus is the one who's working the room.

And, in the doing, giving me at least a dozen more reasons to revere him.

Over the course of the night, he's introduced me to his English department colleagues and their partners, drawing them into our conversation with surprising ease. He may be a god among men, but here, underneath all that, he's charismatic Professor Kane. He's thoughtful and confident. Charming and observant. Quick with a joke or a compliment, keeping the people around us smiling. My face aches because of how long I've been beaming by his side.

I thought I couldn't possibly be more attracted to him, but seeing this aspect of him has challenged that once again—in so many awesome new ways. When the Jet Propulsion Lab rep we're chatting with excuses himself, Maximus catches me staring at him.

He smirks and meets my intimate scrutiny—which has probably gotten sultrier the longer I admire how he fills out his dark-cobalt tux. "What is it? Why are you looking at me like that?"

"Do I need a specific reason?"

"With that particular look? I'd say, unequivocally, yes."

"I guess tonight isn't exactly what I expected," I finally admit.

He smiles, and this time the joy takes up his whole face, causing my heartbeat to stutter.

"Why? Because everyone's gawking like we're the main attraction?"

I laugh softly. "Not really. I'm used to that."

Even at Alameda, I barely notice the looks, from students and professors alike. And really, the whole point of being at this party is to be seen. More, to be accepted by the higher-ups at the university who have the power to make Maximus's career more difficult because of our controversial relationship. Maybe that's why he's been so engaged tonight. This is his livelihood, after all. Not just that. It's his dream. One I nearly ruined by falling so hard and fast for him.

"It's just strange, is all. Seeing you this way." I lift my shoulder. "You know . . . networking."

He leans in to kiss my cheek softly. "Did you think you had the market cornered on fabulous LA parties? You think I couldn't hold my own?"

I giggle when he drags his kiss lower. But as his breath and his beard tickle my neck, I want to be sighing instead. And then moaning. Begging him not to stop . . .

"I'll never underestimate you again, Professor," I declare instead. "And for the record, I might not be so quick to let you out of red carpet engagements now that I know how suave you can be."

He laughs roughly. "Heaven help me."

I feel the texture of the sound against my skin but manage to shoot him a teasing glare. "You might need all the help you can get if my mother finds out you can be an asset in the spotlight."

"Speak of the devil." His humor fades when his gaze lands on my mother's figure across the room.

She's not alone. Arden is with her, his smile gleaming

as he listens intently to whatever she's saying. The fresh tension rolling off Maximus has to be inspired by Arden.

My gaze flicks over to Kell, standing a few feet away from her betrothed. Her body is angled away from Arden, her attention riveted on her phone. I should appreciate their distance and obvious coldness, but something unsettles me about it too. Even from across the room, I can sense they're merely tolerating each other.

All of it pricks uncomfortably at my curiosity. I start to wonder… Did Arden even have a choice in the matter of accepting Kell when the promise of our future was eliminated? If he *did* have a choice, why would he carry on with the charade with my little sister? Or is torturing her during their time together just one of his sick games?

Maximus issues another steely glare in their direction. I press a hand to his shoulder.

"It's fine," I offer, hoping I sound reassuring.

"Nothing about being in the same room as that guy is going to be fine, Kara."

I lift my touch to massage the tight ball of muscle in his jaw. "Relax. He didn't show up to ruin our night. His company sponsored the silent auction they've got going in the library. All the proceeds go to the Seraph Society for helping with elementary school arts and literacy programs."

"Doesn't endear him to me one bit."

Me neither. But I don't voice that aloud. Maximus needs me to talk him down, not give him reasons to face off with Arden at an event that's supposed to legitimize our relationship.

I slide my touch down his tuxedo's arm and take his hand in mine. "How about we go see what they're auctioning off? I heard there was a first edition of *To Kill a Mockingbird* up for bid."

He finally tears his glare from Arden. He blinks, like the words I've said are taking him an extra moment to process. "Really?"

I lift my lips into a smile. "Have I piqued your interest?"

"You've distracted me at least." When he sighs, it's made of so many unspoken emotions—the kinds I can feel when words aren't enough. "And I'm level-headed enough to recognize that's a good thing right now."

And a necessary thing. Thank goodness he can see reason, because I refuse to let Arden ruin a minute of our night.

"Come on." I tug Maximus toward the president's personal library. When we arrive, a handful of people are looking at the different auction items on display.

Maximus lifts his chin toward the book. "That must be it."

He picks it up carefully, studying the intricacies of the cover, running his fingers lovingly over the brown boards held together with the green cloth spine. "I spent a lot of time with this story."

"Did you?"

He nods. "One of my first favorites that I picked up in the store way back."

I smile. "'Remember it's a sin to kill a mockingbird.'"

"And it's a sin, I think, not to own this book," he says

with no small amount of quiet conviction. "What's the bidding at?"

I lean down to study the lined sheet on the table. "Two thousand dollars."

He blows out a breath and sets the book gently onto its stand. "Damn. That's a little too rich for my blood."

I frown a little, already forming a plan to sneak back in here when he's occupied so I can write in the winning bid. There's no hesitation about the decision—or my determination to turn it into reality. I'd sell my soul to make his full. Luckily, all this'll require is my checkbook.

"It's in beautiful condition too. I have one similar to it. Not quite that nice, though."

We both turn at the sound of a woman's voice. The new friend in the room is dressed in an unremarkable black gown. I don't recognize her, but her wide smile is infectious enough to have Maximus and me returning it.

"Are you a collector?" he asks.

She shakes her head, which makes her tight auburn curls bounce below the intricate brass barrette holding them up.

"Not a serious one. Can't really afford to be on a professor's salary." She laughs awkwardly. Her eyes are a little glassy, like maybe the champagne she's clutching could be her third. She shoots her free hand out toward Maximus. "You must be Maximus Kane. You fit the description to a T."

He returns the handshake. "That's me. And you are?"

"My name's Erin. Erin Levin. I just took over the first year contracts and criminal law courses for Professor Vaid. She took her maternity leave early, so I started on short notice. President McCarthy was nice enough to invite me to the party so I could get to know a few people. What a place, huh?"

"It's beautiful," I say, extending my hand to her. "I'm Kara, by the way."

Her eyes brighten, exposing their blue-green depths. "So nice to meet you. You look really familiar. Do you teach at Alameda too?"

I try but fail to mask my surprise. I don't care that she doesn't recognize me from the tabloids. I *am* stunned, in all the best ways, that she'd mistake me for a professor.

"Not yet," Maximus cuts in. "But maybe one day she will. Kara's graduating with a degree in classics this year. She's one of my most dedicated students. She has a very bright future."

He's so sure when he says it that something hums through me. Gratitude, I think, that he's voiced something aloud that I'd never dared to before. That and the warm glow that comes with authentic academic praise—a high that never really gets old, especially when the person dishing it out holds my heart in his hands.

I stare down at the floor a moment, trying to compose myself. "Professor Kane is too generous with his praise."

He takes my hand gently into his. The sudden show of affection is startling, though I'm not sure why. He's been doing it all night. I mean, it is us—a true reflection of how we feel—but we have our parts to play here too. Now more than ever.

"So you found Maximus!" Jesse rolls in, his energy

suddenly filling the whole room.

Erin laughs again. "You were right. He's easy to spot."

"Yeah, you can't miss him. I figured I'd find you in here drooling over the antiques, man."

"And I figured you'd be making new friends," Maximus says with a wry look.

Jesse's boyish smirk and quick glance over at Erin confirms what I've suspected from spying him in action much of the night. Professor North is a consummate flirt. The new professor's returning blush confirms it too, even if Maximus quickly becomes the object of her attention again.

"Professor North was telling me you are quite the Dante aficionado." Her lips are pursed into a shy smile, but her eyes glimmer with the kind of fascination teenagers give my brother. In fact, she seems oddly immune to Jesse's laser-focus attention on her.

"You could say that," Maximus replies, absently gliding our fingers back together.

"I was an English major before I went to law school. I've always had a thing for Dante."

"You should sit in on Maximus's seminar. I know Kara's loving it," Jesse adds with a wink. "His classes always fill up fast, but I'm sure he could save you a seat."

"Oh, wow," she gushes, her blush deepening. "That would be amazing, but I couldn't impose."

Jesse scoffs, dismissing her polite hesitation with a casual wave. "Impose? Maximus, tell her she's not imposing."

Maximus grins at Jesse's playful insistence. "Not at all. If you're already familiar with the material, you wouldn't need to do much to catch up to where we are."

"We just started the sixth circle," I add, even though the woman's preoccupation with Maximus is beginning to rankle me. I feel uniquely possessive over him and his attention—and definitely his lectures, even if I do share them with a hall full of students who will never know him the way I do.

I reassure myself that the party's many guests and the nonstop energy flowing is wearing my patience thin. Shy and unassuming, Erin is no different than any other warm-blooded woman who races to register for Maximus's courses for less than academic reasons. Even the most dedicated scholar isn't immune to him. I never have been...

"The sixth circle?" Arden appears behind Jesse, entering the room smoothly and silently like the snake that he is. "That's my favorite," he murmurs darkly. His gaze is thick and overtly sexual on me, never wavering even as he glides closer to where our little party has gathered.

"Arden." I smile tightly because even though he's a snake, we're playing the polite game in front of strangers tonight. We all really do have our roles to play.

"Kara. You look lovely as always." He leans in to brush a kiss to my cheek, lifting his hand to trace the curve of my earring—the family heirloom I've never had to truly explain. "These are so... so very *you*."

"Cerberus, right?" Jesse says.

The injection of the factoid seems to break the spell of Arden's total fixation on me. He rakes a bored look over the rest of the party, as if he's just realized but doesn't especially care that other people in the room exist. "Yes, Cerberus. We've been acquainted," he answers coolly. "Kara, though? Not so much." He turns his focus back to me, his onyx eyes boring into me like two dark and terrifying promises. "Not yet anyway."

I can feel my skin flush with anger—but with a touch of concern too. The fearful nettles spike through my system, warring with my temper.

"This isn't the time for storytelling, Arden," I say quietly, though I'm perfectly aware that there's nothing private about our exchange right now except the subtext.

He tilts his head in that condescending way that makes me wish he would disappear as swiftly as he arrived.

"Truth or fiction," he says, "there are lessons to be learned with every story, don't you think?"

"Arden." I utter the word through clenched teeth.

It's a warning, but I already know he won't be deterred. Arden doesn't care about our audience or their ignorance about who—*what*—we truly are. He doesn't care about Maximus's possessive clutch on me or the murderous gaze he's casting down on the demon. All Arden seems to care about is stoking that demigod-level rage and reminding me how perilous our situation here on earth is every chance he gets.

"Why are you even in here?" I finally snap, my composure slipping.

The gleam in his eyes flashes with the reflection of my own gaze. The one made of fury that burns like a five-alarm blaze. His smile broadens, as my ire seems to please him even more.

"I just came in to check on progress with the auction items. Did anything catch your eye? I'm sure the Valaris could add something here to their collection to help a good cause."

Maximus squeezes my hand. "Come on, Kara. Let's go."

I'm too invested in my staring contest with Arden to be pulled away, though. The heat in my eyes seems to grow in tandem with his vicious satisfaction. Have I ever hated someone so much?

"You know what, Arden? Something *did* catch my eye."

I release Maximus's hand and turn toward the auction table. With vehement strokes, I ink an amount on the line that will guarantee we leave this party with the book Maximus was so drawn to. He'll balk at the price and the gesture, but I'm so angry with Arden I hardly care. Hell, maybe the precious thing will save the rest of our night.

Because the anger rolling off my beloved right now is threatening to ruin all of it.

As sure as I am of that, nothing prepares me for the curveball that comes next—the stunned drop of Jesse's jaw when I turn back to gracefully exit the room and create space between us and Arden.

Though he recomposes himself with admirable speed, all signs of humor flee his expression. "Oh shit," he mutters. "You weren't kidding."

CHAPTER 19

MAXIMUS

"COME ON." THE GRIP I secure around Kara's hand is as much a command as the words on my lips. I jog my head Jesse's way. "You too, North."

Together we head toward a darkened hallway off the mansion's main room. Beyond the first door I open, there's a mini movie theater. Fortunately, the large screen is dark and the dozen plush chairs are in shadow.

Maybe not so fortunately.

Jesse's initial reaction already had Kara ducking her head. Her blazing irises have dimmed in the minute since, but in the darkness they can't be mistaken for anything else. Not a single flame is missed by my enraptured friend.

"Damn," Jesse murmurs, practically drifting his wheelchair across the tiles to stop in front of Kara. "That's . . . just . . ."

"I know." There's a split second of her grimace before she drags down her hair to curtain off her face. "It's creepy.

Just give me a second to dial things down, and—"

"Creepy?" Jesse grunts hard. "Honest to shit, that's cooler than Catatumbo lightning and the Northern Lights combined."

Kara laughs from behind her hair, but the levity vanishes with her defeated slump. She tilts a troubled glance up at me. It says a thousand things at once, all of them adding to the rocks in my gut. I swallow hard, ordering air to my throat and words to my lips.

"It's okay." I try for reassuring, even as my thoughts are racing for ways to explain this to Jesse. Not just the fire in Kara's eyes that I'd described to him before . . . All of it. The rest of the story that will give this oddity context. But already I know Jesse's not ready for that mind bender—and may not ever be. And Kara certainly isn't ready for me to share it.

"Crap," she mumbles, ending with a shaky sigh.

"It's no big deal, Kara," Jesse mutters. "But, you know . . . it sort of is."

I ignore him, funneling my attention on the woman who's still hunched over the back of a plush screening couch. I step closer, only to realize she's not going to move. She trusts her hair as more of a defense than me. While I understand her choice and the fierce independence that backs it, my frustration is barely mollified.

"Hey," I say, gentling my intent with a soothing hand down her spine.

Kara answers with a sigh, though it's heavier than a rain cloud. The heat has barely dissipated from her eyes, though it's now the texture of potent embers instead of bursting flames.

"I'm so sorry," she rasps.

"It really is no big deal." I dare to lean in and push some hair off her cheek. "It's just Jesse, okay?"

She twists her fingers together. "Right. But if Jesse noticed, who else did?"

Halfway through Jesse's name, her voice cracks again. Before her plea is done, I've got her swaddled in my arms and tucked against my chest. She feels so damn good there, I'm on the verge of being grateful for the circumstances. If only she wasn't so right...

She twists her hands around my jacket's lapels. "And Professor Levin..."

"She was preoccupied with the auction items." I brush an assuring kiss into her hair. "She barely blinked as we left."

"Affirmative," Jesse adds. "She was even smiling. Hell, she was practically glowing."

"So if she noticed anything, she's probably already written it off as a trick of the track lighting in that room," I offer.

"But it's not that," Jesse says. "It's way the hell better."

Kara and I share a second's worth of silent but potent energy. Jesse has no idea how perfectly he's matched the words to the moment—nor can he ever. As badly as I yearn to share the complete truth with my favorite science dork on the planet, dragging him into this danger isn't an option. None of it is his fight to wage or his risk to take.

"Come on." Jesse shakes his head with familiar

fascination. "Help a guy out here. How does that happen? I don't need the masters dissertation. Just some basics... please?"

Unfortunately for him, his curiosity won't be satisfied tonight. While I still don't know what fuels Kara's ocular bonfires, I'm pretty damn sure the Valaris are her special kerosene tonight. I don't want to be right, but I am.

"Ssshhh," I murmur, sliding a hand across the back of her head. "It's going to be all right, beautiful."

"It won't be if I can't turn it off."

"You're exhausted, and your psyche keeps getting pounded on."

"Well, I can't exactly lie down here and grab a nap." She jolts up her head as soon as my answering pause speaks for itself. "Maximus," she chides. "You aren't—"

"Oh, I definitely am. Come over to the couch."

"Maximus—"

"I'm not asking, Kara." Though I do issue the decree with the same courtly swagger that enchanted her earlier. Thankfully, it works this time too. With a smitten little smirk, she allows me to guide her around to the front of the furniture. "Fifteen minutes. That's all I'm asking. Close your eyes and calm your mind. Give me nine hundred little seconds here."

I leave out the reiteration that she really needs it. I'm not going to insult the woman's intelligence. She's fully capable of observing the reflection of her gaze inside mine. But I also leave out the caveat that if she passes out for fifteen *hours*, I'll protect her every minute like a goddamned Doberman.

She opens her mouth again but clamps it shut with a resigned sigh. Her capitulation probably has more to do with the sight of the couch's huge cushions instead of my insistence, but I don't care. I'm only happy to help out, kneeling to ease off her sparkling high heels as she sinks deeper into the soft haven.

"You're sticking around, right?"

"Like a corny lullaby, baby." I grab a plush blanket from the back of a big bucket chair and swoop it over her. As soon as I do, she rolls to her side and tucks her hands beneath her cheek.

"I suppose ten minutes won't . . . be a . . . prob . . . lem . . . "

Her words are barely whispers, tapering off into a sleepy little hum. I take in a huge breath, letting peace wash over me for the first time since our stolen kisses after class yesterday afternoon. For at least the next ten minutes, my precious little demon is safe. Fate's brought Christmas morning a few months ahead of time.

"Is she really out?"

Jesse's query has me looking over to his new position, next to one of the luxury bucket chairs. I walk over and drop against the U-shaped cushion. "Yeah. I think so."

"Well, color me impressed."

Though he's still fixing his stupefied look Kara's way, I shake my head. "Color *me* the idiot boyfriend who made it impossible for her to sleep last night."

My buddy swings his head around, eyes narrowed. "And that's a bad thing . . . why?"

"Because I was passed out." I have the grace to grimace.

"And, I think, snoring because of it."

Jesse chokes on thin air. "Passed out? As in blotto? Trashed? Hammered?"

"All of the above." I grimace. "And probably a few more."

"And I thought the girl with the forest-fire eyes would be my freakiest takeaway from the night."

I pull at the tie holding my hair in its tidy queue. If I've still got ten more minutes of a break, comfort is feeling damn important. "I'm thanking you ahead of time for keeping that little freaky fun fact tucked into the confidential file, man."

"Of course." He's got a smirk at the ready but saves whatever tease is hiding behind his lips. "You're really in it with this woman, aren't you?" He's as locked in to this truth as any scientific statement.

I raise my head. Clench my jaw. "In it? What's that supposed to mean?"

"You know damn well what."

He's got me and he knows it. We both do.

I grit out a soft curse and rake back my hair again. Jesse loosens his steepled fingers.

"It's . . . complicated," I admit after a pause that stretches far too long.

He tosses back his head and groans. "You did *not* just go there."

"Did it. Meant it. And believe me, you don't want to know *how* complicated."

"How about you try me?"

"How about we pretend you didn't ask?"

"It's a simple question, Kane," he rebuts. "Are you in love with her or not?"

"Tea is for savoring, not spilling," I mutter.

"I'm not asking for all the dirty details, though you know I won't turn them down. But right now, I'm asking one simple question. How do you actually *feel* about her?"

I crisscross my own fingers. A better option than letting him see my full stew. "Simple question," I concede. "But not such a simple answer."

An admission I had no trouble giving Reg and Mom this afternoon. But would I have spewed it so easily, knowing Mom would nearly faint and Reg would be dialing up her version of the National Guard?

Not that Jesse will resort to either. The man knows my entire romantic dossier. Now he has confirmation of just how different Kara is, in more ways than the obvious. With more intimate intel on top of that, he'll insist on helping in every way he can—including, but not limited to, facing any of my divine relatives or diving into hell itself by my side. Because he's Jesse. My ride or die.

The man has one of the most brilliant minds I know. He's undoubtedly ascertained that I'm protecting his intrepid ass. Doesn't mean he's happy about it. Not by a far stretch. He makes that clear as blood on glass with his defeated snarl.

"So that's how it's going to be now? Out with simple Max. In with fabulous, famous, 'complicated' Maximus?"

"Jesse." It's far from the apology I intend or the one he deserves. But my system's a hive of stress and fear, giving birth to more anxiety by the second. It's my only constant right now.

"It's fine." From somewhere in his trendy jacket pockets, he pulls out the long, sticky plastic rope that's his version of a stress ball.

"It's *not* fine," I argue. "But it's just the way things have to be for a while."

"I get it." He whips the wide end of the rope, landing it to the back of another bucket chair with a soft *thwack*. "Optics. Branding. You have to stay red carpet ready, after all."

"Damn it. None of that is relevant to this."

"Says the guy who's been holding court in McCarthy's living room in a pretty custom suit?"

"Yeah," I counter. "Exactly that guy—who knows it's often easier to hide in the light than the shadows."

"Hiding!" Jesse's so baffled, he nearly pitches it into a question. "What the hell from?" He's unnervingly quick about reading the new strain in my posture. "Or *who* the hell from?"

I push out rough air from my nose. "I met my father."

For possibly the first time ever, the guy goes totally speechless. Doesn't stop him from trying for words, though—and eventually they come out in a croak I've never heard from him before.

"You're absolutely serious."

"I absolutely am." It's not a revelation I'd planned on feeding him, but it's enough to dazzle him out of asking for anything more. I hope.

"You really know how to toss a guy into the centrifuge,

buddy." He shakes his head slowly, like that's exactly what just happened. "You must've been tripping."

"Just a little," I deadpan.

"So . . . when? And where? Did Kara have anything to do with it?"

"Yes and no." I deliberately skirt his other queries. He's already gotten the juice from the main bombshell. Details would be the equivalent of escorting him into the nuclear reactor. "Apparently our families have some connections. Mutual friends, so to speak." It's a stretch, but I'm trying like hell to use language Jesse will understand on this one.

"No kidding. So does she like him? Do *you*? What's he like? And where the hell has he been all this time?"

I wince. "That brings us back to the complicated part."

"Of course it does," he grouses.

"I'm sorry. I wish we could go home, order a pizza, and inhale it while I give you every detail."

"But then you'd have to kill me?"

I crunch a frown as my whole gut twists. "It wouldn't be me, man."

The guy's genius brain picks up exactly what I need it to. I know it as fact the moment his face pales and he drums all ten fingers against his wheels. "Well, fuck."

"That's become one of my favorites lately too."

An uncomfortable moment stretches by. I'm still racking my brain for subjects other than the themes that have taken over it. Discovering—and dealing with—my family. The intricate politics of Kara's whole clan. The impact of all this on Mom and Regina. Figuring out a new normal beneath the glare of paparazzi lenses—and the more vexing flare of Hades's fixation.

I lower my elbows to my knees and then my head into my hands. But I'm not there for long, because I'm saved by my woman's adorable little sigh. I return to her side on the couch as she blinks in sleepy confusion.

"Maximus? Where am… Oh." She interrupts herself once her gaze takes in the rest of the room. "Oh, yeah. I'm…here."

I run my knuckles down the side of her face. While I've memorized every one of her expressions already, nothing takes the place of getting to relearn them with my own touch. "Feeling a little better?"

While she's stunning, she's not vibrant. Her attention seems foggy. Her lips are pressed and pale.

"Kara?" I prompt when nearly a minute goes by without her reply.

"I'm okay," she says at last.

"You sure about that?"

"It's just a headache," she murmurs. "Honestly, Maximus. Stop stressing. I think I just need some fresh air."

She gentles her grip on my wrist and flows her fingers across the back of my hand. At once, all my fingers are rays of perfect warmth. Even my palm burns like the sun creating those rays. No matter how many times this happens between us, I'm struck as if it's the first sunrise—or lightning jolt, or energy surge, or brush fire—she's ever pushed into my blood. Like all those times, I never want it to end. I never want *us* to end. Even the consideration of that possibility shreds my mind to violent purpose and my senses to unthinking fury. Which, of course, she's honed right in on.

"Maximus?" she asks sheepishly.

"Yes, beautiful." I gently kiss her knuckles. "You're right. Outside is a grand plan."

A smile teases the edges of her lips. It has to be the most perfect sight of my night.

Correction. That honor goes to the look on her face as she swings her legs over and pushes all the way back to her feet. The second she's there, she grabs my hands and draws me up too. "I was really hoping you'd say that."

"Because . . . ?" I purposely lead her with the comeback. She looks a little too eager for a stroll around the pool deck and gardens, despite how prettily they're lit up tonight.

"Because we've been invited to another gig."

I stop. "Tonight?"

"Umm . . . yeah." She's sheepish again, but I'm much fonder of this version, especially when she adds, "Out at the beach. Jaden and a friend are throwing a party in Malibu. I'd really like to go."

"Your brother?" It's a no-duh question, but it spills out anyway.

"Well, he's definitely not here," Jesse comments. "I'd have noticed his name on the auction sheet for the VIP afternoon at the Porsche test track."

I crunch a frown while realizing the same thing. "How'd he get out of this gig?" I ask Kara.

"Because he's sly. Rerek Horne is co-hosting the bash, and he's supposedly invited some major casting agents, so

Mom let it slide."

"Who's Rerek Horne?" I live in a book bubble, but I also live in LA. I have a decent working knowledge of Hollywood's movers and shakers. This one isn't familiar.

"A family friend," she says, exposing more truths in her simplicity than I probably want. "He moves more... discreetly... than most." Despite her cagey phrasing, an impish grin takes over her mouth. "It's all about the grip and grin, remember?"

"Well, I like gripping." I demonstrate just that by lowering my hands to the sweet curves of her hips. "And I'm sure, with proper motivation, I could be talked into grinning."

"Motivation, hmm?" She tiptoes up to press a breathy, sexy kiss to my cheek.

"On that note, I'm so gone." Jesse maneuvers his chair into a fluid one-eighty. "I need to go slam some peaty scotch. Something to wash out all the sugar that's flowing in here."

Kara giggles quietly into my bicep. When she comes up for air, she sends a dazzling smile Jesse's way. "I'm sure Jaden and Rerek have plenty of scotch flowing at the party," she offers. "And he wouldn't mind us bringing—"

"A third wheel?" Jesse jibes back. "Thanks, but I've got two fine ones of my own right here." He balls up his sticky snake toy and tucks it back into his pocket. "But you two kids get out of here and go have some fun. Build a sandcastle in my honor."

"Sure. That's totally going to happen," I jibe. "Seriously, though. You should try to swing by. I'll message you the address."

"Aw. You *do* love me."

I smirk. "If you say so, man."

Despite our banter, Jesse's parting wave is noncommittal. But I secretly hope he'll make the trek to Malibu. Tonight hasn't exactly been low-key, and I'm not totally sure what to expect at Jaden's party, especially because Kara still seems to harbor mixed feelings about attending. While I hope my instincts are off and this gig will be weirdness of the standard Hollywood kind and not the unpredictable underworld kind, Jesse's never failed to be the best kind of social backup.

My friend wheels from the room, leaving the door open in his wake. My attitude sobers once I refocus on the gorgeous demon at my side.

"How are you doing?" I ask her with husky concern. "You feel up to leaving now, or do you want to rest a little longer here? I can bring you another plate of food if you're still hungry."

Kara lifts her face, full of adoration, as she scratches gentle fingers into my beard. "I'm ready when you are, Professor. Besides, I'm in the mood for some trashy party food."

I answer her tease with a longer, deeper kiss. She tastes so damn good and feels even better, wrapped tight and close against my thrumming body. I suddenly wish my powers extended to teleportation and I could beam us onto the Malibu sand this second.

When I finally—and reluctantly—let her go, I ask, "Do you need to check in with Veronica before we go?"

Kara crinkles her nose with luscious precision. "Last time I checked, Mom was holding court just fine on her own. But I do need to grab my purse—and one more party favor."

"Party favor?"

But I'm left hanging with my puzzled words as we approach the mansion's front foyer and she sashays off with a mischievous wink. I walk to the wide front drive and hand off a ticket to the valet. I imagine Kara reemerging with everything from a kiddie party bag with candies and toys to something like the designer gift satchel she brought home from the Piper Blue movie premiere.

She comes back out with neither.

Instead, after I help her into the truck, she pushes a mylar-wrapped rectangle into my grasp.

"Don't tell me to take it back in," she says. "You and that book are meant for each other."

"What the… Kara?" I manage to stutter around the giant ball in my throat.

Though I hold Harper Lee's words like the rare treasure they are, I cup the face of my women with even greater care. "Well, don't tell the book this," I whisper. "But I've already found the one I'm *really* meant to be with."

Her light laugh is the best jewel of my night. I draw it into me, stringing it onto the sparkling strand in my soul, by taking her lips with a consuming sweep of mine. I don't stop until she's trembling, sighing, and grabbing at my clothes with her addictingly ferocious force. It's several minutes before we drag apart. I'm lost in her scent and softness and hooded, seductive eyes.

And now, her sinfully sexy voice, as well.

"Stow that book and start driving, Professor," she dictates against my lips. "Before we get into a lot of trouble in your boss's front driveway."

CHAPTER 20

Kara

LOW-KEY R&B TUNES COMING from the truck's speakers match the shift in the evening's mood. Maximus and I are both quiet for a while, savoring the feeling of not having to be *on* anymore. The break also gives me a chance to sort out my thoughts. Well . . . half-thoughts. Snippets of conversation I wasn't supposed to be overhearing though unintentionally did. Because I was napping and not full-on dozing, despite how I convinced Maximus otherwise. Because of the subject matter that ensured I had to hang on to at least half my consciousness.

You're really in it with this woman, aren't you?

What's that supposed to mean?

You know damn well what.

It's complicated.

It's a simple question, Kane. Are you in love with her or not?

He hadn't said no. But he definitely hadn't said yes.

Staring at the angles of my lover's profile, made

even more beautiful and bold when we zoom beneath streetlights, isn't helping me discern the answer any clearer. And unlike Jesse, it's not like I can just ask. Not right here and now.

But why not? I don't need a choir of angels and a bower of roses. This moment, with summer wind in the air and his fingers linked in mine, is better than any of that fanfare. He has to know at least that much by now. He also has to know, in more than a few corners of his instincts, that my heart's tumbled as deeply into this fire as his.

And there's the very reason my whole heart is in my throat. If he wanted to say something, he just would . . . right?

"Kara?"

I visibly jolt at his calm interjection. "Uhhh . . . hmm?"

He hits me with a pointed glance. "I was just saying I'll probably cut over and take Topanga to the coast rather than battling the midtown crush."

"Right. Good plan."

"You sure about that?"

"What makes you think I'm not?"

"Demon girl." He squeezes my hand gently. "Come on. Talk to me."

I feign interest in the darkening landscape beyond the window as he takes the exit for Topanga and heads for the canyon cut-through. "Talk? About what?"

"About the fact that you've been fond of talking in questions since we left McCarthy's place?"

"Have I?"

The second it leaves my lips, he chuckles. I join him

because I don't have a choice. The memories I'm not supposed to have are turning me into the world's worst date.

"Sorry," I murmur. "My mind was in another place." An absolute truth I can borrow for making my point. "It's been a really long day."

"After a really stressful night." His face tightens. "Made worse, in no small part, by my shenanigans with Z."

"Necessary shenanigans, remember?"

Without taking his eyes off the road, he yanks my hand up and plants a firm kiss to my palm. "But no less trying for you."

After his talented mouth leaves my skin, I keep my hand open, savoring the feel of his strong whiskers and forceful jaw. "I'm just fine."

He darts over a look that conveys his difficulty believing me. "I can turn around anytime you say the word. This party isn't mandatory."

"I know, but it'll be at least another year before my brother takes interest in hanging out with me again." I pivot to face him fully. "More importantly, I want him to meet you."

My new positioning reaps an instant reward in the form of his wide smile, pushing a deep dimple into existence at the corner of his mouth. The look is almost too irresistible, and I write a raincheck to myself for kissing him in that delicious divot as soon as we get to Rerek's place.

"So you want your little bro to like me, eh?"

"Has nothing to do with what I want, because he *will* like you."

I finish that with a confident smile, and it doesn't wane the rest of the trip. Though I suspect Jaden's invitation was inspired more by his curiosity about Maximus than any strong desire to reconnect with me, it's still a connection I welcome. It's also some downtime that we need after another intense day.

Maximus finds a parking spot about a hundred yards up from Rerek's front door.

"Stay right there," he orders.

I'm barely done opening my door, but I know better than to test him. The last time I heard him sound this way, he was kicking a couple of jokesters out of his medieval lit class. Though I have a decent idea about his intention this time, I still let out a surprised yelp when he gets to my side of the truck and then reaches in for me.

"Maximus," I scold once he carries me across the road but shows no sign of slowing down. "Come on. I can walk the rest of the way."

"In those stilts?" He nods toward my feet and the glittering four-inchers strapped on them. "In this gravel?"

"You ever walk a red carpet between Piper Blue and half the cast of a new Marvel flick?"

Any witty reply he might have is stunted when we reach the front entrance and Maximus eases me down to my feet once again.

Like many of his neighbors, Rerek's front entrance is miniscule but classy. There's a small balsa wood planter, multi-tiered, that at first glance is filled with typical California succulents and field grasses. It's centered around a small stone and glass fountain that's supposed to make people think Rerek—or at least his decorator—has been somewhere like Solvang, Santa Barbara, or Laguna Beach. Maximus actually stops to admire the artsy setting, but I hurry past it. I know what the rest of the world doesn't—that the grasses are cultivated from vain sinners forced to part with their hair and the cute pebbles in the fountain are trophy teeth taken from history's most notorious traitors and murderers.

I rush up the steps and wait, now a little jittery, for Maximus to catch up. The last time I graced this entry, I'd been in a more accepting headspace of all things demon. But even then, Rerek was never like other demons. I hope, yet doubt, that's changed much. Still, as Maximus and I walk through the already-open front door, I hang on to Jaden's recent theory about Rerek mellowing out. I'll know whether that's true the moment I see.

Inside, a definite aura of underworld energy fills the place, despite its all-white decor that's interrupted only by gaudy throw pillows and pathos-drenched sculptures from a thousand eras ago. But no way is everyone in this place an actual demon, unless there's been an odd Tinseltown recruitment campaign that I don't know about. If that's the case, then Hades has definitely targeted all the beautiful people. They're here in every shape, color, and size, primped in their trendy party finery—which should have them fawning all over each other like the trained courtesans they are.

But that's where the real disconnect begins.

There's nothing lively about this bunch. As I gaze over the throng, mingling with high-end cocktails and plates of expensive canapés, I wonder what golf match they must be waiting on at this late hour. It's strange—*really* strange, for a crowd of people who should be vying for buoyant social media exposure—but true. I'm barely sensing pulses from any of them, let alone thoughts and feelings. But they *are* alive, proven by their relaxed sways to the music that comes from the ceiling speakers.

Maximus cocks one brow my way before muttering, "And I always thought Jesse threw weird parties."

I side-bump him with appreciation for the humor. "Let's find Jaden." As I say it, I focus on the beach just below the outside balcony. "I have a good idea where we can start."

Besides, the bonfire out on the sand looks too fun to resist—and after the insanity of the last couple of days, some fun sounds like total perfection.

We manage to avoid any awkward introductions on our way to the back deck, which connects to some shallow concrete steps down to the sand. The moon is full and the breeze is brisk as we abandon our shoes and step out on the sand toward the two silhouettes outlined next to the bonfire.

They don't see us yet, laughing while staring into the dancing flames of the big blaze. But my impression has yet to be validated. I'm not sure Rerek Horne has ever enjoyed a real laugh in his whole life. While his wavy black hair, lean stature, and Italianate lips are similar enough to Jaden's, Kell's, and mine that he's often mistaken as a Valari, the similarities are only skin deep—and I'm happy to let it stay that way.

I've never understood Jaden's draw to the demon, who seems to have been in a centuries-old funk since most of the Egyptians stopped believing in him. He and Jaden connected back when we were kids, when Rerek was on a victory high after orchestrating the Fukushima meltdown. It'd be a lie to say we all weren't a little concerned. A headstrong half-demon son, heading into puberty as besties with a full-blooded chaos demon . . . What could go wrong?

"Aha!" Jaden's easygoing exclamation bursts out as Maximus and I step closer. His greeting comes with a generous I-might-be-a-little-high hug. "Look who's rolled in from the land of academia. Thought you'd never get here. Last time I checked, you guys were turning out of the canyon. Seems eons ago."

I hug him tighter, hoping that last part gets muffled by my hair, before he breaks off to plunk me down in the sand. Maximus is relaxed and happy tonight, and I want to keep it that way. The last thing he needs is an explanation about Jaden's black-ops-level hearing abilities.

"And look what else we've got here. Her lucky escort!"

Oh, yes. He's buzzed.

"Maximus, this is my brother, Jaden. J, I'd like you to meet—"

"*The* Professor Maximus," Jaden intercedes before hauling my date into a hearty bro hug. "Good to meet you, dude."

"Uh . . . yeah. Sure," Maximus mutters. "Same."

"I'm so psyched you guys could make it. Rerek is too."

I sneak a glance around him toward the spot where

Rerek arcs his hand in a wax-off wave. His black, semi-wiry hair is longer than I remember, serving him well by hiding the tops of his ears, their size exaggerated by his noticeably long neck. His whole form is the same way. By most human standards, his body would be called gangly, though he handles it all with the cocky elegance of a rock star. He's actually smirking like one, exaggerating dramatic cheekbones that clash with his generous mouth.

But that's Rerek. The guy revels in his contrasts. Doles them out like his chaotic calling cards. That's why my return wave is brief and cautious. Really cautious.

"Hello, Rerek. It's been a while."

"I think your brother is feeling nostalgic, Kara. I believe I may be too." Rerek pairs the remark with a look as warm as the brandy snifter cradled in his palm. Reflections from the fire lick up its sides and into his pastel irises. "But you're right, I think. It really has been too long."

Every syllable is an unnerving drawl as the demon ambles over, regarding me with new intensity across his enormous ice blues. I've always wondered if his eyes seemed bigger because so few demons have pastel irises. Now, this close to him, I know. His eyes really are that big. And discomfiting. And prying.

Maximus stabs a hand through his hair, looking awkward but delectable in the same moment. I shift my weight too, reining in the craving to climb him like a hungry squirrel up a pine tree. It's a much preferable feeling to the sensations brought on by Rerek's persistent perusal, which I know is designed to incite discomfort. Is blinking as foreign to him as smiling?

Jaden leans and pats the center of Maximus's chest. "That's Rerek. He's like a brother."

"Speak for yourself." I sock him in the shoulder.

Jaden chuckles. "Fine. He's like *my* brother."

I don't miss the slight wince in Rerek's guarded stare, now fixed on my brother. "Brother. Hmm."

I inhale deeply, hoping it helps my gritted smile to stay in place. "Rerek." It's my textbook surfacey chide, usually brandished on reporters who aren't aware of boundaries. "You know it's bad form to openly gawk, yes?"

Rerek's secret passion for Jaden has never been much of a secret, at least to anyone belonging to a family with our kinds of intuitive gifts. He knows that too, but that doesn't stop him from rolling his eyes with a silky smirk after brushing a few ashes off his velvet jacket. "Come now, Kara. There's a lovely line between gawking and appreciating a creature of splendor."

Examining his subtext—a brand of not-so-brotherly affection that is often felt but never discussed—feels daunting. And I've had my fair share of daunting for this week *and* next.

"Nice threads," I say, hoping to shift the conversation for everyone's sake. Except Jaden has already distracted Maximus with a sidebar about firewood and trucks.

Rerek adopts an urbane pose, feathering his fingertips over his satin lapel. "You like it?"

"Very much." This time, none of my sincerity is forced.

"I've had it since the sixties. That makes it vintage haute

couture now." He relaxes his stance and wrinkles his nose. "Though I see I'm not the only one who got the fancy fashion memo for the night."

He nods toward Maximus, who purposely ditched his tie and dress jacket back in the truck but still looks like ten million dollars in his tailored shirt and impeccably fitted slacks. As the ocean kicks up a stronger wind, his shirt gets plastered across his broad pecs and the ridges of his abs. His hair lifts away from his face, giving the firelight free rein over his bold features. Just when I thought he couldn't captivate me more than usual... For all those reasons, I can't stop staring.

"Oh, my my my." All too quickly, Rerek's knowing murmur breaks into my reverie.

I shake my head, pushing off another schism of discomfort. Rerek *is* a lot like our unofficial brother. Because of that, he's never actively messed with Hollywood, though the town has done just fine in the chaos department all by itself. Still, no creature that's helped with centuries of human catastrophes should be so urbane about it.

"My my my what?" I ask, still struggling for a semblance of charm.

"Just commenting on perceptions, darling. Your lust is dripping like wax from a dungeon candle."

"Oh dear," I mumble, beyond glad that Jaden still has Maximus's ear.

Rerek wiggles his toes through the sand but frowns when a new gust scatters the grains onto his black pant leg. "'*We are asleep until we fall in love.*'"

I laugh, buying myself time for an acceptable reaction. Why do I feel so strange and violated, when Maximus and I are on every mortal magazine cover and every immortal watch list?

But there's no time for time for processing that. Thankfully, at least on the outside, I'm able to maintain a show of serenity to match Rerek's. Past a calm smile, I reply, "I had no idea you were a Tolstoy buff."

My masquerade is successful, if his short chuckle can be believed. "Little one, whom do you think kept the man company when he told the literary elite to fuck off?"

"Oh, goodness. Well, that must have been a fun feather in your cap."

"Leo didn't need any help from me," he assures. "The man already had a head full of demons by the time I showed up."

"Yo, R-dog. I'm empty!" Jaden interjects, hoisting his tumbler in emphasis. "And thirsty."

"And that just won't do." Rerek struts over to my brother and links their elbows. "What do you say we find something sinful to imbibe or inhale?"

"Might want to check everyone's pulse while you're at it," I remark. "It's pretty dead in there."

Rerek scowls. "Well, that just won't do," says the man who gladly cops to half the world's insanity.

I'm happily diverted as soon as Jaden disconnects from Rerek and pulls me into a hug. "Thanks for showing up. I mean it."

I smile into his shirt, which smells like ocean and smoke.

"Thanks for the invite. I mean that too."

He winks and flashes the smile that's landed him a thousand magazine covers before he disappears into the darkness between here and the house. I watch their shadows in the gloom and then their silhouettes against the wide cement stairway up to Rerek's living room. Since the pocket doors are all open, the party music flows out our way. It's a pleasant mix with the ebb and flow of the waves and random spark pops from the fire.

Maximus presses his torso to my back. His hands around my shoulders and his lips to my ear, he offers softly, "Beach blanket for your thoughts."

A smile melts the last of my tension, especially as I follow his pointing finger to a pile of big velour squares that Jaden and Rerek left behind. "Well, now you're talking."

"No," Maximus counters while helping me spread out the top blanket in a spot upwind of the fire's smoke. "Now *you're* talking. What's going on?" He finishes the question by pulling me down into his lap and pressing a tender hand to my face. "We came here to unwind. So far, you've only been pretending to."

I dig into his train of thought by doing the same to his forearms, playing with the alluring hairs between his elbow and wrist while organizing my thoughts. "Rerek can be unpredictable. He puts me on edge. I guess Jaden thrives on that kind of thing. Me, not so much."

"The guy seems pretty easygoing."

I attempt a laugh. "Easygoing isn't how I'd describe a full-blooded chaos demon, even on his mellowest day."

Maximus absorbs the revelation with shocking calm, though the slight lift of his brows is oddly comforting.

"All right. That's starting to make a little sense now."

"In what way?"

He scoops his hand to my nape and rubs there, as if we're just enjoying a Sunday picnic in the sun instead of discussing demons by firelight. "I thought his name sounded familiar. It's a nickname for the Egyptian demon Apep. He's Ra's nemesis."

I nod, acknowledging the myth that happens to be the truth—and wondering, for perhaps the hundredth time, why Maximus accepts these crazy truths so easily. Often better than me. "He switches out the name every hundred or so years so he doesn't raise any alarm bells in the mortal world."

Maximus is thoughtful for a moment. "According to ancient texts, the only advantage he had over Ra was his ability to hide in the shadows."

"The shadows?" I lean in, now fascinated with what he's saying. Mostly because *he's* saying it, but it's because his account makes sense. I'm not sure I've ever seen Rerek out in broad daylight. "You mean coffins and caves? Like a vampire?"

"Caves, yes. Dark mountain passes, yes. But coffins?" The edges of his lips quirk. "I think you've been watching too many horror movies."

Really? Thank goodness you didn't know to stop and admire the murderers' teeth in the entrance fountain.

I keep that to myself, at least for now. Instead, I tease

back and wriggle around to secure a closer snuggle. "Hmm, well… Only after I've done all my homework."

A rough breath leaves him. "Ahhh. Such a good student." He runs his hand down my spine. "You must work very hard."

"Have to," I say, inching my mouth toward the alluring angle of his jaw, tickling my nose in his beard before adding, "I've got this one professor… He takes no prisoners."

His hard swallow doesn't escape my attention. "Sounds like a real hard-ass," he mutters. "No prisoners at all?"

"None that have lived to tell the tale." I cock my head up enough to show off my mischievous grin. "You either prove your worth or walk his plank."

Once more, his generous lips twist upward. I gaze in delight at what that does to his deep dimples before fanning all the way up to his alluring blues. Within a few seconds, they're as dark as the sky above, reflecting the fire's flying sparks as his version of shooting stars.

What he says next comes through a voice I've never heard from him before. A mix of murmur and whisper that covers me in shivers and heat at the same time…

"But what if he falls in love with one of his prisoners?"

CHAPTER 21

MAXIMUS

I KEEP TELLING MYSELF her silence might be a good thing. That, or I've truly gotten carried away with the moonlight and the fire and just fed her some line.

No. I've gotten carried away with *her.*

Everything about her. Everything about how I feel when I'm with her. Free and brave. Open and real, like the confession that's just spilled from my soul by way of my lips.

But nobody promised me the truth wouldn't be terrifying. Because right now, it is. Especially because she's still saying nothing.

The agony doesn't compare to the few seconds I wait to kiss her, ordering my mind to memorize every square inch of her fire-lit beauty. The silken heart of her face, almost sizzling with visual evidence of our connection. The honeyed warmth of her eyes, glowing with unabashed adoration. Damn it, even the delicate sweep of her nose, leading my gaze down to the sweet pillows of her lips.

My God. *Her lips.*

I want to lie here for hours, lost in fascination with them alone—but they're moving in strange ways, as if she's attempting a smile, until she catches herself by biting them with insecure little nips. Then a stuttering sigh. Then the most perfect words…

"What if the prisoner falls in love with him too?"

I force myself to breathe. Then rake my free hand up her spine until I'm bracing the back of her head. Her hair is a handful of silken luxury, surrounding my fingers as if it were spun explicitly for that purpose. Right now, that's exactly what I choose to believe—the same way her mouth fits so perfectly against mine.

Because she *is* perfection.

This is perfection.

The affirmation becomes a pulsing, pressing mantra in my senses. Unrelenting. Inescapable. And so damn right.

Yes. Yes. Yes.

The beat pushes harder. Stronger. I succumb to it, sliding my tongue between her plush, pliant lips. She accepts me with a ready sigh, gripping a hand into my hair too. When she twists and pulls harder, I willingly let her lead. I'm on my back on the blanket, with the most breathtaking beauty in *any* realm atop me. She's bathed in shades of orange and red and yellow, as if summoning inspiration from the netherworld itself, but I can't think of her as anything except my beautiful, carnal angel.

She's so much more now.

Especially after the words. My admission. Then hers.

Not exactly traditional confessions but better in so many ways. Better because they've come from pure places in us both. Places I wasn't even aware of until this extraordinary woman changed my world with her smile and her touch...

A touch that moves me even more in this moment.

That lights me up, just like the tiny sparks that dance along her face, as we explore each other with deepening wonderment. The light gets even better when she yanks another blanket off the pile and spreads it out, ensconcing us in a velour cocoon. Stars dance between our fingers as we touch again, and when Kara leans down for a new kiss, a miniature solar system lights up between our mouths.

While the entire galaxy explodes through my spirit.

Just like that, I finally understand Dante's obsession with one woman. Why he made her his divine guide, his ultimate purpose. His never-ending love.

We press more urgently into each other. Quickly, we're devouring each other's mouths, but the kiss still doesn't feel deep enough. She fills me, but I crave more. I'm her sponge, taking in every drop of her passion. I'm her mountain, ready to surround her with shelter and lift her to new summits. Most of all, I'm her convert, pledging my worship for the rest of my existence. Ready to exalt her in every way she'll let me...

"Fuck." I force it out after twisting my lips free from hers with a tormented groan. "Oh, fuck. Kara. *Kara*."

"I know," she rasps into the base of my neck, blasting a firestorm of fresh lust through me. I swear, she can read more than my emotions. How else does she know every perfect way to touch me, every spellbinding way to talk to me? "I know," she repeats in a whisper, trailing her entrancing mouth down the center of my torso, undoing my shirt buttons as she goes. "I know . . . I know."

"Ah . . . I'm not sure you do."

She can't possibly understand these flames in my veins, this pressure from every beat of my pulse. And the agonizing battle of holding it all back from my groin.

"Maximus." Her every syllable is a study in soft agony. When she raises her head and our gazes meet, I know for sure that she does get it. There's no way *not* to know it, as the blazes in her irises keep flaring higher . . . and brighter . . . "*Maximus*. I'm burning up . . . "

"Oh, I know."

Fortunately, my sarcasm is good for us. Giving in to light laughs is what we both need to fill up our lungs and uncross our eyes. But—surprise, surprise—my little demon is twice as gorgeous now, seeming to actually pout as she rests her chin above my navel. It's as if she's debating which direction to go but refuses to let me in on the dilemma.

Keep going.

Don't *keep going.*

"And now *I'm* burning up." I direct the desperate growl to myself as much as her.

She gets the nuance, if her cocked head and quirking lips are telling the truth. "Misery does love company," she murmurs while pushing aside more of my shirt to expose the breadth of my chest. "Though I'm not sure if this helps or hurts."

"If it's hurting you, it's gone."

I'm not sarcastic about it this time. Not a note. "Kara. I'd cut my own heart out if its beats caused you pain." I form my hands over hers, bringing them back up to the space at the center of my sternum. "In a world where I'd have to exist without you, no knife would cut deep enough anyway."

At once, she pushes up and atop me. The blanket falls away from her. Her stare matches the moon for wide, stunned brightness.

"I love you, Kara. Truly," I whisper, grateful that the sound isn't swept away by the wind.

She smiles. Aside from the jewel of her heart, I can't think of a more incredible gift.

Though I admit, her glistening tears come close. Then her words top everything.

"And I love you too. *Truly*."

Before I can pull some needed air into my lungs, she scoots all the way up to recapture my lips. I take greedy advantage, sweeping in to possess her mouth just as she possesses my soul. She tastes like blissful tears and beach salt wind. She feels like a dream and torments me like a maddening sea siren. Her kisses. Her body. Her touch.

Torture that turns into agony as she glides her hand down to my belt buckle and has the closure flipped open before I can breathe again.

"*Kara*."

"What?" Her sough is as unsteady as mine, though infinitely sexier. "Don't tell me you don't need this as much as I do. I kind of know differently."

A true statement, even without her unique window into my mind. Because as she unzips the door to my pants, she's got more than enough evidence of my . . . *need.*

"Not arguing, beautiful. But we can't—goddammit."

I'm cut off by my own croak as she wraps her fingers, small but sure, around the part of me that's nearly too big for her reach. That dilemma happens right after she mewls into my beard while pumping me several times. As I jack my head back, the earth spins beneath my skull. I'm connected to that terrestrial rhythm in ways I never thought possible, suddenly aware of its miraculous pull on the cosmos overhead and vice versa. My blood starts matching the beat, and I'm hyper-aware of that too. Of the pulse rising through me. The vibrations *she's* inspiring.

Desperately, I cling to the sliver of logic still left in my brain—and use it.

"My love . . . "

A new sigh, longer and happier. "Yes, Maximus?"

"We—we have to remember where we are . . . "

"On a private beach? Under the stars and wrapped in each other? All we're missing is the yurt. I can live with that."

"We're only a hundred feet from a house packed with your brother and his buddies in it." Coincidence backs me up in the form of a song cranked louder inside Rerek's place. The kind of sultry R&B tune filled with a hundred poetic euphemisms for exactly what I want to do with this woman. Right now.

"You mean a house packed with people who probably sprinkle dirty thoughts on their breakfast cereal every morning?"

Now I'm the one bursting with a soft laugh. "And who says I don't?"

She must know the answer, because without wavering her gaze or slowing her strokes, she whispers the words that have me forgetting Jaden, Rerek, the party, the *world*. Even my stress about the rest of it—my father, her mother, and the uncertainty around the whole damn mess—disappears in the light of her sweet confession.

"*I'm* saying I love every part of you with every ounce of my soul, Mr. Kane—and I can't wait any longer to show you so."

CHAPTER 22

THROUGH THE NEXT SIXTY seconds, I learn a pair of new life lessons. First, love definitely lends a girl courage. Second, if I'm going to use that boldness to seduce the human side of this man, I'd better be ready for the glory of his other half too.

But I'm nowhere near prepared. Not for the power of the look on his face, a mix of mesmerizing awe and adoration.

Not for how he holds my face in his mighty grip, calling down the stars to collect in his unblinking gaze.

Not for how his massive body thrums against mine, his every muscle alive with unimaginable power . . . and his every thought filled with nothing but me.

I'm mute, motionless, and a little dazed. This has never happened to me before—and that surprise must finally show, because his tawny eyebrows suddenly draw together.

"What?" he coaxes gently, despite his growing length

beneath my palm. "Hey . . . what is it? Do you want to wait?"

I shake my head, broken free from my paralysis. "No. It's just—"

"What?"

I bite my lip but release it fast. "Tuning myself in to you right now . . . it's intense. Like looking into a mirror of all my senses."

The stars in his eyes gain new glows. "And you're surprised?"

"I guess not. It's just new."

"And that's strange?"

"Yeah. A little."

"Why?"

Back to biting my lip. Then back to a smile, though this one's not as huge. There's no way to say this tactfully, so I let the spill happen.

"Because nothing can ever compare to you. This. *Us.*"

"Oh, Kara." The glows in his gaze become a wash of warmth across his skin. Every magnificent, muscled inch of it.

Reluctantly, I let go of his cock. With a lot less hesitation, I swing up and over to straddle it instead. Though the filmy layers of my dress are still caught between our bodies, I'm completely concentrating on what we both crave right now. What we both *need*. Then he bucks beneath me, evoking a moan from the bottom of my throat.

"I think you'd better start getting used it," he husks. "Because if you haven't noticed, I don't have a lot of willpower when it comes to you. I want this with you . . . often . . . completely . . . forever."

His vow, full of such promise and fervency, has my heart overflowing and my blood simmering. Before I tear my stare away from his rippled abdomen and lift it back up, reconnecting with the fixated focus of his breathtaking blue eyes.

"Right now, I have other ideas about what you can give me, Mr. Kane."

He rocks back his head once more, his soul-deep sigh swirling with the bonfire sparks in the summer air. Nothing can prepare me for the perfection of him right now. His body, so sleek and sculpted. His hair, a thick riot across the blanket and out into the sand. His joy, unhindered and free. It's an intoxicating force, wrapping around us both like a living thing, blooming into something even better when it joins with the rise of his arousal.

It's become wild, racing thunder on the air—or is that just his resonance in my mind? That answer's moot once he grabs for my skirt, furiously shoving the peach froth aside, until his long, demanding fingers get to the last barrier between us. My silk panties.

Though I'm shocked his low rumble doesn't melt the whole garment off, he takes care of the challenge anyway. With one determined tug, he's provided enough clearance for our flesh to slide together, blissfully reunited.

"Oh!" I gasp, pleasantly shocked by the urgent nudge of his swollen crown.

"Sorry," he grates. "No. I'm not sorry. Fuck, I need you, little temptress. Need . . . *this* . . . "

"Yes." I barely choke it out as we slide together,

merging more perfectly than the waves with this sand. As he stretches me wider, finally seating home deep inside, my whole soul recognizes how much that makes sense. He's the moon to my tide. The magnet that's changed all my gravity. And I never, ever want that to change.

I brace myself to his shoulders as that force intensifies and then even more as we rock together, finding a rhythm that's as new and amazing as it is familiar and affirming. Desire crowds the last of my logical thoughts just like the clouds imposing on the stars overhead. A smile breaches my lips when those thunderheads growl, quivering the sky itself. I'd be addicted to this man and his passion even without the meteorological kink, but it's definitely an extra aphrodisiac.

Just like the way he rolls at the height of each thrust.

And grips my hips with sensual demand.

And fills my gaze with unbridled adoration. My ears, with his low groans of primal need.

And soon, my body with his scorching release.

As soon as he nears his climax, I'm ablaze too. I burst and swear and tremble from the force of it. My overwhelmed tears are joined by some heavy drops from the impatient squall overhead. The storm dissipates before we're even done with the thick of our torrid tryst, but that doesn't stop me from twisting my head, looking both ways on the beach.

"Hey," Maximus murmurs, his own stare intense on me. "You okay? Did I hurt y—" He catches himself, already knowing the answer to that. "Did I . . . satisfy you? I thought, when you were shaking all over—"

"Oh, you thought right." I seal the assurance by smashing

a long kiss to his welcoming lips. Once I've untangled my tongue from his again, I add, "I was just hoping I didn't have to scramble for a visit from your dad."

He laughs. "Or your mom."

I drop my jaw. "Bite your tongue!"

He snarls suggestively, undulating his hips. "I'd prefer it if *you* bit it."

I narrow my eyes, which are likely brimming with naughtiness. "So now you *want* me to be a vampire?"

"Well, I—" he interjects in on himself. "Don't tell me they really do exist too."

"No idea." I give his lower lip a playful bite. "But maybe sometime I'll try some creative interpretation."

After he turns my little taste into a wet and sweltering tongue tangle, he pulls back with his eyes closed and his lips in a satisfied curl. "Just listening to you say 'creative interpretation' has me wanting to bring back those thunderheads, beautiful."

I giggle before nuzzling my mouth to his ear. "Creative interpretation."

His rough exhalation and swift thrust lifts me by several inches.

I gasp but manage to goad him further. "Creative interpretation."

"You're such a bad girl."

"Creative interpr—*ahhh*!"

My shriek corresponds to his powerful sweep, lifting and flipping until I'm the one with sand in my hair and the whole sky in my view. At once, my scream gives way to a mesmerized moan. The coastal sky has never been more incredible, especially because the man of my soul is part of the vista.

The demigod of my destiny. The fulfillment of my fate. The lover who gives himself to me in every bright and burning way, until every thought is his name and every sensation and desire is his to own.

The stars bear witness to our lovemaking. The sand cushions the urgent press of our bodies, twined together now with little care for anyone who might see us. And as quickly as the storm cleared, Maximus's fevered drives summon a soundless flash of lightning, piercing the tumultuous sky.

The frenzy between us numbs us to the ensuing rain. The tempest matches the wild energy between us, making every second feel right. Fated, even. Before the lusty haze of my thoughts can ruminate any more on that, my writhing, scorching climax takes over. And Maximus owns every second of that too.

For another hour, we lie in a tangle of damp blankets and half-shed clothes, trading quiet kisses and admiring the enduring coals that survived the storm. *Our* storm, I tease, newly committed to appreciating Maximus's sway over the elements during these intimate moments.

In the fading light, I'm quietly grateful that my mother hasn't managed my life so heavily that I'm clueless about the stuff that contributes to a happy, normal relationship. It's stolen, silly moments like this. Laughter shared during experiences that no one else will understand.

I'm thankful that Maximus gets it too. For one of the few times in my life, I'm also grateful for the abilities that give me that assurance. We snap a few grainy pictures of ourselves in the dark. We're tired and messy and totally happy. For someone whose life has been defined by the last photo snap, capturing these moments—raw and unfiltered—means more than I can say. What's even better... They belong to us. We'll never have to share them with anyone else.

"We should head back, I think," Maximus finally says. He sits up and starts to button his shirt. "We've been gone a suspiciously long time. Your brother has to have noticed by now."

"Mm, not yet," I moan, burrowing into the warm place he's left behind on the blanket. I'm determined to savor every last second of our happy little bubble. Too soon, it'll be over. We'll be back in the world of glitter heels and Tinseltown deals, balanced with academia propriety and politics. Both such ridiculous games—but until we get the underworld's final ruling, these games are compulsory for us.

Fortunately, Maximus doesn't let me get too morose about that. "Fire's almost out anyway." He sweeps sand over the dying embers with his massive paddle of a foot. "And you still haven't gotten your party food fix."

"Well, there *is* that."

I accept his hand so I can fully stand and straighten out my dress. He obviously approves of me prioritizing the five thousand layers of the skirt, fixating on my chest without a flinch. Everything's fallen out of the silky bodice, meaning it's impossible to hide how his approving growl turns my nipples into pinpoints. I swat away his teasing advances to right myself once and for all.

"Hey there, mister. I thought you were eager to get back inside."

"Not exactly eager." He brandishes a look I'm not used to receiving outside his lecture hall. His lips are firm, but his stare is penetrating. "More of a polite compulsion. Make no mistake, there's a savage in me that never wants to leave this beach."

I'm not sure what's sexier: the complete conviction beneath his soft statement or the way he kneels again to press a reverent kiss atop one of my sand-covered feet. It's barely a brush of his lips, but my bloodstream doesn't know the difference. Or my nerve endings. Or every pore of my skin. Even with a mansion full of people possibly able to see everything we're doing, I'm on the brink of begging him to whip everything out and ravage me all over again.

After a steady breath in and out, I control myself long enough to brush the sand away from his beard and lips. "Hmm. A savage, you say?"

He arches a brow. "Do you doubt it? Do I need to prove—?"

"You do *not* have to prove it. I know this savage very well." I push at his chest, taking his warm hand in an attempt to tug us closer to the destination. "Besides, I have a feeling I may see again him *very* soon."

As we approach the access point to Rerek's place, I'm already dreading having to put the strappy stilettos back on.

Maximus turns me around and lowers me to one of the concrete steps.

"Oh, I think you definitely will," he answers to my musing. "Unless you want to play student and professor when we get back to my place," he adds with a devilish smirk.

I giggle. "Well, I do love when you read the cantos with your pretend glasses on. Definitely does things for me."

He chuckles as he works to fasten my straps. A little of the lightness of our night seeps away, though, as my thoughts take a dark turn. They're doing this more and more lately, especially if the subject approaches anything that has to do with hell.

Arden. Rerek. Now Dante, unfortunately.

Maximus rises and kisses me softly. "Where did you go, beautiful?"

"It's nothing." I'm almost harsh about it, which isn't his fault. But even Maximus's gentle kiss is barely enough to pull me back. "Just . . . a visit to the underworld, even between those pages, isn't exactly something I've wanted to think about lately," I explain.

"Hey." He strokes a hand over my hair. "I'm sorry. I didn't mean to drag that into . . . wherever it went."

I attempt a smile. "Was I that obvious?"

"Maybe not to others," he replies. "But let's just say you'll have to try harder to hide from me. Though I really hope you don't."

I can only manage a nod, dually overwhelmed by his earnest sincerity and the fears I'm still trying to outrun.

Stories that were just stories until I was faced with the actual threat of hell.

"I know you think it's just a beautiful piece of poetry, Maximus. But whether Dante imagined it all or knew it to be true, *I* know that hell isn't a myth." I can't control a small shiver. "Growing up, I heard too many stories to doubt it." Another ice bath through my veins escalates the shiver to a shudder. "And it's not a pretty place to go. Dante got that part right. I'm sure of it."

His brows crowd in on each other. "How many of those kinds of stories have you been told?"

"Too many. Enough to have established a healthy fear of the place." I avert my gaze. "Or maybe not so healthy. Though it definitely made us eat our peas and go to bed on time."

I'm not sure how to take the new energy of Maximus's stare. It doesn't match anything in his psyche, which is still drenched in his adoration for me—though his intense blues say something different. I almost wonder if he's just read my dismal thoughts in return, but his look doesn't match any normal reaction to it. I don't see pity or sadness or consolation. I simply feel . . . seen. And despite the mental subject matter, it feels wonderful.

The moment's gone as fast as it came. At once, he's back to the sincere charm that had me silently fawning over him back at President McCarthy's house, especially as he tends to my feet, now well secured in my torture heels.

"Well, *I'm* terrified your brother isn't leaving us any of the good party food."

"Or the good scotch," I add with a little laugh.

"Nothing but the best for you, my love."

And here I am, thinking he couldn't make me feel more treasured tonight. The words, and the way he issues them like a promise, are so much more fun to linger on as we climb the stairs back into the house, hand in hand. My leg muscles are sludge after being wrapped around him for the better part of an hour, but every one of my steps is a study in gliding confidence. It's impossible to feel any other way. I'm on the arm of the man I love, and I can't wait for the day I can be a part of all his plans. His days, his nights, his now, his forever.

Soon, I pray to any divine power within earshot of my soul. *Please . . . please . . . soon.*

CHAPTER 23

MAXIMUS

"SO."

Jaden Valari might be lit on at least a dozen substances right now, some legal and some not, but the stare he fires at me across Rerek's long kitchen is one hundred percent sober.

"So?" I take a hesitant swallow from my glass of scotch, enjoying the expensive booze's spicy caramel taste but little else.

Jaden leans forward like an indolent lion, bracing his arms along the quartz-topped island. "I'd ask what your intentions are toward Kara, but I've already gotten that part with crystal clarity."

"My intentions?" I wince, not catching his meaning. Even in the most traditional sense, the challenge seems old-fashioned at best. Especially for a playboy demon who can't seem to be bothered by much.

"Ah." He smirks. "I guess K-demon forgot to mention I can hear shit practically into Santa Monica."

I do my best to mask a stunned choke. Kara can pick up on every feeling in the room, and Kell can smell all of it. It should come as no surprise that Jaden has his own sensory specialties.

I clear my throat. "She definitely left out that part."

He spreads out his arms, looking like Malibu Jesus even with a full cocktail tumbler in his grip. "Don't worry, it's easy enough to tune out when I decide to. There are some sounds a guy can't unhear, you know?"

I actually don't know, but I offer a confirming nod all the same.

"None of us had a choice about our birthrights," he goes on, dipping his head with a wistful air. "Okay, nobody really does. I get that too." He takes a long swig of whatever concoction is in his glass and raises his head. A hock of hair keeps obeying gravity, a thick triangle hanging between his eyes. Doesn't matter. His dark-gold stare bores right into me. "Can I ask you something?"

I nod again, maintaining neutrality. "Sure."

"If you had the chance to *not* be Zeus's bastard kid, would you take it?"

Damn. That's definitely not where I predicted this going.

I recover swiftly. "Irrelevant question. It's not a possibility, so why waste time dwelling on it? I've got to move on in spite of the circumstances."

He chuckles. "Wow. So you and my sister really *were* made for each other."

I'm taken aback by the affection in his voice. The Valaris are possessive, cunning, and protective. Of all my interactions with them, though, I've never witnessed anything close to warmth. I suspect Jaden's impaired state might be to blame for the sudden camaraderie. Maybe I shouldn't be taking advantage of that, but if Jaden is really ready to open an extra window into the woman I love, no way am I the idiot to turn that down.

"So you're not in your mother's and sister's camp, then?"

A puzzled V forms between his eyebrows. "What do you mean?"

"I figured everyone was Team Arden until circumstances made that path impossible."

He pulls in a long breath. "I've never even met the guy. Not that I'd need to. Full-blooded demons are—" He stops short, cutting a sharp glance to the side where Rerek is chatting quietly with Kara out on the balcony. "Let's just say they're not to be screwed around with. I've always worried how Kara would manage it. She's not like Kell and me. She doesn't play the game." He lowers his arms, again spreading them across the island. "Okay, she doesn't play it *well*. Let's put it that way. I'm afraid belonging to Arden for any length of time would have changed her forever, and probably not in a good way."

I swallow hard, hating any vision that includes Kara bound to the scheming incubus. I thank everything holy he never had the chance to call her his own.

"Now with you," Jaden continues, "I mean, ask anyone. It's an overused cliché, but she's practically glowing."

"Literally or figuratively?"

He chuffs out a laugh. "I'm guessing both, depending on the situation. Seriously, though. I can't remember any other time, even when we were kids, that she looked truly, totally happy. We don't run in the same circles, but to be honest, part of my mojo on inviting her tonight was to see if this was all real with you. She's always donning the party hat and putting on a great show for everyone when it's necessary, but Kell and I saw through her charade a long time ago. There's always been something missing about her performance."

I set aside my drink and lean against the counter. "Something like . . . real emotion?"

"Bingo. But you already know that."

Of course I do. Kara's my most vital treasure, and I'm no stranger to the themes here.

"I do," I divulge. "I grew up having to shove down most of my real feelings too. Honestly, I simply thought I was fucked up. A freak who'd never be normal."

I hesitate more on that last part. Now that I've been on a couple of field trips with Z and have been educated about the resolve—and ruthlessness—of my real family, I see my mother's story and all the agonizing decisions she had to make about it through a different lens. In a much brighter light.

"Well, you're *not* normal." Jaden eases the whack of that one by chuckling again. "But you're also not a freak."

"Not totally sold on that one yet, but you get an A for effort."

"*Pffft.*" He hikes up his hands again. "Save the grades for the students who care, Professor. Trust me, I'm the last guy you want in the front row of your lecture hall."

I tilt my head, giving him a curious scrutiny. "I figured there was a reason you never graced campus."

"It's called the School of Hard Knocks. And I'm majoring in Hollyweird media spin."

"Veronica must be so proud."

"Like it or not, there's an art to it. Spins aren't spontaneous," he counters. "Basic physics, right? They need a little jab to get started. And around here, you're an idiot not to control the media jabs. Control the narrative, my friend. Write your own story."

His words hit home. *Write your own story.* Wasn't that exactly what Dante did during all the political upheavals of his time? Even after being exiled, he didn't give up on issuing his *jabs* for social change across Italy. I'm not after such a lofty goal, but the advice makes significant sense. "Control the narrative," I repeat. "Because if you don't, someone else will."

"Huzzah." Jaden hoists his drink. "Say what you will about my mother, but if you could hear her late at night from the other side of the house working her magic, you might feel differently. Just because she's learned to play the game better than all of us doesn't mean she's not tired or terrified by it. Especially lately . . . "

He interrupts himself once more, feigning interest in the depths of his cocktail. "Don't think for one second Kara's happiness hasn't come without a price to the whole family."

I reach for guilt and regret but come up short of anything close to convincing. Finally, I mutter, "I do get it. And for what it's worth, if I'd known the whole truth about . . . well, everything . . . I would have—"

"Done exactly what you did anyway."

"I would. But I'd also gash out my whole soul for your sister."

He doesn't respond verbally but simply extends his glass to clink against mine. It's a moment of quiet understanding, and I'm glad that under his cavalier and breezy exterior, he seems to care for Kara. Now, partnered with that concern, he can at least know that I care too. Deeply and wholeheartedly.

"The lady has requested a slice of bacon and pineapple pizza."

The interruption, coming from the entrance closer to the living room, is a double-edged sword. While I'm grateful for Rerek's intervention, I carefully sidestep him. Now that I know the truth—the likely version of it, anyway—about this chaos creator in glam rock clothes, distance makes more sense by the second.

"And now I might really have to kill you," Jaden mutters.

"Don't look at *me*," Rerek protests. "Tropical produce was created for cocktail rims, darling, not pizza. Thank you very much."

Kara ducks in from around the corner. "Did someone say pizza?" At once, her eagerness is the best medicine for my tension. "Clear the way, people. Starving girl incoming. I need some melted cheese and pineapple more than my next breath."

Jaden finishes off a facepalm with a long, low groan. "Who are you, and what have you done with my sensible sister?"

"Don't answer that," Rerek drawls, swirling the tip of his index finger toward a spot over Kara's shoulder. "Just go out, come back in, and say the exact same thing." He sweeps his stare around, addressing his smirk at Jaden. "It's such a treat to watch you get all wound up."

His statement oozes innuendo but doesn't faze anyone for a second, least of all Jaden. Clearly he's used to the thinly disguised flirtations from his friend. Whether they've ever been acted on is anyone's guess but nobody's business. Right now, my concern is more about the other aspects of Rerek's nature. The ones he's likely perfected over decades, if not centuries. The chaos that's hardwired into his blood and bones.

Kara steps over, inserting herself between the island and me to pick over what's left of the hors d'oeuvres. "Ugh. Not even some leftover cheese globs."

Jaden lifts a lazy grin. "Why don't we toast instead? To my gorgeous sister and the demigod who's making her happy."

Kara turns and nestles into my side. We all raise our glasses, only to be halted by another object in the air. Rerek's commanding hand.

"I believe I can top that one," he declares, bringing his stare to rest on Kara and me. "Here's to you adorable daredevils, breaking all the rules in the name of true love."

"Here's to breaking the rules, period." Jaden whoop-

whoops with his free hand and guzzles from his glass with the other, seemingly oblivious to the weird new air in the room.

Kara illustrates her uneasiness with pursed lips and a silent turn-down of the toast. I don't have the benefit of her unique intuition, but I've already had enough of Rerek's cagey machinations. Something feels too smug about his supposedly celebratory and romantic sentiment. I soothe a hand around the ball of her shoulder, a silent acknowledgment of what we both seem to be picking up on. Something's not right.

Suddenly Rerek seems to be in on it too. His eyes glitter with mischief, like we've both issued a fabulous invitation—except I fear the event is chaos and he's about to be in his element.

"Is everything all right? Did I say something?" he croons innocently.

My voice is as steady as my stare. "Sounds like you meant that toast as much as you'd mean 'bon voyage' to a *Titanic* passenger."

Rerek spreads a huge smile. "Ahhh! The ship of dreams but the cruise of nightmares. Fond memories indeed."

I straighten to collect myself from the casual chat with Jaden and brace myself for something less friendly.

Rerek smiles even wider. "Now, now, Professor. Have I offended you?"

Kara clunks down her drink and locks her arms around my bicep.

"It's all right, beautiful," I murmur without deflecting

my gaze from Rerek. "We're all gentlemen here. We're not going to break the furniture."

Rerek grimaces. "I love a good mess. But no. Fisticuffs are so barbaric."

"I'd still be grateful for an elaboration on what you did mean by all of that."

He shrugs. "I suppose I'm just sentimental. Anyway, I really should mingle. This *is* my party, after all." As if his words have emerged as magic light orbs to guide him away, he turns around and strolls back out toward the main party area.

"Rerek?" Jaden calls, clearly just as baffled as we are about this. "What the fuck is he up to now?" In one fluid move, he slides off the counter and follows his friend.

I watch him leave with a careful regard, keeping Kara tucked securely to my side. "Maybe we can sneak out now."

Kara gives me a look like she wants to laugh but doesn't dare. "Jaden will be back, likely sooner than later. Even from the other room, I could tell he was enjoying talking to you."

I draw in a huge breath, fighting my inner conflict. I'm ready to put Rerek's house in my rearview and have all of Kara's attention again, but quashing her desire to spend time with her brother would be like denying her very essence and the huge heart at the core of it. The immense kindness that's part of my admiration for her.

With a resigned sigh, I slip my hand down into hers. I'm about to grab another drink for her, but it's forgotten as soon as music swells louder in the next room. It's a classical waltz. The selection is as odd as everything else about the party, which doesn't surprise me at this point.

"Oh, wow. *Now* it's a party." Kara gives me a spirited smile, made more gorgeous by a warm breeze that flows in to pick up her dark hair. The wind plays with the layers of her dress too, wrapping the peach fabric around her subtle curves. "Hey. You want to dance?"

"Yeah." I chuckle. "This one's a real rager."

She gives into a laugh this time, ensuring her face is illuminated by the dancing flames from the glass fire pit out on the balcony. She's a California fantasy come to life—light and dark, natural and joyful, sexy and smart—and right now, the stunning siren I can't help but kiss . . .

Except when I'm cut off as I lower my lips over hers.

"Sorry to barge in."

As we swivel our faces, her hair mixes with my beard. The spicy scent of her shampoo is a damn aphrodisiac in my nose, which doesn't help my diplomacy in responding to Rerek's sanguine smile.

"Yes?"

He dips his head to me but extends his hand to Kara. "May I cut in?"

For a second, I'm confused. What the hell is he cutting in *on* except me kissing her?

Luckily, Kara senses enough of that to squeeze my arm in reassurance. "Just a little dance," she says, nodding to indicate she's pulled at least that much from the demon's mind.

I step back, keeping my protective glower to myself. His request is innocent enough. The two clearly share some history I'd like to learn more about. Maybe soon. Maybe even later on tonight. Just not now.

The room grows too warm. I suspect it's from the new sizzle in my blood and the inescapable crackle in my senses. Nothing about this party has felt right, but playing nicely with the underworld is priority one right now.

I impale her with one more intense look, asking a silent question. *Are you all right with this?* She answers me by popping up to press a sweet kiss into my beard.

"Save my spot, okay?" she whispers.

"Doesn't belong to anyone but you."

As Rerek deftly guides Kara into a waltzing swirl, Jaden approaches from my other side.

"Why didn't he ask you?" I grouse.

"Because I'd have to say no, and he'd be a thousand kinds of bent about it. Besides, I can't dance. I mean, at all. I'd end up scuffing his shoes and stomping on his feet."

My penetrating stare is a silent call for Jaden to tell me more.

"I'm bound by the same vow as Kell and Kara." He dilutes the statement with a shrug. "And it's fine. Females are fascinating, and I'll be content with whomever they throw at me. Rerek hasn't said it, but I get the sense he'll be ready and waiting as soon as my duties have been fulfilled. But I don't anticipate that being anytime soon, so for now, we're friends."

"Veronica knows this too?"

"If my mother had her preference, I wouldn't be mated at all—or at least until I'm much older." Another shrug, corresponding with his casual side eye. "If you haven't figured it out by now, males outnumber females down under. I mean, by a lot. That's another reason why Mom's stressing hard about Kara and Kell—and why your arrival in all this is a bigger deal than it seems at first."

And perhaps why Hades was so fixated on invading all my thoughts about Kara. Just thinking about last night's encounter with him is another introduction to tension, with more on the way.

"Well, they'd all better get used to it," I finally utter. "Because I'm not going anywhere."

Jaden flips his head back, tossing the hair out of his eyes. "I don't think anyone's questioning that part."

His assurance doesn't stop me from setting my vow on repeat in my mind while keeping watch over Rerek and Kara. Neither of them are saying much, but her discomfort isn't cramping her style. Her frame is flawless, her footwork poetic. Even her profile captivates my imagination. I greedily take it all in, from the smooth plane of her forehead to the place where her neck blends with her collarbone, and everything in between. She makes me wish we'd really come in from the beach and just left for my place.

As soon as she whips her stare around, eyes snagging mine before Rerek turns her again, I realize how thoroughly my fantasies have taken over my brain. And likely hers as well.

I let her revel in my embarrassed smirk before Rerek twirls her away again, with her lush hair sweeping above and her skirt layers swirling below. Between them, her body is nothing but regal movement and innate grace. They're dancing on their own along the far side of the room now.

"What the hell is he doing with her?" Basic jealousy would be easier to conquer than this bizarre amalgam in my heart and mind. Uncertainty and suspicion have become my constant wingmen lately.

Except the look on Jaden's face mirrors my worry, which doubles my own.

Rerek and Kara waltz closer to the balcony, even farther from us.

An agitated rumble vibrates my chest. Heaven help me, I've gotten so paranoid—and maybe a little delusional. Because as I watch, Rerek's angular features and lean frame start to phase in and out of view. It's as if he's been thrown into one of Gio Valari's old movies, except his whole physical presence is flickering in slow motion.

Forget paranoia. I've careened right to baffled, wondering if my senses are playing a prank—until Kara's gaze pops wide too.

Then I realize Rerek isn't the only one in the room who's phasing in and out of existence. The rest of the party guests start up with the freakish effects too.

"Holy shit," I mutter. Every one of them has grown fuzzy edges and sketchy visibility. On. Off. On. Off. The calculated bursts continue across the room, making me question if this is all even real.

"You're seeing this, right?" Jaden mutters.

"Yeah. I'm seeing this."

And nothing about it is okay. Something bizarre is

going on here. Something not confined to this room or this house. Something that sets off every alarm in my intuition.

A single glance toward Jaden tells me he didn't orchestrate a fraction of this freak show.

But Rerek... He's seemingly unaffected as he leans over to utter something to Kara. Something as smooth as oozing lava.

At once, she tenses in his grasp. With matching speed, my heart crashes against my ribs.

I curl a fist into Jaden's shirt sleeve. "What's he telling her?"

Jaden inhales and then exhales. As his breath begins to leave him, a tremor claims his entire form. "Get her out of here." Every rise and fall of his rasp conveys his underlying fear.

"Why? What's—"

"You want a full transcript or my sister's safety?" he snaps. "Get her the hell out of here. Now!"

I believe him. I can't afford not to. I pivot around and lurch into action. I make it all of three strides before the first couple I encounter is breaking free from their own dance, redirecting at me like they've been newly drafted for party security. The couples to their right and left change course in the same way, pressing in with surreal speed. Everyone's waif thin but pushing back at me with shocking strength. At once I understand why.

The crowd of pretty humans are more than weird holograms. The lapse in their glamorous guise reveals more of the truth with each passing moment. Now I'm getting bigger glimpses of their true selves.

Minutes ago, this was a luxe party peopled with beautiful faces and sculpted bodies. Now the mansion is wall-to-wall with demons, in every sense of the word. Their bones drip with jagged skin. Their mouths are toothless maws. Their eyes are fathomless—and soulless.

But every one of them has underestimated my love for the woman in their host's grip.

I lift a hand toward the target I've mentally painted on the chest of minion number one. I already envision how to domino him into his partner. If I think a few seconds ahead of each shove, this will go fast and easy.

But my hand gets no higher than my waist.

I growl and try again. I still can't move.

What the hell?

I'm still alive—breathing, sweating, flexing, cursing—but everything from my neck down is like a hexed statue. Behind me, Jaden's locked in the same invisible cement. We're stuck here as Kara now visibly fights to be free from Rerek's hold. But it's as if the demon's arms have become concrete too. She can't do anything but reach for me, eyes afire with fear, fury, dread, and desperation.

My only reply is the agony of my soul. Out of every torture method Rerek is surely familiar with, he's handpicked the one that brings me the most awful anguish. The fear of losing Kara.

I know it just by looking at him that he's savoring every disgusting moment of this, laughing like a kid who's gleeful about bigger thrills to come. And that's when I know. *I know.*

We haven't just walked into a trap.

We've been ambushed.

CHAPTER 24

*H*USH NOW. DON'T FIGHT *it. You knew this was coming.*

Rerek's eerie warning echoes in my thoughts. Every syllable burns its way up my throat, aided by the bile consuming everything between it and my belly. The heat licks all the way up to my eyes too, but something tells me that's not a concern in this crowd.

Every person in the room, aside from Jaden, Maximus, and me, is fading in and out of view like holograms losing the power source that conceals their otherworldly ugliness.

Never in the history of Hollywood have looks been more deceiving.

The crowd is fully closed in on Maximus and my brother. They've done something to both of them, holding them in place with some unearthly evil. I protest with a shrill cry of anguish, already knowing it's no use. My mighty lover, who can crush walls and summon thunder, is suddenly, terrifyingly powerless against the half-real mob.

There's nothing half-real about the awful rips in my heart—the terrible gashes that keep going, breaking open every seam of my soul. I watch, helpless and furious, as Maximus turns into a man possessed. He shoves and punches and tears. Swears and snarls and roars.

Rerek's just as determined, with his iron grip and his stance fused to the floor, keeping me right here. Right where he wants me.

But growing up in the Tinseltown rat race has taught me some lessons better than others. Like nobody having the exclusive rights on tenacity.

"Rerek! Stop this!"

My verbal slash earns me little more than his flinch. I have his full attention now, though, evidenced by his open-mouth hiss. The illusion of his humanity is erased for a moment, revealing a creature with cratered skin, a hooked nose, and gaunt eye sockets.

"I'm afraid that's not part of the plan, Kara."

The plan? I go still.

Hopelessness stabs, hard and deep. It intensifies as I consider all the awful options of what his plan might be. Worse—who's orchestrating it. With circumstances as dire as they are, the candidates are horrifyingly few.

"Hades." I go ahead and hurl it, hoping Rerek will deny it and eliminate my biggest dread. "It's him, isn't it? Tell me, damn it. Did he put you up to this?"

Rerek's black eyes brighten with intrigue. "Did *he* put *me* up to this?" He scoffs. "Come now. As if I need encouragement to wreak havoc."

I almost believe him. Almost.

"Then why this? And now? We've been friends. You care for Jaden." I lock my lips to cloak the tremble in my voice. I'm ready to keep ticking items off the list of reasons why he wouldn't want to betray me, but his attention is torn from me again, back to my brother.

Dread sets in now, burrowing with awful, icy fingers. I should have been suspicious this morning when Jaden invoked Rerek's name out of nowhere. But my guard came down because of the unexpectedly warm invitation, likely encouraged by Rerek himself…

Rerek, who's always been so cool about never messing with our family.

Rerek, who'd never harm any of us for fear of alienating himself from my gorgeous, charismatic brother.

"No. Rerek, please no," I rasp, my stomach burning again. The horrible pressure behind my eyes joins suit, and there's no way to prevent the appalled tears from tumbling down my face. I hurtle my glare into his, yearning for my optic flames to become a real explosion for once. *Please, just this once…*

But if the Almighty has ever been tempted to hear me, now isn't the moment. Even the Divine of the Heavens knows when it's time to step back and let hell have its turn. To let Hades have his toys.

And sometimes, in some instances, to let him share them.

I examine Rerek's features. His pastel gaze is bright and

satisfied. His lips are smirking, accentuating the cruel cut of his cheekbones against his deceptively smooth skin—in the few seconds before it melts again, distorting back to his true self. There's something else about his energy now too. Something inside matching his hideous outside. Palpable excitement.

I hate it.

I hate him.

"Damn you," I seethe.

Rerek laughs. "Oh, Kara. What in all of the universe makes you think I care what you feel when I'm about to have what I *want*? Or rather *who* . . ." He swings his heated stare, swirling with azure and periwinkle, toward Jaden. "This was the way it had to happen. The only way. So sordid and messy. A chaotic adventure. And best of all, I no longer have to wait. Patience is not one of my virtues, which may come as a surprise to you."

Heavier tears spill and run down my cheeks. *What have I done?* The powers that be have become the powers that refuse to stop, adding my brother to their tally of Valaris who'll pay the price for my rebellion. Unless I can warn him first . . .

"Run!" I scream, scratching and writhing at the cage of Rerek's grip. "Jaden, damn it. *Run!*"

But I'm wasting my breath. My brother's still trapped with Maximus, unable to move, let alone run. All three of us are hostages. Caught, captured, and all but chained down by these bizarre insurgents—and whoever fuels their power.

Their leader.

The fallen angel who authorizes every move they make, every breath they get, and every feeling they have. The ruler who owns their souls for the rest of time.

Hades.

At the moment, he's giving all of them, Rerek included, less and less of their mortal shrouds. Soon, I'm no longer staring across a room filled with trendy wannabes. Their faces darken and shrivel. Their clothes dissolve to tatters. Their energy becomes a dirge of desperation. They're an army of eternal slaves, moving because they have to, their voices swelling with greater grief by the second. I grit my teeth, fighting the urge to scream myself, as their hopeless, endless sorrow seeps deeper and deeper into my psyche.

Stop. Make it stop.

Am I going insane? How I hope so. This hurts so much. Too much. All the pain and penury and heartache . . .

Stop. Make it stop!

Then I recognize Maximus's dread coiled in with all the others. The weight of it balls in my chest until it collides with my heart. Agony floods me. I'm weak. I'm broken. I'm terrified.

And that's when I know . . .

This is the moment . . .

At first, there's nothing but a whisper of sound. A feather across my frontal lobe, making my head jolt up. It's such a contrast to the barrage of grief, I'm disoriented—for about two seconds. It takes only that long for a new sound to dominate the air.

Maximus's bellow.

"*Hades!*"

There's a third sound, visceral and violent, as if the structure around us might shatter and crumble. The lights flicker then pop. Paintings fall off the shivering walls.

I'm not crying anymore. I'm too scared.

Especially as the veneers crack on all of the room's morbid statues.

"What...in all of..." But my voice hitches as the alabaster confines continue breaking open and fall away, allowing larger, living creatures to emerge from their shattered shells. I never thought my eyes could flare this wide, but they do. I watch, stupefied, as a rearing ram statue becomes a living, moving, red-eyed ram. Next to that, a large owl emerges, wings tipped with flames, before taking flight. The next gives birth to a massive hound that splits apart at the neck so its three heads can emerge.

Taking form next to the hound, as if the flickering hologram show is working in reverse, is a man.

No. Not a man. The comprehension runs me through at once, a blade that twists my guts and sears my soul.

"No!" I cry out, which does nothing to slow the intruder's strides toward me. He's slender and groomed, urbane and smooth. He has an easygoing stride, like a guy simply strolling to work in the financial district.

No. Not a guy. Not even a man.

Not. A. Man!

I order myself to keep remembering it. But I also can't stop staring at him, my senses plunging beyond bafflement. Why is he so...normal? He should be taller. Filthier. Darker.

Shouldn't the ruler of the underworld have three vicious faces with a bat-spawning beard? Shouldn't he be garbed in black instead of a deep-red suit that accentuates his brutally chiseled features?

"Kara. We meet at last."

As his summons permeates my thoughts, I recognize my observations of his physical presence for the stupid assumptions that they are—lame attempts to alter this nightmare by fixating on things that make sense. Like nearly everything else in my life, nothing about this makes sense. Until three weeks ago, I just accepted the fact with grim certainty, never hoping for anything different—until everything *was* different. Until I touched a demigod and my heart woke up.

But now, sleep beckons again, pulling at me from the lips of the demon who comes nearer. His every step sends up clouds of silver smoke, though his strides splinter the floor as if he's walking on a frozen lake.

"Look at me, love."

I whimper, tortured by his compelling command. Still, I lift my head. I have no choice. I'm forced to subject my gaze to the fathomless red furnaces of his.

The connection diminishes Maximus's bellow to nothing but a whisper. Slowly, the god's clasp replaces Rerek's around me. It's gentler but just as confining. Hades hushes more of my tortured sobs, even as the ongoing invasion of his insidious voice compounds my anguish.

There's nowhere to move, outside or in, as the king I've defied becomes the dictator of my future. My muscles are dying coals. My blood is an ice floe.

Only in the deepest core of my heart can I cling to any warmth, from a flame I protect like a prisoner in an Antarctic dungeon.

It's the light of love. The blaze of my beautiful demigod. The fire not even Hades can take from me—nor, I swear, will ever see. It's evident he doesn't even now, as he clamps a hand to my temple and stalks his way into more of my mind. I fight him with all the psychological force I can muster, but he's here now. Stomping through my mind. Gouging my senses before consuming them with his captivated murmur.

"My word. You really *are* fascinating."

The sound is strange and surreal, vibrating only in the confines of my head—just like my unending scream, as he carries me off to a fate I know nothing and everything about.

CHAPTER 25

MAXIMUS

"HE'S TAKEN HER."

Jaden's revelation is a brutal husk, reflecting my own agony. But hearing it in spoken form doesn't ease one soul-eating shred of it.

Desperate to rewind, rewrite, and reclaim the harrowing moments, I reset my mind to the moments after Kara and I came in from the beach. I force-feed the memories back into it. Every awful, ignorant second. Every disgusting detail. I don't stop until everything's inside, festering like a pile of plague-infested rags. But so much worse because I can't incinerate it all away. Nor do I want to, because those blindly simple moments could hold vital clues to getting her back.

It's all I can think about. The flames of the wish are fed by the kerosene from my soul until my vision goes black. I'm going to die. If Kara is truly gone, I hope so.

But my heart is still beating. I'm still hemorrhaging with

rage, throbbing with misery. I open my eyes, and I can still see everything. At least this place *looks* like a hellmouth now. Hades's arrival took out all the windows. There's shattered alabaster everywhere. I yearn to crush it to dust.

And now, thanks to me, torrents of rain are soaking everything. A spear of lightning bisects the deck. It might be impressive under different circumstances. Like if I were making love to Kara instead of grieving her abduction.

Right now, all I want to do is howl until the rest of the roof comes down. Hurl my fists through the walls that are still upright. Most of all, wrap all my fingers around Rerek's neck. But the traitorous shit, along with the rest of his freakish friends, dissolved along with Hades and Kara.

Dissolved to where?

My throat convulses as I yearn to thunder the question at Jaden. But his face is gaunt. His eyes are bloodshot. Clearly his imagination is consumed by the same visceral terror I saw in Kara on the beach. His mouth moves as if he wants to bellow things too.

The waves on the shore worsen as I endure another slam of helpless fury. I don't try to tame the breakers, but I don't claim a shred of satisfaction from them. They're the same as the lightning and rain. Products of my rage, not partners in it.

My only true partner has been stolen. Ripped from me by the hell scum whom I made the mistake of underestimating. In his wake, Jaden and I stare at nothing but half-soaked floors littered with broken plaster and discarded party flutes. He's already on the move after shakily testing whether he *can*, rushing into the area being pelted by the rain. "Nothing," he groans. "There's literally nothing here!"

I wish he were wrong. But if the gods can move around entrances to their beachside bar like balls under a cosmic sorcerer's cup, then Jaden is likely right. We're really just standing here in the sideways rain with nothing but statuary shards for clues.

Clues I start gathering as fast as I possibly can, dropping to both my knees to do so. "Help me." I nod toward another pile of the white wreckage. "We have to salvage as much of it as we can."

"Why?" Jaden challenges, though not enough to disobey me. Thank God, because I'm stumbling through a nightmare right now, guided by nothing but my desperate dread. Wondering if I'll ever wake up.

Kara.

I vocalize the thought too, pushing it out in an adoring whisper. I imagine she's still here as I cup her face, holding her firm for my deeper penetration...

Kara, sweetheart. Hold on.

I don't give that one any volume. The plea is as lame as it feels. Hold on to *what*? And *where*? So much I don't know. So much I can't do.

Waves are crashing closer and closer. The destroyed balcony will be driftwood before dawn. And a deeper reality sets in that I have to actually accept this into my brain as fact. She's gone. Truly gone. In my blood, I already know she's been taken someplace that won't be easy or even possible to find.

"Maximus. *Hey.*" Jaden's inflection is a clear indicator he's on repetition five or six of the hail. He clutches the top of my shoulder. "Recalibrate, man. Hell really doesn't wait for anyone. We'll get her back."

His drizzle of veiled hope provides a much-needed shot of energy for my body and hope for my heart.

But . . . "How?"

"No idea, but I'm guessing you're going to need some help. We can try to glue this place back together, but I don't think it's going to get us much closer to finding her."

A sliver of hope is better than none, and clinging to it is the galvanizer I need right now. Time is of the essence.

I scramble in my pocket for my truck keys. "You're right. Let's go."

Jaden nods, also using the motion as a directional toward the front door. My careening senses are grateful. We race through the rubble toward what used to be Rerek's artistically cool front entrance.

I'm there in no time, but when I don't hear Jaden's footsteps anymore, I stop in front of the fountain in the vestibule. Jaden's still there, but a wholly new sound erupts from him as he drops violently to the floor. He grunts hard and topples harder, as if he's hurtled into a clear glass door. But there's no such barrier. There's nothing's there but air.

"What happened?"

He's still flat on his back, muttering curses. With a fresh groan, he pushes back to his feet. On his new approach attempt, he extends his hands to make cautious friends with the air first. Except once again, his palms *thwack* into the invisible wall. After a more gritted profanity, so do his coiled fists.

"Is he fucking kidding?" He laces his fingers at the back of his head and jams his sights toward the ceiling. "Are you *fucking* kidding me?"

I take a tentative step toward him. "Hades is doing this?"

He shakes his head with savage fury. "Rerek."

I pause, processing his revelation. "He helped Hades get to Kara. You were the prize."

Jaden lowers his head. His nostrils are flared, his eyes enraged. "That chaotic cretin is going to learn just how awesome a *prize* I am."

I inhale hard, hoping to suck in some of the powerful punch from his anger. But suddenly I'm twice as paralyzed as before. If I couldn't save Kara from these forces, how the hell am I going to save Jaden?

"Hey. Don't worry about it," Jaden snaps, as if he's able to hear my thoughts now too. Likelier, I'm wearing all the stress across my face. "Just go." His voice is raw with rage and resignation. "I'll deal with Rerek. You . . . well, just find her."

"But—"

"You have to get her back. I'll do whatever I can from here, but it won't be enough. I can practically guarantee that."

I'm exhaling now, yearning to turn it into a blast capable of taking out everything on the patio. But the invisible clock in my head ticks louder, subduing me into a terse nod. "If I have to turn hell inside out, I'll find her," I vow.

"You may have to," Jaden mutters. "But right now,

you've got to get out of here. Rerek could be back any second. You shouldn't be here when he does."

I pause once more, wanting to ask if he'll be okay, but the urge gets stowed for more selfish reasons. It won't do any good, and Jaden's better prepared to deal with his sentence as Rerek's prisoner than Kara is as a hostage in hell.

A hostage?

Is *that* even right?

The question pummels me as I rush back to the truck. What does Kara mean to Hades? Why did he go to such lengths to take her himself, when he could have employed any number of minions to carry out the task?

Is she his prisoner? Or is she his captured rebel, taken to experience his personal punishment for her sin against him? If so, then what kind of punishment? And for how long?

Driving through the night, with the wind whipping my hair and the rain lashing my face, I can't stop myself from imagining all the possible answers for that. How many ways can Hades, king of misery and suffering and sorrow, choose to hurt the woman I love?

Panic surges again, hot and terrible and suffocating. I rechannel it, revving the truck's engine far past the speed limit. I push a button and bark at the truck's Bluetooth to call the only other person who's been a true lifeline in tragic times.

Jesse picks up after the third ring. "This better be good."

"It's not." I drag in as much air as I can, acknowledging the crack in my voice now that the cabin speakers surround me in a familiar, safe voice. "Fuck. It's just . . . not."

"Jesus. You sound like shit. What's going on?"

"Can't explain right now. I'm on my way home."

"All right. I'm downstairs. But the suspense is already killing me. What happened? Is it Kara? Did you guys have a fight or something? Were you being an ass—"

"No." I practically yell it. "It's nothing like that."

Jesse sighs, seemingly resigned to the sparse details. I'd tell him more, but I need the next twenty minutes to figure out exactly what to say and how. Until then, he'll have to wait out the suspense.

"I'll be there in twenty."

After I end the call, my every thought magnetizes once more to Kara. For the rest of the drive, I focus my mind—and my heart—on a different activity. Something I haven't done in a long damn time.

I pray. With the force of every neuron in my head and fiber of my heart.

Because she's the fire I worship. The single soul in this world, and all the others, who has dared to go to the depths of mine and gifted me with hers in return.

I'm going to find her.

I'm going to bring her back, even if it means diving to the bottom of hell.

Even if it means trading my own soul for hers.

ACKNOWLEDGMENTS

Special thanks to my beta readers, Lauren and Jennifer, for providing early feedback on the first draft. Thank you to Scott Saunders and the entire Waterhouse team for their enthusiasm, talent, and dedication throughout the editing and publishing process. Big thanks to my husband, Jonathan, and my mom, Colleen, for always helping push me through the tough spots. Last but not least, I owe a debt of gratitude to my co-author Angel Payne. Maximus and Kara's story could not shine so brightly without your poetry and imagination on every page.

— Meredith

What an amazing adventure this has been and continues to be! I owe so much fierce, fiery love and thanks to the incredible Meredith Wild. I continue to be floored and honored that you've invited me along to be a part of Maximus and Kara's journey. Thank you for being a truly awesome creative partner and a deeply cherished friend. Here's to the magnificent "storm" ahead!

As all the cute ponies say: friendship is magic! It's unbelievably true in my world, and I want to say a massive

thanks to my sisters who keep me perpetually sane—and supplied with all the corny motivational stuff when I need to hear it most! Victoria Blue, Carey Sabala, Cynthia Gonzales, Shayla Black, and Jenna Jacob: you are such jewels in my world!

So much gratitude to our editor, Scott Saunders, who helps make the words dance with such patience and expertise.

The Waterhouse Press team: I am beyond grateful for each and every one of you, in so many ways. In marketing & publicity: Jonathan Mac, Robyn Lee, Haley Boudreaux, and Kellie Jo Chen. In graphics, design, and social media: Amber Maxwell and Dana Bridges. In operations, distribution, and technical support: Jesse Kench, Yvonne Ellis, Jennifer Becker, and Kurt Vachon. You all are truly the dream team! Thank you for everything.

Martha Frantz: You are my sanity essential. Thank you for keeping everything running so smoothly!

Stephanie Arrache: Thank you for continuing to make sure that all things Jesse are accurate and awesome. You are my freakin' hero!

Thomas and Jessica: you are the center of my world and the fire in my heart, each and every day.

— Angel

ABOUT MEREDITH WILD

Meredith Wild is a #1 *New York Times*, *USA Today*, and international bestselling author. After publishing her debut novel, *Hardwired*, in September 2013, Wild used her ten years of experience as a tech entrepreneur to push the boundaries of her "self-published" status, becoming stocked in brick-and-mortar bookstore chains nationwide and forging relationships with major retailers.

In 2014, Wild founded her own imprint, Waterhouse Press, under which she hit #1 on the *New York Times* and *Wall Street Journal* bestseller lists. She has been featured on *CBS This Morning* and the *Today Show*, and in the *New York Times*, the *Hollywood Reporter*, *Publishers Weekly*, and the *Examiner*. Her foreign rights have been sold in twenty-three languages.

Visit her at MeredithWild.com

Photograph © Sharon Suh

ABOUT ANGEL PAYNE

USA Today bestselling romance author Angel Payne loves to focus on high-heat romance starring memorable alpha men and the women who love them. She has numerous book series to her credit, including the action-packed Bolt Saga and Honor Bound series, Secrets of Stone series (with Victoria Blue), the intertwined Cimarron and Temptation Court series, the Suited for Sin series, and the Lords of Sin historicals, as well as several standalone titles.

Angel is a native Southern Californian, leading to her love of being in the outdoors, where she often reads and writes. She still lives in Southern California with her soul-mate husband and beautiful daughter, to whom she is a proud cosplay/culture con mom. Her passions also include whisky tasting, shoe shopping, and travel.

Visit her at AngelPayne.com